Trivialized Pursuit

Trivialized Pursuit

A Love & Games Romance

Mia Heintzelman

TULE
PUBLISHING

Trivialized Pursuit

Tule Publishing First Printing, July 2023

The Tule Publishing, Inc.

First Publication by Tule Publishing 2023

Cover design by Dot Covers

ISBN: 978-1-959988-63-2

Dedication

To Mommy and Daddy, the social butterfly and the bookworm.

CHAPTER ONE

ROX

Q: Derived from a French word meaning "to block" or "to obstruct," what word's first recorded use was by Michael de Montaigne?

A: Embarrassment

"SHOULDERS BACK, CHIN high, smile, and don't throw up," I tell myself as I scoot my chair closer to my freshly Lysoled dining table and flatten my hands on the cool glass surface.

I inhale a deep breath, then smooth the lines of my sensible sleeveless pink blouse. It's a conservative, not-too-low-cut, bright solid that, according to my "TV Interview Prep" checklist, meets the recommendation for high-definition television.

It's a visual medium, and I'm supposed to want viewers to focus on me, and not my busy clothes.

"This is all part of the plan. It's going to be like any other interview."

Breathe.

This is just a video chat with a new friend. *On a nationally syndicated news program. With tens of thousands of viewers waiting for me to screw up.*

"*Why* did I agree to do this stupid interview?"

A little voice in the back of my head reminds me this is about the store, not me.

I'm here to keep Love & Games' name in the news. Literally. Three months ago, my sister, her best friend Nadia, and I saved our business. Now we just need to remain socially relevant. And keep growing at an exponential rate. Spread the word. Keep our faces out there.

But if in the process I happen to catch the eye of some well-rounded, devastatingly handsome stranger who loves his family and is open to genuine commitment and intimacy…

I peek over at my *Book of Lists* and turn to my checklist of the day, where "find an amazing eligible bachelor" did not make the bullet-point cut.

Again, this is about the business.

My heart rate kicks up as nervous energy zips through my veins. A groan claws its way from my throat, and I suck in several deep breaths to stop myself from checking my watch for the umpteenth time. Instead, I open my laptop and double-check my makeup, then my teeth for signs of egg and spinach omelet bits before digging my hands in my hair to zhuzh up my curls.

"It's only five minutes," I tell myself.

A notification jolts from the side of the screen, both startling and reminding me to log on to the video call the studio set up.

"I'm going," I mutter. A quick glance at my checklist

with all its boxes filled does little to relieve my anxiety. My fingers tremble as I type in the meeting ID and passcode. I check my selfie light one more time, making sure my laptop is positioned to show only the brightly colored business on top. *Not* the polka-dot pajama party on the bottom. Because that would be counterproductive.

One viral video is enough.

Then I peel the black electrical tape from my webcam.

As soon as I click Submit, a little circle spins, further winding me up, when my screen splits in two.

You've got this.

"One of the game shop owners involved in that now-famous Monopoly kiss-gone-viral is with us today via satellite," news reporter Jennifer Ling says.

I have no clue whether they've patched me in yet or if I'm live, so I smile awkwardly.

"Earlier this month, Channel 5 Action News brought you face-to-face with the blissful couple who confessed their love with the world watching. This week, we bring you the co-owner of Love & Games, and the mastermind behind the romantic-comedy-inspired stunt that saved a small, women-owned business."

She continues to detail the events of the video, beginning with my sister's boyfriend Declan's live post, asking Harper to meet him thirty minutes before the city Monopoly tournament if she returned his feelings. The screen cuts to a clip of the movie *Never Been Kissed.* It's my favorite scene of Drew Barrymore standing on the pitcher's mound, waiting to be kissed for the first time.

Jennifer Ling chuckles good-naturedly as the movie clip

ends and the video of Harper and Declan kissing appears on the screen.

"Roxanne Sloane is the sister of Harper Sloane, the woman people have affectionately named the Monopoly Queen, seen here *showing up* for the man she calls *the love of her life.*" The raven-haired news reporter flashes her megawatt smile straight ahead. Behind her, there's a huge monitor with her face beaming on one-half of the screen.

On the other half?

Me.

With a glob of Vaseline glazed over my teeth to hold my shaky smile in place—advice from the helpful Monopoly Queen herself.

You never know who'll be watching. Or who you'll meet… Harper had purred earlier on the phone, baiting me. The operative silent words being that I'm never going to meet a guy if I don't go somewhere and do something new. Even if this pointless interview benefits the store.

Just smile and be yourself.

So easy.

Which normally it is. I'm good at putting my best foot forward in the public eye. But this is my dining room table, and knowing Jennifer Ling, the won't-be-scooped reporter known for exposing tax scams and pest-infested eateries, she's probably gunning for something a little less rodent and a lot more reality TV. I'm both dreading and dying to know what her angle is going to be with me.

Restless, I tug the hem of my blouse and cheese into the camera.

"Welcome, Roxanne Sloane. It's great to have you with

us."

Jennifer clears her throat, and her blunt-cut bob dusts her slender olive shoulders as she draws them back. Not even a peek at the paper stacked in front of her before she narrows her gaze, sucks in a breath, and plasters on her serious journalist face.

"Thank you for having me."

I shift in my chair, bracing myself for one of her classic curveballs. After the media storm attached to anything Love & Games, I became the *famously* single sister of the Monopoly Queen. *Lucky me. The world knows I'm a workaholic who can't get a man.* At least Ling won't be able to stump me with any *Are there any wedding bells in the near future* questions like she did with Harper and Declan. *They met in January. It's the end of June. Like, what's the rush down the aisle?*

"Tell me, Rox… May I call you Rox?" She chuckles.

Okay, she's just buttering you up. Stay on your toes.

I nod like a grade-A newbie. "Yeah, yes," I stammer. "That's fine."

Ling pauses for what seems like forever, and I make the mistake of looking at myself on the screen. The fresh honey highlights I got last week for this occasion aren't warm and beachy like I imagined. Mixed in with my shoulder-length dark brown hair, the stark selfie light casts a putrid green, almost chartreuse glow. *Decidedly not my best look.* Add in the new Bliss & Makeup Co. pink stain currently chapping my lips and the mink lashes Nadia swore would make my eyes pop, and I'm a flaming hot YouTube makeover mess.

Literally, given that I forgot to put on deodorant.

I sit up taller, resolved to focus on the reporter instead of nitpicking my image.

"So, tell me, Rox. How does it feel to know the video you orchestrated has fifty-six million views?" Her voice is measured and choppy in that newsy way reporters use to make things sound super dire and important.

And it works.

But at least she's going with the viral video route. This isn't going to be so bad.

The last I checked, the number of views was at some crazy inconceivable number, but fifty-six million? *Holy flaming shit did that video work.*

"Wow," I say, but I feel heat rushing up from my neck to my cheeks as my mouth falls open. I'm still shaking my head, my hand pressed to my chest as I twist to angle my good side to the camera. "Actually, I haven't looked at it in a while. I didn't know, but that number is *wild*."

Yeah, this isn't bad.

"Wild is right, Rox. What does attention like that do for a small business? Tell us what inspired the video." She tips her chin up to look at me over the bridge of her pin-straight nose and clasps her hands.

I'm just glad we're veering into talk about Love & Games.

"Ms. Ling—"

"Call me Jennifer, please." Her smile teeters on genuine and I feel myself softening.

For the next few minutes, we go over everything step by step, beginning with the BusinessFunder account I set up to crowd-source funds to save Love & Games. All it took was the perfect rom-com movie groveling scene brought to life. The people liked, subscribed, and clicked in droves. The rest is viral history.

"Love sells, and we were hoping some of it would also sell games," I say.

Jennifer Ling clasps her hands. "That was some quick thinking."

"Risky, but thankfully it worked."

"Speaking of love and games..." She attempts to segue into Monopoly and my dating life, and I quickly redirect to the merits of Trivial Pursuit, my favorite board game, thinking about how well this interview is going.

Well, if this is the worst of it, then I'm good.

Soon, the conversation volleys at an easy rhythm for a bit until she brings us full circle.

"Do the numbers translate to sales?"

"Thankfully." I laugh.

But she continues to probe until I outline all the things a viral number of views affords a small business: increased traffic, an undeniable spike in sales, local celebrity—for Harper and Declan. Our BusinessFunder crowd-sourcing account is still getting donations. Not to mention we're receiving invites to snazzy parties, fan gifts, and brand spokesperson requests. "Interviews like this one," I quip, even if I am still unclear why our story is assigned to an investigative reporter...

"Other than the messages from guys offering to be my sugar daddy"—I cringe, recalling some of the creepy DMs—"the publicity has been freaking great." So much so that, after more than a year, I'm finally feeling at ease with the trajectory and solvency of our business.

Enough to shift—at least a fraction—of my focus and attention.

Find love.

My immediate thought goes to Dad. It took him four marriages and there's still no guarantee he's found true love. Actual love. I don't want to go through multiple marriages to get it right. I'm willing to take time, figure out what the heck I want the first time. Especially if the history of Sloane women giving up after a single setback is any indicator.

I've got one shot. I'm not throwing it away on just anyone.

"It must be a lot to handle."

Jennifer's voice jolts me back to reality, and I smile.

"Definitely. It's been a whirlwind, but it's a welcome one. We're so grateful to our growing community," I say, beaming. My nerves have eased up on me. My shoulders are relaxed. The early afternoon sun streaming through my blinds has neutralized the selfie light, and dare I say it, I'm actually looking hot on camera.

Hot enough to—hopefully—steal some unsuspecting, but well-adjusted, emotionally mature, settled viewer's eye.

"Yes..." Jennifer trails off and tucks a bone-straight onyx strand behind her ear, focusing on the papers in front of her for a sec.

But then she lifts her gaze to me again, and there's amusement stewing in her espresso eyes.

"Speaking of your BusinessFunder donations, I'm sure that you've already used most of the funds as listed on the public account toward your lease, utilities, accounts payable, fixed assets, and inventory."

Something passes over her face I can't quite place.

Where is she going with this?

"Absolutely." I swallow, nodding slowly. "Because the donations received are taxable income, we've offset all but our recurring expenses."

When she takes a long pause again, my mind spirals.

Jennifer Ling is a self-proclaimed scam-buster. I've seen more than a few of her of tax exposés... *Shit! That's what this is. She's reviewed our tax returns and found an error. She's probably teamed up with some auditor friend and this is it. Jennifer Ling is going to publicly crucify me and Love & Games. We're going down.*

A shudder washes over me. My heart knocks around in my chest. Panic flares in my gut. All the air in my lungs lodges in my throat, and there's a strong chance I might faint.

"As you know, I'm the chief reporter for Channel 5's Top Tax Scams." My pulse thunders. *Here it comes.* "I hate to be the one to inform you about this, but during my preparation for the interview it's come to my attention that a shadow account has mirrored your BusinessFunder account."

Wait, what?

"What?" My eyebrows trench and I feel my entire face twist in confusion.

"Your account is listed under Love & Games Store with your University Avenue address. However, I've discovered an account with the name Love & Games *Shop* on University *Lane*," she clarifies. "There is no business filed with the Secretary of State under the latter. Nor is there a street with that suffix."

And there it is.

The curveball.

All the air in my body plumes out of me. My shoulders sag at my sides as I shake my head. *What the actual fuck?*

Behind her, the giant television plays a live news feed. The screen isn't halved with the two of us anymore. For a few seconds, it's just my face taking up the whole screen. There I am. Looking feverish with my mouth wide open. Eyes overbright, a flush of red-hot shock swarms over my skin.

Of course they freeze-frame me looking deranged.

Mother... No, no, no, no. Harper and Nadia are watching this, probably freaking out, too.

I open my mouth and *try* to speak. I really do, but nothing comes out except for an ear-piercing squeak.

"I'm sorry to be the one to tell you all of this." Jennifer Ling dips her chin solemnly.

When I'm finally able to string words together, I eke out, "So, someone is trying to steal our donations?" I have this niggling need to wrap my head around this new information overwhelming me.

On cue, Jennifer Ling nods sympathetically, her thin lips pressed tight. Her expression is heartfelt and solemn, but I can almost see her writing her Pulitzer acceptance speech.

"There is a silver lining, though, Rox." *Seriously?* "After some digging, I've found a way to stop the bleeding." *Have you now?* She nods like she's reading my mind. "Immediately after I discovered this unthinkable situation, I reported it to the IRS and the Federal Trade Commission. An investigation is underway as we speak."

A mirthless laugh pushes past my lips.

It's a strange feeling of pained relief. There's an ongoing investigation which will surely prove those thieves wrong, but what about the donations we haven't transferred yet?

"What's going to happen to the funds that were rightfully donated to us?"

Quick to respond, she squints and nods. "Absolutely. Great question. Unfortunately, the funds in both accounts are frozen until the investigation is complete, but we have every hope all capital raised will be returned to Love & Games Store."

I fold my arm over my chest and prop the elbow of the other on it, massaging my temple. *That's the silver lining?*

Naturally, Jennifer sniffs through my thoughts.

"As a courtesy, Channel 5 Action News has arranged for JWC Business Solutions to complete an audit at no expense to Love & Games."

An audit?

God, why did I let down my guard? This is Jennifer Ling. Of course she's got something up her ridiculously expensive sleeveless blouse. It's not enough she's broadcasted to the world that we've not only been duped, but donations stolen, assets frozen by the freaking FTC. And now we're being audited? *Audited?*

What if I'm missing a receipt or my math is off?

No. No, no, no, no, no.

Every white-collar crime drama I've ever seen reels across my mind. Hyperaggressive, tough-talking suits drilling us for paper-filing blunders or typos. What if I entered the wrong filing status?

The shell-shocked image of me flashes across the screen again as Jennifer Ling wraps up my world-shattering segment. I thank her for having me and sign off. Not just disconnect. I shut the whole dang laptop down and close it. For a moment, I deflate against my chair, still in a state of shock.

This was not the plan.

I'm officially freaked the freak out.

CHAPTER TWO

MURPH

Q: The Fourth of July commemorates which document?

A: The Declaration of Independence

A LAUGH BELLOWS above the restaurant chatter, pulling my gaze away from my phone. Every table bustles with the vibrant, carefree easiness of the holiday crowd. Local and tourist sun-followers alike, all dressed in some variation of red, white, and blue beach wear. It's summer in San Diego. What better excuse does anyone need to enjoy a surf'n'turf interrogation brunch on an airy patio overlooking Mission Bay? I, for one, can't wait for my parents and Nadia to get here, so we can begin the festivities—and quickly end them.

I scan the room, never settling on anyone or anything for too long.

"You sure I can't get you anything while you wait?" A young, brown-eyed server with a pile of curls on her head pauses in front of my table. She's got a large round serving tray stacked with steaming-hot plates balanced on her shoulder, but she smiles sweetly, glancing at the three empty chairs around me.

"No, thanks." She sinks her teeth into her lower lip, presumably giving me a chance to change my mind. "They should be here any minute."

"Anything at all?"

Again, she fixes a pointed stare on me for a beat too long.

Normally I'd take the bait. Let it reel me in for a night. This girl is cute, and as much as I wouldn't mind dipping out, doing all the things her words and eyes suggest, it won't save me. One way or another, Mom and Dad will weave their usual *why don't you settle down with a nice young lady* talk into the conversation. *Might as well get it over with.*

I decline the offer—implied or otherwise.

Whatever is so important my parents canceled their trip to New York this summer, I need to hear about it.

Tipping my head to my water glass, already dripping with condensation, I flash her a small smile. "Thanks, I'm good for now."

She lingers a second longer, but then her attention falls to my phone, and I follow her gaze as it scans the Channel 5 Action News headline, *Love, Games, and Scams.*

"Not gonna lie, I've watched that video like a dozen times, and Jennifer Ling is a piece of *work.*" She shakes her head. "The way she did Roxanne Sloane, buttering her up before she dropped that bomb on her… It was just dirty if you ask me."

I nod absently, letting my faraway gaze slip past her.

"Okie doke." The server shrugs, shaking her head. "I'll be back to check on you in a few minutes." Then, she moves on to deliver the food to the next table, and I'm left with a far-too-familiar uneasiness.

Protective instincts swell inside me, smoothing and hardening my expression, tugging at the cords of my neck.

Rox Sloane and I have a simple relationship. There's attraction there for sure, but we've never crossed that line. The way I see it, she's my sister's friend and business partner, which makes her part of our lives. *And off-limits.* Not that relationships are my thing. Between my otolaryngology practice and owning a home, I've got enough strings.

I think we both know she wants the fairy tale.

So, unless it involves our sisters, Rox and I don't make it a point to hang out or call on any regular basis. Though, I hope she knows if she needs me, I'll drop everything.

Right now, she may not be ready to admit it, but I see the cracks. The tiny fissures splicing through the tough-as-nails facade she's put up, and I'm worried about her. I won't overstep her boundaries, but everything in me needs to make sure she is okay.

I care too much not to.

My thoughts drift to Mom all those years ago, bedridden, and weak, too proud to ask for the support she needed. And Dad, only thinking of himself when he should have been beside her whether she voiced it or not.

Family—or even complicated friendships—they shouldn't have to ask. *Rox shouldn't have to ask.*

I shove the thought aside and click the X in the top right corner of the video to close it. When I swipe over to messages, I'm surprised not to see a *"running late"* text from Nadia or a missed phone call from my parents. I close my eyes, pinching the bridge of my nose between my thumb and forefinger.

But then I spot my sister beelining for the table.

"Thank *God* I made it before them." Nadia plops down on the seat next to me, releasing an exhausted sigh. "I hope I'm not too late for mimosas."

I shoot her a sidelong glance. She's wearing a red-and-white polka-dot sundress. Her short blond hair is parted and tucked behind her ear, and she's wearing full makeup, which means she took her time getting ready. But as oblivious as she can be to other people's worries, seeing her eases a little of the tension tangled in my shoulders.

"Glad you decided to show up." I shake my head and toss her a small smile.

"Happy Fourth of July to you, too, ding dong." She rolls her bright blue eyes and shoves her hand into her purse before fishing out a tube of pale pink gloss. As she twists off the top and glides it across her lips, she groans. "Don't even start. You know I hate these brunches as much as you do."

"Doubtful."

Her upper lip curls because we both know she won't win this argument.

Nadia is the free spirit of the family. My unpredictable baby sister. At thirty-two, she goes and does as she pleases, and Mom and Dad don't give her the slightest pushback. When Nadia broke the news that she and the Sloane sisters were starting a business—and followed through with it—she absolved herself of all future parental demands. If one day she settles down and bears children, they might lasso the moon and name it after her.

"Whatever." Nadia squints at the menu, probably hunting for something post-worthy. "What are you ordering?"

I rub my hand over my face again and look back at the restaurant entrance. Mom and Dad are *five minutes early is on time* people. I can't think about my stomach with all the worst-case scenarios gnawing at me.

"Have you talked to Mom this morning?"

"Yeah, she said they're slow moving today..." Nadia trails off. She doesn't lift her gaze from the menu long enough to notice the way my posture slumps, the slight tension draining from my body. "I think I'm going to go with the shrimp tacos and the blueberry lemonade mimosa."

With that all worked out, she sets the menu on the table and stares out at the water, but I sense the strained silence.

"Any idea what this brunch is about?" I ask.

When she meets my gaze again, she heaves a sigh.

Every twist of her expression tells me she knows what I'm doing. "Can you not give them a hard time today?" She says *them*, but we both know it's not Mom and me who butt heads.

"Yeah." A humorless laugh huffs out of me as I scratch my chin. "Yeah, I'm the one giving *them* a hard time. Sure. That's it."

Vivian and Allen Sikes are snowbirds who usually spend the warm months in New York and the cold season here. Both retirees—a senior editor for a publishing house and a cardiologist, respectively. They're upstanding community members and empty nesters with two successful adult children, the white-picket-fenced house, and a feisty golden doodle.

When it comes down to it, Mom is unassuming and pries too much, but I know it's because she cares. Dad is stoic and quiet, harsh when he speaks. Further reason we rarely do.

To the outside world, they are this picture-perfect couple who proved they can have it all. They mastered their careers, then had children later in life, and came through it happily married for almost forty years. People look at them like some example to follow. I've seen them my whole life from the inside. To me, their loveless marriage is the one thing I don't want.

"You're such an ass sometimes," Nadia says.

Because I really don't want to get into this right now, I change the subject. "How's everything with Love & Games since the news broke?"

Her shoulders sag and she lets her head fall back with a sigh. "Serious? Now you're trying to act like you're so concerned?"

I don't validate her comments with an answer. She knows damn well how I feel about her and the Sloane sisters.

"Fine." She crosses her arms over her chest and tosses me a smirk. "Harper's all freaked out about this auditor coming tomorrow. She's doing these elaborate window displays and reorganizing our entire inventory like this person's going to give us demerits for being messy and not alphabetizing the board games."

"So, other than that, the three of you are okay?"

Nadia dips her chin and pins me with a pointed stare. Her lips twitch as she bites back a laugh.

"All *three* of us are doing fine…" She trails off, laughing at my expense. "If you want to know how Rox is doing, why don't you just ask? Or call her yourself? You act so ridiculous about her." She flicks her eyes skyward.

I stare at the city sprawled out beyond the bay.

"Fine. How is she? Has the backlash from the interview taken a toll on her?" Heat creeps into my cheeks. Inwardly, I'm wincing that my sister can read me so easily.

When I turn back to Nadia, movement over her shoulder snags my attention, pulling like a loose thread.

It's Dad's jutting chin and slightly curved broad shoulders that pierces through the crowd first. He's aloof and unsmiling as usual, but the way his heavy brow wrinkles draws my attention to his labored trudge.

He looks right past me to Nadia, and that's when I catch sight of Mom. Her prominent cheekbones climb up to her sparkly blue eyes at the sight of us. She's got on her favorite royal-blue track suit with sneakers and her thin gray hair is curled today, but I can't pull my attention away from the oxygen tank as she struggles to drag it behind her.

A war between fear, fury, and numbing sadness wages inside me.

Has it been that long since I last saw them? When did she become so fragile and small?

My throat tightens around thoughts of the unthinkable. Of all those worst-case scenarios that ran through my mind, this wasn't one of them. Somehow, I keep forgetting that while I'm getting older every year, so are they.

Obviously, I know death is an inevitable part of life we all must grow to accept, but the thought of losing them always seemed so far off.

Fuck.

Agonizing fear splinters through me as a wave of icy panic washes over me. An urge to protect them, preserve them somehow. I scramble to my feet, taking wide, hurried strides until I'm in front of them.

"Oh, now, don't you dare give me that face, Teddy," Mom chastises me, using her pet name for me. After my middle name, Theodore. "I'm fine. I'm just not as fast as I used to be, and my lungs need a little help. Don't get old." She chuckles.

I force a smile and carefully wrap my arms around her, hating how much I wish I could freeze time. My pulse picks up as I chew the inside of my cheek to keep from crying. My heart feels like someone is wringing all the life from it.

"Murphy," Dad finally acknowledges me as I hook Mom's arm on to mine, guiding her to the table. "It's good to see you, son."

My throat constricts as my eyes latch on to him.

I'm hardwired to meet his words with animosity. The sight of him has never failed to bring all the anger I've been harboring toward him to the surface. Somehow, my focus always zeros in on him ever one step ahead of Mom. Never holding hands. They don't have fun or kiss. Their lives are as separate as the beds they sleep in.

In the back of my mind, the days he left her in that hospital bed to fend for herself while she fought off pneumonia and hypoxia with strangers taking care of her, he'd showed exactly how much she meant to him. What Mom and Dad shared had never been a marriage, and I couldn't let go of the idea it was a business arrangement in which he never held up his end of the bargain.

If that was what marriage was, I didn't want any part of it.

It made me ache for my childhood when I'd been blissfully ignorant about marriage. When other parents who hugged and kissed and showed affection made my stomach turn. Before I ever considered divorce might have been a better option.

But today, my heart keeps arguing none of that matters now. When it comes down to it, it's the *only* thing that matters.

"Hey, Dad," I mutter, even though it feels like it's going against the grain.

When we're all seated again, the server makes her way back over to take our food and drink orders. We all take our cue from Nadia when the woman raves about the shrimp tacos, and order the same along with waters, beers, Nadia's blueberry lemonade mimosa, and a strawberry lemonade for Mom.

Nadia must register the pain gripping my chest because she reaches over and kneads my shoulder.

"It's okay," she reassures me. "We're all together now."

I nod and listen as Nadia updates them about Love & Games, giving them all the details about Rox's interview. She's animated with wild hands and expressions, dramatically answering Mom's questions about Jennifer Ling.

Dad actually looks interested when the conversation turns to me, and I tell them I'm being honored this year at the Academy of Otolaryngology Conference in Las Vegas at the end of July. I expect Mom's proud excitement; she loves hard and unconditionally. But to see Allen Sikes's stony expression warm with a genuine smile…

It makes me feel like maybe I've been building walls between us for too long. Maybe I couldn't see past my resentment. Maybe I stopped seeing *him* somewhere along the way.

"Teddy, that's amazing," Mom coos, continuing with her request. "Now which days are you going to be gone? You know our fortieth anniversary is coming up on Sunday the twenty-fifth. If you and your sister are free, we were thinking of having dinner some place nice, like La Dinette or Francesco's. Nothing too fussy, just the four of us…"

Nadia snickers because we can both fill in the blanks.

"Or, if either of you are seeing anyone important, of course, they're welcome, too." Her gaze flits between the two of us like she's dissecting our reactions for hints about secret relationships.

I have to bite my tongue not to laugh aloud.

"Let's see, the conference starts that Wednesday, the twenty-first, through Saturday. I booked an extra day, so I'm coming back Sunday morning."

The disappointment etched on Mom's face when neither of us offers information about significant others is classic. "Well, that should be fine. We wouldn't make reservations earlier than six or seven in the evening. That'll give you some time to rest a bit."

"I'm in," Nadia adds quickly.

The funny thing is, Mom's still itching to dig a little deeper. So, when she shifts in her chair to face me and asks, "Why don't you settle down with a nice young lady, Teddy?

Or, young man, if that's your preference. We're up with the times," Nadia and I cringe, then burst out laughing when Mom looks put off.

I drop my head in my hands, my shoulders shaking.

"Thanks, Mom, but there's no one special at the moment," I mutter with a wide smile. Except, even as I say the words, I'm not sure why Rox's face pops into my head.

CHAPTER THREE

ROX

Q: Commonly performed by a certified public accountant, what process is conducted to review a company's financial statements and internal controls?

A: An audit

I LOOK OVER the top of my book at Harper. She's put up—and taken down—the same bright yellow SUMMER FUN & GAMES sign a good dozen times since we got to Love & Games *two hours* early. To do nothing more than move game boxes around, vacuum, and dust. Like, seriously. What does she think is going to happen today?

"Can you please stop rearranging stuff?" I shoot my sister a deadpan expression.

We're all nervous. We get it.

Harper looks over to Nadia behind the counter at the register to cosign, but as usual, her asymmetrical blond bob is in her face, eyes glued to her phone to keep her mind off her nerves. *Like a normal person.*

"Sorry." Harper heaves a frustrated sigh. Her hands are planted on her hips, but she doesn't stop scanning the space for the *one last thing* she can do before this so-called *detail-demon* barges in here to condemn us for all our failures as business owners.

Yeah, this ought to be fun.

Not that I don't get where Harp is coming from. It's Monday and some random business advisor will be here when the store opens to conduct a full *business assessment.* I don't even know what that entails. We weren't given an exact time. We don't know who is coming, and Jennifer Ling called it an audit. For all we know, it could be the whole dang IRS at our front door. So, like I said, I get it.

It's nerve-racking.

But it's not the health department or The Home Edit women. We're not being judged on cleanliness or how well we color coordinate our organization and storage systems. *Although, I will say, it doesn't hurt that we've got the form-meets-function thing down.*

The store itself is the one thing we have going for us.

Love & Games is magical with its bright, oversized wall graphics and classic board game motif. It's got open shelves heaped with stacks of game boxes, books, and action figures. The atmosphere is playful, but cozy. It's a one-of-a-kind wonderland the three of us conceptualized and brought to life at my kitchen table over wine coolers.

What I'm worried about is what Ling told this guy. *Or gal.*

I might not show it, but I'm shaking in my hot pink ballet flats, too. I just don't go into psycho-cleaning mode hyped up on caffeine to deal with my worries. Dating how-to books and romance novels are my go-to vice for anxiety. But how can I get past the same paragraph of *The Blame Game* that I've read FIVE times when my sister is literally short-circuiting in front of me?

We're not in trouble.

"Relax." I slowly lower my chin to my chest as I survey my sister's wild espresso waves, big forest green eyes, and dark circles over the bridge of my nose. "Not gonna lie, learning about the BusinessFunder scam on broadcast television wasn't ideal." *Understatement of the year.* I press my palms against the air. "But...maybe this is a good thing."

The other two-thirds of this business ownership release a collective groan.

"After everything we've been through almost losing the store, it might be nice to have an unbiased third party corroborate what we already know." They look at me expectantly. "That we're *fine.*"

The death glares crush me. Anyone who has watched Jennifer Ling's tax scam exposés knows she doesn't hop on a bandwagon with nowhere to go.

"Just hear me out." I let my gaze dart between my sister and Nadia, making sure they're listening. "That video may have gotten us the attention we needed to crowd-source the funds, but *we* did the work. *We* paid off all our creditors and used the media storm to our advantage to market the hell out of this business. *We* did that. I'm not letting anyone take that away from us. Period."

Nadia's shoulders sag, but she nods.

"Oh, and if I'm not mistaken, it's the *Monopoly Queen*

who cleared our entire inventory of Monopoly board games by doing photo ops and autographs. Am I right?" *I'm totally on my soapbox right now, but we are not about to stop planning the store's fifth anniversary just because some rando will be here in...* I check my watch and start moving to the front door to flip the sign. "So what if the rest of the donated funds are frozen? We've got this."

"You're right." Harper flashes me a beaming full-teeth smile, indicating my pep talk is indeed working. "Thanks. I needed to hear that. Between the business and Declan acting all weird lately, I'm a freaking basket case."

I tilt my head in question, but she holds up her palm and shakes her head.

"No, it's nothing to worry about... I think I'm just reading too much into everything," which is just extra vague. She pinches the bridge of her nose. "He locked the bedroom door for a few minutes the other day. Not even. Maybe seconds, but it totally threw me..."

With my hand on the lock, I pantomime taking a deep breath and exhaling the stress away before I turn to unlock thc door.

We will talk about this later.

I open the door and freeze. Nadia's head pops up from her phone. "What? Are they here? How many?" she asks, panic streaking her stormy blue eyes.

I should just tell her it's one advisor out on the sidewalk. Not tall, but easily taller than me in heels. A mess of dark waves tapered around the edges, smoldering green eyes, and a five-o'clock shadow—which, technically, isn't a beard, but close enough.

Of note, he's giving me European vibes.

French, specifically.

It's the perfectly cut suit. The kind you know doesn't come off the rack. A thin black tie and crisp white button-down against tanned skin.

Oof, and those lips.

They're set into a slight pout, like at any moment he could fix them to mouth, *Je t'aime…*

So, yeah, I should probably share that information with my overly anxious business partners, but I'm too busy drooling.

Because I'm the finance end of Love & Games, I figured I'd be quarantined to the back office with some droning numbers guy inundating me with spreadsheet after spreadsheet and talking my ear off.

Not the case. So *not the case.*

I swallow. "Good God…" The words spill out of me onto the floor along with my jaw.

Before he can make it to the door, Harper sidles up beside me. I think she's going to tell me to stop gawking, but then she gets a glimpse of what I'm seeing.

"Amen to that," she murmurs in solidarity.

He doesn't have to reach for the door because Harper holds it open for him to enter. Again, a greeting would be fitting, but the two of us just stare.

My mouth is dry, and I can't stop imagining I'm in the middle of a meet-cute in one of my contemporary romance novels.

"Hello, I'm Jacques Chastain." *Definite romance-novel-hero name material.* He extends his large hand to me, but I've forgotten how to use words *and* my motor skills. If I'm not hallucinating, there's the tiniest hint of a French accent.

Oui...

I might die. I know what I said about taking my time to figure out what the heck I want in a man the first time. Mentally, I'm already flipping the pages of my *Book of Lists* to the top five on my "One Shot" list: attractive, loves his family, loves Trivial Pursuit, wants a lasting, loving relationship. Me and the guy will have the *zing*. As in, just being near the person stirs up all kinds of butterflies, tingles down my spine.

Immediately the air feels charged and I'm overheating.

This is my bookish workplace romance fantasy come to life. He's already hot. Check. If he knows how to play Trivial Pursuit, I will at least let him make me French toast, or fries. Ooh, or beignets. Baguettes!

Holy...

When neither Harper nor I move an inch, he lowers his head and a devastatingly beautiful smile spreads across his face.

I have to thank the heavens and the stars for Nadia, who is immune to masculine charms, being the charmer herself. "Welcome. I'm Nadia, one of the owners. I'll show you around." She flashes him a sweet smile before rolling her eyes at us as she leads him on a small tour of the space.

The bell above the door jingles, breaking the spell.

A handful of customers enter and immediately commandeer Harper, leaving me alone near the door. From where I'm standing, I get a firsthand view of my sister. She's totally in her element as she poses for selfies and offers to sign the last Monopoly game in stock.

Eventually, I get my act—and my vocal cords—together and go talk to Jacques, who is surprisingly down-to-earth. He doesn't immediately whip out our financial statements or drill me about the Ling interview.

"So, how is it working so closely with your sister?" His expression smooths slightly, and he seems genuinely interested in learning about us as much as the business.

Slipping my hands into the back pockets of my slim fit jeans, I lean against the counter facing the register. "I love it. My sister, Nadia, and I are tight-knit. We trust each other. We trust this dream we're living." I chuckle, embarrassed by how corny I sound, but it's true.

He shakes his head, his eyebrows bouncing up. "I don't know how you do it. I'm not close to my family at all. I can't imagine being stuck with any of them in a professional environment where we're required to behave."

I flash him a soft smile, but I'm already unchecking the "loves his family" box, which is a big one.

While I'm kind of bummed about it, I love the fact our conversation zigzags freely between business and idle talk. I tell him about the Vegas weekend the girls and I have planned for my thirtieth birthday at the end of the month. He goes on about his horse, Luc. I'll admit, as he talks, his throaty voice fills my mind with many lurid images of corded, muscular forearms and a clenched butt.

He's still distractingly hot, but…not a single butterfly or tingle. Zero zing. Other than the obvious appreciation for his physical lottery luck, no sparks flickering. *Shit.*

Honestly, I'm beating myself up.

I'm so tired of chasing goosebumps and sparks. Why can't I build something real with a guy like Jacques? He isn't wearing a ring. He's romance-hero gorgeous. Why should I discount all that because he's missing two boxes on my list?

Okay, two huge *boxes.*

I'm jinxed by genetics. I don't want do-over marriages or a life of solitude—even if the latter sounds less exhausting.

That's the downward spiraling thought process zipping through my head as Jacques and I dip into the stockroom.

At least let him like Trivial Pursuit.

"Whoa!" Jacques skirts to a halt in the doorway. His mossy green eyes are wide as he surveys the board game back stock towering dangerously close to the ceiling.

Right. I need to focus on what's important. Games, not so much the love.

"I know." I wince. "It's a lot."

The unwavering deadpan directed at me sends a giggle bubbling in my throat. I bite my lip not to laugh in his face.

"Let me get this straight. Love & Games can't keep Monopoly in stock, but you have... How many editions of Trivial Pursuit is that? Ballpark, I'm seeing at least, thirteen, fourteen—"

"Twenty." I toss him a defiant, chin-raised, firm-eye-contact stare. "It's the most important, well-rounded board game there is. You actually learn something worth remembering when you play. It's not my fault people fail to appreciate its world-changing quality."

Jacques wants to laugh. His lips twitch and he still hasn't looked at me, but he nods. "Okay. I'm more of a Scrabble guy, but which edition here is your favorite? Maybe that's a better question to start with."

I blow out an exasperated sigh. *Uncheck.*

He clears his throat and slips a manila folder from underneath his arm, flipping to a tabbed page midway down the stack. "You've got *five hundred* Trivial Pursuit games in stock. The next closest item is Clue with only fifty..."

The way he trails off, I know he's trying to make a point.

I *see* his point.

Perhaps I was a little overzealous when we were building our inventory. But what's the alternative—throw them out, donate them? A deep discount feels like a dagger to my trivia-loving heart.

I stubbornly fold my arms across my chest, chewing the inside of my cheek. "For what it's worth, we didn't buy them all at once," I hedge, but even I hear how weak my argument is.

"And they're taking up valuable space on the shelf..." He peeks over at me, seemingly to determine if anything he's saying is sinking into my thick skull. "Where there could be more Monopoly games people are actually *buying*." His voice goes low and careful, like he knows this is a sensitive subject for me.

The man has no idea.

We were this close to losing this business. I'm trying to redeem myself here. There's no way I'm going to do it as the *Monopoly Queen's sister* or by discounting the merits of Trivial Pursuit. *Literally.* I've spent the last few years working on this business, and making sure Dad was finally happy and Harper got her man. At some point, I need to step out of my sister's shadow and focus on me.

For a beat, I gnaw on my lower lip, but all I come up with is "There won't be another Monopoly tournament until next year."

It's the principle.

Jacques closes his folder and turns to me. "Believe it or not, I'm here to help." It's soft and genuine. I feel the tension in my shoulders and neck loosen. "Maybe this is a good time to go over the trends I noticed while reviewing your financials."

With a conceding nod, I lead the way back to my office.

We sit on opposite sides of the glass desk, facing each other. My attention snags on his elbows propped on the edge of the desk, his fingertips tapping lightly against his cheek.

"First, let me say your resourcefulness in saving this business is commendable. You didn't give up." He answers my soft smile with a matching one. "Now, I know you didn't seek my services, but I'm here and I want to help if you'll let me. In your survey, you said your goal was to grow the business. My goal is to help you do just that."

He continues to explain how he assesses business viability, looking for ways to help maximize strategic options and see the companies he works with emerge stronger with a more solid foundation for growth. He looks for financial stress trends to be eliminated to enable immediate recovery.

Which sounds all good and fine, but I'm lost.

Love & Games is in a good place. Yes, having our extra safety net scammed sucks, but our sales are through the roof. We've finally put ourselves on the map. That's got to count for something.

We're fine.

Aren't we?

"What are you saying?" My tone drips with trepidation and a little resentment that I need to ask a third party about the stability of our business. My pulse quickens and heat swarms over my skin. "What were the trends?"

He clasps his hands and tips his chin up, but my stomach is all tied up in knots.

My heart is in my throat when his gaze lands on mine.

"Look, don't get me wrong. The three of you have done an outstanding job. The way you've cut spending and prioritized your payables is the best start to a stable business." He pauses and I hear the *but* before he says it. "But your cash flow is limited, the money you're making isn't covering your overhead on each sale, and as we just saw, you seriously need to liquidate inventory."

Shit.

His words hit me like a freight truck, and I'm biting a scream. Here I thought an assessment would confirm business is booming, that the changes we've made have course-corrected us. That the influx of traffic and sales since the viral video, while I knew it wouldn't last, had at least given us enough of a boost to build something sustainable.

Once again, I've been holding on to a false sense of security.

Heat creeps into my cheeks and my scalp prickles with shame. I can't go through this again.

Then he hits me with his take on a genuine silver lining. An action plan aimed at immediate results. "Reevaluate pricing and unload excess inventory—starting with Trivial Pursuit."

I slowly blow out a breath and nod.

"I'm game."

If Harper can make Monopoly a must-buy, I can do the same with Trivial Pursuit. There aren't any tournaments I know of, but I'll think of something. Whatever it is, the bleeding stops right here and now.

Before Jacques can say another word, I'm up off my chair, headed for the stockroom, where I grab as many classic editions as I can carry. The man is literally laughing at me, but when I set my mind to an action plan, I don't need to think about it.

No distractions.

"What are you going to do?" he asks, trailing behind me as I stride to the front of the store where Harper left her SUMMER FUN & GAMES sign.

He helps me set the boxes on the floor, and one by one I remove the hodgepodge mess of games Harper displayed earlier, replacing them with the most beautiful blue and gold boxes to hit Hasbro Nation.

The funny part is that his laugh is contagious. He's got one of those warm, throaty laughs, funnier than the joke.

Good-naturedly, I shoot him a scrunched-face grimace and stick my tongue out at him, which only makes me laugh harder. I'm doubled over, my hand pressed to my chest, gasping for breath when the bell above the front door jingles.

"Welcome to Love & Gam—" I clamp my mouth shut when I take in the man standing before me.

Murphy "Murph" Theodore Sikes, M.D. Nadia's brother, whom I have crushed on for all my twenties. Sadly, it's a condition unlikely to stop in my thirties given the swarm of butterflies in my belly.

For all intents and purposes, if Jacques is romance novel princely material, Murph is the quintessential bad boy. Rake. Broody. Smoldering charmer who does the lazy lean in a doorway. The all-around player with the typical aversion to commitment, all rolled into one.

Or, as I like to think of him, *forbidden.*

Yeah, checking off all the boxes for a torrid one-night stand—which I'm certainly not in the market for.

But goodness if he isn't dangerously easy on the eyes.

Tall, lean muscles, product-whipped sandy blond hair. Looks like a beachy sex god with tropical blue eyes and a fresh-from-vacation glow. *Like, come on!* It's unnerving, really. Most of the time he's in scrubs, but his style trends toward comfort. Jeans and useless white T-shirts that do little to hide the tapestry of tattoos on his sculpted body.

Tingles race down my spine.

"Hey, Rox." He drags his tongue over his pouty lower lip before sinking his teeth into it, and my knees turn to liquid.

No do-overs in the forecast, I remind myself. There hasn't been a first to do over, but it's a good rule to keep at the top of my mind.

I clear my throat as his gaze skates over my skin.

"Hey."

We're both staring at each other awkwardly, so it's understandable that Jacques excuses himself to go talk to Harper and Nadia. I assume. Can't be sure because Murph has all my attention. Part of me wants to put on my fun, carefree mask and act like this isn't weird, but curiosity takes over. I'm dying to know why Murph is here.

The air is charged with uncertainty.

I hike up a curious eyebrow at him.

Warmth spreads through me as he lowers his chin to his chest. "I know you said you were fine." He nods, smiling. "I just wanted to check on you all—see for myself, if that's okay…"

You all… He's here to check on his sister, the three of us. Like a package deal.

It shouldn't, but disappointment drags my shoulders down.

His gaze darts past me over toward Harper's, Nadia's, and Jacques's voices before his seaside-blue eyes begrudgingly settle on me again.

Looks like my plan to limit distractions and focus on the business is still intact.

CHAPTER FOUR

MURPH

Q: What song by former boy band singer Nick Jonas was inspired by his real experience with then-girlfriend Olivia Culpo?

A: "Jealous"

ROX LOOKS LIKE she wants the floor to open up and swallow her whole rather than stand here with me.

Honestly, I don't blame her. We both know I'm stalling.

Why couldn't I just make up a reason for stopping by the store, ensure she looked okay, then leave like I'd planned? Why didn't I believe her when she said she was "fine"? Better yet why am *I still here?*

"So…" Rox quirks a soft smile.

Everything about this moment feels awkward, forced. I should leave. I did what I came here to do. I checked on her, and Rox is better than *fine*. She's apparently all laughs with men she just met.

Heat flushes through my tense body, my pulse racing.

I toss a glance over Rox's shoulder at the man she'd been

laughing with when I walked in. They were *just* laughing. They weren't even close enough to hint at anything more, but that doesn't make me want to wipe the smile off this guy's face any less.

Everything about him rubs me wrong. I know his type. Smooth, overly eager, ladies' man, ready to do extra to win over some unsuspecting woman. He's a tallish, decent-looking guy with dark hair and a style sense that apparently includes skinny ties. I'm strictly jeans and T-shirts out of scrubs. To say we're different is putting it lightly.

But then there's the way she'd looked at him...

Like he's worth every second of her attention. Like she can't tear her eyes away. Like he stepped out of her romance novels...

Is this the kind of guy Rox is into?

"Is that the guy?" I cross my arms in front of my chest and jerk my chin toward the counter where he's standing with Nadia and Harper. "The business advisor the news station sent over," I clarify.

Rox pivots to follow my line of vision, but she doesn't turn back around. Not right away. She stares at him a bit too long to be insignificant. Not that she owes me an explanation. We're just friends, but I can't discount the flash of anger that sears through me, watching Rox with him.

A tightness settles in my chest like my ribs are squeezing together.

I tell myself what I'm feeling is normal. That anyone would be irritable with a strange man around three women I care about. That I'm just as protective of Harper and Nadia. But I talk to my sister all the time. Harper is dating my best friend. If I want to know how she's doing, I can ask Declan.

Everything with Rox feels different.

"Yeah, Jacques Chastain from JWC Business Solutions. It's his company," she finally mutters, clearly impressed. She turns her focus to the game boxes on the display table in front of us. Absently, she straightens and stacks them in a pyramid.

There's a faraway look in her coppery brown eyes.

I catch myself studying her delicate features, searching for hints of where her mind's gone. She's got a beauty that sneaks up on you. Fresh face without much makeup, but then there's sunlight imbued in her honey-colored eyes. I get lost in the way her dark brown waves and face-framing golden highlights contrast against the light pink flush to her olive skin. I'm distracted by the slight pout of her pillowy pink lips.

But this is my best friend's future sister-in-law. My sister's business partner…

She tosses me a sidelong glance after a beat.

"Are you sure you're okay?"

The question throws me off. What does she want me to say, *No, I'm killing time because I selfishly don't want to see you flirt with another guy*? That she's important to me, but I can never be what she needs? Because sadly, I already know what the other side of happily-ever-after looks like. There's no such thing. But I don't want to be the asshole who tells her the Tooth Fairy and Santa Claus don't exist.

Settle down.

Mom's words flood my thoughts, muddying everything I thought I knew.

Every inch of me resists the notion of settling. Of a loveless marriage. Of growing old without growing in love. The way I see it, is sharing a lonely life better than being alone? How can I imagine more when I can't separate the thought of settling from settling down?

But seeing Mom and Dad at brunch this past weekend, it shifted my focus somehow. They're still together, propping each other up all these years. I've made judgments about what marriage, what love means, what it's worth... But what do I know?

"Yeah, I'm good."

A small voice inside me keeps pressing the issue, though. Pointing to the throbbing veins at my temple. Zeroing in on the urge to clench my fists when I look at this guy. The voice calls my spade a spade.

I'm fucking jealous as hell.

What can I do about it?

The muscles in my jaw harden as I attempt not to stare Jacques down. It's really none of my business who Rox dates or *laughs* with. I'm not the best fit, but this guy with his skinny tie... He may be dressed the part, but he sure as hell isn't fairy-tale material.

I tear my gaze away, needing to focus somewhere else—*anywhere* else. I center all my attention on one box on the bottom of the pyramid, straightening it, then doing the same on each level.

"We're not hiring, but if you want to volunteer to do our display tables, I think I can work something out..."

We both laugh. Anyone can see I'm stalling. I know I should leave and let her get on with whatever she was doing when I walked in, but my feet are cemented to this spot.

"Would you put a good word in with the boss for me?" I smile.

The thing is, I know what Rox wants. She's always got a romance novel or a book about dating and body language in her purse. From what I've gathered based on Nadia's offhand comments and the things Harper tells Declan, Rox's recent dates have damn near been interviews for the position of husband—complete with checklists and scales of attraction. For Rox, finding love is an intense process that involves research to find the best candidate.

When it comes down to it, I don't do relationships. If it requires anything more than a warm body lying next to me for the night, I lack the desire and the skills. So why even apply?

Love isn't my thing now, likely never, but especially not with Rox Sloane when I'm never going to check the boxes on her list.

But can't we be friends?

"Listen, I've got a lot on my mind, but I worry about you all, though." I scrub a hand over my face. "You didn't ask me to, but I stopped by to make sure you really were okay after the interview. That you felt comfortable with this *person* here. But I guess you really are *fine*." I drag the word out.

Rox's expression softens. Her smile widens as she beams up at me. "You're not going to let this go, are you?"

I shake my head, smiling guiltily as I nudge my shoulder against hers.

"Just so you know, I'm only humoring you because I

don't know if I can handle any more *how are* you all *doing* texts." She heaves an amused sigh, flicking her gaze skyward, but her tone is light and teasing. "Let's just say I've had better days. Scratch that, better *weeks.*"

"That bad, huh?"

Rox kneads the back of her neck like the weight of her worries is crashing down on her. I should offer support. Say something comforting. Reassuring. But all I can focus on is the delicate curve of her neck as she bares her throat to me. The faint moan that slips from her lips as her bright eyes sparkle up at me.

This is the convoluted, complicated part of our relationship. It's like there's a magnetic field around us when we're near each other. As hard as I try to pull away, something keeps pulling me back.

"The funny thing is—"

"Ohh." I chuckle. "You're massaging your neck, and there's a funny part?"

She groans, shaking her head, but her smile is warm and contagious, and I mirror her smile.

"Last week, I was looking forward to the holiday, feeling good." Rox's laugh is musical and airy. "I bought a new dress, made plans to see the fireworks. It's my birthday month—you should come, by the way. We're going to Las Vegas, or The Meadows, if you don't speak Spanish—just a little trivia for you. I'm turning *thirty.*" She groans the word like it's a cutoff. "I even got serious about signing up for another dating…" She trails off, sinking her teeth into her lower lip, but I mentally finish her sentence.

Dating app.

That's when it hits me. I've known women who've doubled down on their dating efforts based on some bucket list timeline. Rox is actively looking for someone because she's turning thirty. Her birthday is putting a rush on her process. It's the only reasonable explanation she'd even consider a guy like this Jacques.

"Sounds like you have a lot on your plate," I murmur, weighing my next move. She must know she's too special to rush into anything based on an invisible ticking clock.

Rox blows out a breath and nods, the corners of her mouth tugging upward. "Anyway, I thought things were finally turning around for me. For Love & Games," she continues, oblivious to the tightness in my chest. "But between that interview, seeing my face freeze-framed and plastered all over social media, the business assessment. Oh, by the way, I'm a meme…" She laughs, dropping her head into her hands. "I'm just…not *fine*." She giggles, backtracking. We both know that word is inadequate for what she's going through. "I'm making do. Is that better? Will that work for you?"

I press a finger to my lips and nod slowly, hating the pressure she's putting on herself.

"You're literally the worst, you know that?" *Her smile is the best.*

"Seriously, though. What can I do to help you *make do*?" I throw air quotes around her words, aiming for casual. Friendly. Because that's what we are. I may not be what she needs, but I can be her friend. That's what I know how to offer.

Her eyes widen and she's staring at me open-mouthed

again like I've just confessed I love Almond Joy *and* Mounds.

"Why do you keep staring at me like that?" I ask, laughter shaking my shoulders. "I came here to check on you. I was worried. It's simple as that. Now, I'm asking if I can be there for you… You know, and my sister and Harper," I scramble to correct myself. "The same way I know you'd be there for me."

She nods, her lips twitching at my noticeably fumbled attempt to make this about the three of them.

"You've never done…" Rox circles her hands between us. "This."

I blow out a lungful of air and scrub my hands over my face.

"It's not every day a reporter ambushes you, live on television." Because I don't want to read any deeper into this and she seems intent to do the exact opposite, I pick up a Trivial Pursuit game box and quickly change the subject. "It's about time you put some of these bad boys on display."

"*Right?*" She takes the bait. It isn't shock this time. Rox's expression borders on pure amazement. "Finally, someone who appreciates a classic board game with substance."

For a few seconds, I stand there, examining the familiar box. "You wouldn't by chance have the original Pop Culture edition, would you?"

"You wouldn't by chance want to buy one hundred and fifty of them, would you?" she counters playfully.

Over the next few minutes, she recaps the findings from Jacques's preliminary assessment of the store's financial statements and tells me about the action plan she's set to implement immediately. Namely, over the course of the next week, she's going to work side by side with Jacques to analyze and change the prices of the shop's entire stock of games aligned with his profit analysis results. But she's made it her prime focus to unload surplus Trivial Pursuit games, which she contends will increase their cash flow.

"Sounds like a few more items got added to your plate."

"Yeah."

Her voice is faint, barely above a whisper as she goes over the details, but my mind is stuck a few sentences back.

Side by side.

Annoyance flares in my gut again. I know it's probably me being protective and irrational, but I have to do something.

"Listen, I won't hold you much longer, but there's this little spot a few blocks down from here. Nothing fancy, just a loud dive bar with good food and drinks. Elixir's owned by a cool, down-to-earth guy. They have seasonal sporting events for March Madness, the World Series…"

She nods, but the weight of her stare feels like she's considering where this could go.

"I don't know if I told you, or if Nadia mentioned it in passing, but pretty regularly, I go for their trivia nights."

Rox stares, deadpan.

Whether it's because she's shocked that I'm into trivia or if she's still waiting for me to stop beating around the bush, it makes me nervous.

"Anyway, I was thinking maybe you might want to…check it out with me. Bring some friends," I rush to add.

The question seems to take her by surprise. *That makes*

two of us. She releases an audible gasp. She's all unblinking, wide eyes and open-mouth stare again.

I clear my throat and stand taller.

"Sorry, I..." She scratches her scalp.

"Relax, I'm just asking you to come check the place out. Yes, we could have some drinks and fun playing if you're any good," I tease. "But if you wanted to sell off your Trivial Pursuit stock, what better place to do it than in front of a room full of a bunch of trivia heads? You could pass out flyers or coupons for your..." I lean down and pick up the bright yellow sign next to the stack of game boxes, reading the hot pink words aloud. "SUMMER FUN & GAMES SALE."

When I meet Rox's gaze again, her expression smooths, and she blinks out of her trance like the idea is sinking in, and I'm guessing by the way she tilts her head, she recognizes the merit of my off-the-cuff suggestion.

"When is it?"

"They, uh...Elixir used to have them every Friday night before the location booked for other events, but now it's usually every other week." I survey her for a second, gauging her response. "So, what do you say? Are you in for this Friday? Starts at seven."

When she hesitates, settling her attention back on arranging the blue game boxes, the tension in my chest returns.

But then she cocks her head to me.

"I'll think about it, but...I still can't wrap my mind around the fact you, Mr. Laid-Back, easy breezy, mellow Murph, likes Trivial Pursuit let alone trivia." She laughs. "And you regularly attend trivia nights. Like in public..." Her mouth falls open and she shakes her head with amusement before exploding her fingers. "Mind blown."

Maybe I'm feeling protective of her with this guy. Or the fact she clearly thinks I'm not progressive enough to hold my own in a social game of wits, but I'm squarely on defense.

"I think you'd be surprised at my hidden talents."

Shit. Reflex.

Rox holds her middle, gasping for air. "You know what… See, this is why I can't talk to you." She's in stitches. "Bye, Murph. Some of us have work to do."

I turn to leave, cursing my choice of words as I reach the door, when Harper walks up beside me with worry clouding her eyes.

"Everything all right?"

She scrunches her face, waving off my concern. "Yeah, it's probably nothing, but I was wondering if you'd noticed Declan acting different lately. A little on edge, or just…off—not himself?"

Harper eyes me expectantly, gnawing at her lower lip.

"No, but I tell you what, both of our dockets are full this week. I'll try to catch him in the lunchroom or between surgeries. If not, I'll invite him to grab drinks. See where his head is."

Harper swallows, her relief visible as she leans in for a hug. I squeeze back, but my attention snags on movement at the register. My stomach hardens at the sight of Rox and Jacques talking, and I just want to get out of here.

Harper loosens her arms, but she doesn't let go. Her smile is teasing as she lets her gaze dart between Rox and me. "So do something about it."

I step back, slipping my hands into my pockets, and quirk a small smile.

The thing is, if I was the relationship type, I might.

CHAPTER FIVE

ROX

Q: Name the founding father who charted his thirteen-week plan to practice such important virtues as cleanliness and temperance, thus earning him the nickname of *the godfather of lists.*

A: Benjamin Franklin

THE SECOND MY front door closes Wednesday night, I strip off my work clothes, tug on black yoga pants and a T-shirt, and twist my hair up in a bun. Both the pizza and my friend Gwyn will be here any minute, and I need to be comfortable. After a day spent doing price adjustments on our *entire* inventory, I need a girls' night in the worst way. We're supposed to be watching *My Best Friend's Wedding*, playing Trivial Pursuit, and catching up over wine, but I have a feeling there won't be much screen time.

For one, Gwyn and I used to be super close, and we've sort of drifted apart since I've been busy building Love & Games. A little chitchat is long overdue. Filling each other in on what we've missed trumps scripted HEAs every day.

Especially if there's even the teensiest hint I'll find a guy and slow down so we can double date and travel together.

And two, I haven't talked to her since before Jennifer Ling set the dominoes of my life tumbling.

I'm going to need all the sustenance and libations.

But just in case I'm reading tonight all wrong and Gwyn just needs to unwind, I stack the nineties metal box and the Friends Trivial Pursuit editions on the table alongside the glasses of pink rosé, a tin of brownies, Red Vines, and popcorn, leaving space for the pizza.

"Okay," I mutter, sucking in a deep breath and slowly releasing it as I scan my living room for last-minute touches. "I'm ready."

As soon as I plop down on the couch and grab the remote, my phone trembles on the coffee table. I crane my neck to the front window to check for headlights. Seeing none, I reach for my phone and shift back into the cushions. It's not Gwyn telling me she's running late or the pizza place with a new estimated delivery time.

I press the speakerphone button. "What's up, Harp?"

"Omigod, omigod, omigod," she chants. Her breathing is stuttered as it whooshes into the line, but her voice is low and muffled. "Rox..."

Between her dire tone and the concern in her voice when she says my name, I immediately freak out. My pulse races as a wave of panic washes over me. I jolt upright, propped on the edge of the couch. "What's wrong?"

"I'm hiding in the pantry," she says in a hushed tone.

Naturally, my mind goes to the worst-case scenario. I'm two seconds from grabbing my keys and hauling ass over to her house with pepper spray and a rattail comb in hand. *Don't underestimate the weapon power of a sharp hair tool.* "Is someone in the house? Do you need me to call the police?"

"No!" she whisper-yells. Then there's a dull rustling noise, followed by a faint click.

Now my mild heart attack is over, the tension in my muscles drains.

"Okay, but why are you whispering?"

"You know how I said Dec was acting all weird?" She doesn't let me get a word in edgewise before she answers her own question. "I did something stupid and took a magazine survey. One of those 'is he cheating' multiple-choice ones. I panicked, so I snuck into the room. Checked his pants and coat pockets, then his drawers, and there it was." She's talking so fast, slurring her words as she whispers, but her tone is frantic. "In the back of his sock drawer. A small. Velvet. Box!"

A breathy, silent scream fills the line.

"Before you freak the hell out, did you look inside of it? It could be earrings," I point out, mentally calculating the *seven* months they've known each other. How do you go from questioning someone's fidelity to marriage in five seconds flat?

I'm like ninety-eight percent stoked for her because she's found her person, which, *Yay!*

But also, *Yikes.*

Okay, wait. It may sound shitty, like I'm jealous of my sister when she totally deserves her happily-ever-after, but that two percent isn't unwarranted. Harper and I are the daughters of Harrison Sloane, a certified hopeless romantic on his fourth marriage. In numbers, that means three of them ended in divorce. Based on the pattern, the fourth is still yet to be determined.

Not great odds for us.

And that's just the half of it. Dad's ex-wives—her mom, Rita, my mom, Vanessa, and Jade—never got remarried and never changed their last names back from Sloane. I'd say that's *another* glaring pattern. Just like Jacques looks for financial stress trends in businesses, patterns pop out for me. Sloane women don't get do-overs.

And numbers don't lie.

I've actually been thinking about this a lot since I got the last invitation to Dad's wedding in January. Seeing him with Everly on their wedding day last month… I couldn't shake the cautious optimism I felt for my newest stepmother, the same way that two percent weariness for Harper won't stop niggling at me.

Harper and I both have two choices: keep marrying like Dad or end up alone like every other Sloane woman.

We've got one shot.

It must be the right one.

So, I'm just saying, if it's a ring, I'm going to be genuinely happy for my sister—and maybe just a little scared. *And a microscopic, teensy weensy, smidge sad for me. I want my shot, too.*

"Okay, so I know I'm not supposed to look, but Rox! It's freaking gorgeous. Three carats, pavé diamonds along a white-gold band… He did so well," she gushes. "I don't want to get ahead of myself, but I'm thinking of a New Year's Day wedding. Wouldn't that be so cute, getting married on the anniversary of the day we met?"

"Adorable," I say, biting into a Red Vine.

Everyone says when you know, you know. You can't put time limits on love. Meanwhile, I'm over here perma-single and my only prospects are a hot French guy who gives me zero zing and a devastatingly delicious man-child who sets me on fire just by walking in a room. Unless we're counting creepy guys in my DMs…

I want to know.

And not when the time is right. I want my time to be now, too!

"Congrats." I'm genuinely happy for Harp, but also reaching for my glass of rosé. Gwyn will understand.

Like she senses her name on my tongue, the doorbell rings just as I take a sip. I take a large gulp then set my glass down to grab my wallet with my free hand just in case it's the pizza. I amble over to open the front door right when Harper says, "I have to go, but don't tell anyone."

But it's too late.

Turns out it's not just the delivery. It's Gwyn looking fierce in a red jumper with her long dark brown hair cascading over her tanned to perfection shoulders. She's armed with the pizza in one hand and more wine in the other.

We're going to need every drop.

As Harper ends the call, Gwyn dips her chin to survey me over her expertly threaded and shaped dark brows.

"Okay, so, what are we not telling anyone?"

Two pizza slices, one full bottle of wine, and a whole lot of colorful language later, Gwyn is up to speed on everything. Four things are official: Harper and Declan had better send Gwyn a wedding invitation. Jacques Chastain has a new—fiercely dressed—cyberstalker. As usual, Murphy Sikes is on thin ice, and after showing her my socket-shocked meme, Jennifer Ling officially has an enemy. *You don't mess with Gwyn's girl. Period.*

"Are we happy for Harper?" Gwyn asks over a mouthful of popcorn.

I nod no less than a dozen times. "Absolutely… Of course we are. You know how I am about moving too fast. I'm just cautious…"

Gwyn's expression pinches, and her wild fringe of faux lashes takes flight as she blinks repeatedly. "Uh, no…I heard hesitation."

My phone vibrates against my thigh, saving me. "Hold that thought." I check the screen, and I'm surprised to find a text from Declan.

> *"Please, don't share any of what I'm about to tell you with your sister. I'm going to ask Harper to marry me. I already spoke with your dad and Rita, but I'd love to have your blessing too since I know how much you mean to her. I could use your help getting her out of the house next Saturday around noon."*

When I finish reading and lift my gaze, Gwyn, who has apparently been reading over my shoulder, tosses me a pursed-lip head shake. "See, that's what I'm talking about."

"What?" I snap, way too defensive.

The ring is one thing, but Declan's text makes everything real. He's going to propose next weekend. In ten days, I'll be the only one wading through the fish in the sea—Nadia doesn't count since she's not even looking. She isn't a Sloane, so it'll probably just magically happen for her, anyway.

"What if I don't find anyone and I end up alone? I'm turning thirty. Do I just stop looking, settle for the first guy who comes along?" I roll my head from side to side, loosening the muscles in my neck. "I mean, does love only happen in fairy tales? Do *you* still get the butterflies and tingles with Christian?" I ask, referring to her Insta-perfect Puerto Rican boyfriend.

Gwyn straightens against the arm of the couch and shifts to look me dead in the eye.

Important note: she is *not* Team Murph.

"Before you go feeling sorry for yourself, you are not settling. You are not desperate. You're a goddamn catch." She holds up a long, pointy stiletto-shaped red nail. "And I know you've been looking at that damn *Book of Lists* of yours, but if Murphy Sikes can't see that, then it's his loss. *Shit.* Inviting you to freaking trivia night when he should thank his lucky stars you pay him any attention at all," she mumbles the last part to herself.

If the shoe was on the other foot, I'd be saying the same thing to her. Telling her what a bombshell she is. Cursing any man who can't see what a badass catch she is. So why is it so hard to toot my own horn?

"Where is it?" She crosses her arms over her chest.

I don't have to ask what *it* is. I blow out a small, mortified sigh, lean toward the other arm of the couch, and pull out my blush-pink journal with the embossed gold script from the crack between the cushion, and hand it to her.

It's mostly an outlet. A way to alleviate my anxiety. A

tangible way to feel in control of my life. I don't let anyone see it, let alone read it. But given the state of my hot mess life…

I gnaw on my bottom lip so hard I taste copper as she opens the book. My heart is in my throat. She fans past "Life Goals," "Dream Travel Destinations," "Love Languages," and my ever-growing "To Be Read" lists. She briefly pauses at my fully checked "Twenty-Five by Twenty-Five" list, scanning through things like go to the movies by myself, own a genuine diamond, and establish excellent credit. I hold my breath when she flips to the "Thirty by Thirty" list.

There're still three unchecked boxes.

The first, "Have a Wild Dirty-Thirty Party in Vegas," is pretty much set. It's planned and I'm halfway packed. It's the other two that haunt me every waking second of the day. "Start and Grow a Successful Business" and "Find Real Love." We've been in business five years and Jacques is helping us, but I can't check that one off with confidence yet. And real love…

Yeah.

"I'm working on them." I study Gwyn's face for signs of judgment.

We both grab a Red Vine at the same time.

"I'm just reading, but are you really? Are you on a dating app? Gone on an actual date recently? Or are you still reading about dating?"

There's no judgment in her tone, so I start to answer her, but she holds up the finger again like the questions are rhetorical and flips the page.

To my "One Shot" list.

A wave of panic washes over me as I watch her gaze drop past my top five to the other thirty must-haves for a "real love" man.

When she sighs for the fifth time and closes the book, I can't take it any longer.

"What?" It comes out a whimper.

Gwyn arches her back and twists her hair up into a knot. "So, I'm assuming you think this *one-shot* guy is Murphy." She refuses to call him Murph on principle. She doesn't believe he deserves me based on his fuckboy dating history.

"I don't know," I grumble, dropping my head into my hands. "Yes, he's a player who doesn't do relationships. But you didn't see him at the store Monday. When he walked in and saw me with Jacques—"

"Every time you say his name, I want beignets." She laughs, then waves at me to continue. "Okay, go on."

"Exactly, Jacques is hot. I should pursue someone who's emotionally available and a friend, but I can't get past the no-sparks thing. I feel *nothing* with him." Gwyn nods. "But like I was saying, when Murph walked in and saw me with him, I compared the two of them. Jacques is my fantasy, but Murph *is* the list."

"Mm-hmm." I can almost see Gwyn's wheels turning.

"Murph was concerned about me. He was endearing. I think a little jealous, too." I cringe. It's risky letting myself be hopeful, idealizing him. Perfect people have no flaws.

When Gwyn doesn't jump on the jealousy tidbit, my pulse quickens. "What are you thinking?"

"So, are you going to trivia night?"

It does sound fun. As much as I hate to admit it, passing

out coupons and selling games to a bunch of trivia lovers could help Love & Games.

I shrug.

"Let me ask you a serious question," Gwyn says. "Be completely honest with me. *And* yourself. If Murphy pursued you, would you go for it?" She tilts her head, surveying me.

My gut reaction is to say no. But deep down, even with everything I know about his relationship history, if Murph wanted me, I would jump at the chance.

I give her a sheepish nod.

Gwyn holds her hand out for my *Book of Lists* and grabs another Red Vine before she flips to a clean sheet. She fishes a sparkly pen out of her purse and scribbles something at the top of the page before she holds them both out to me.

"Write this down." She instructs in full-on business mode.

She's titled this new list "Get My Man," and already added a checkbox on the line beneath it. I try not to focus on the words glaring back at me as I click the pen and prepare to take notes.

"One, if he calls, ignore him," she dictates, totally in her element. "Two, if he shows up at the shop, act busy and laugh with Jacques like it's the funniest thing ever. Three, go to the trivia night, sell some games, and promote the heck out of your business. Murphy's presence should not stand in the way of you getting your money."

She pauses when I shoot her a questioning glance. *Does she really want me to write all of that?*

Her raised-brow stare jerks to the paper before crash-landing back on me.

Apparently so.

She waits until I jot it down before she continues. "Christian and I have plans Friday, but I can stop by for the first thirty minutes for moral support—and the drinks." She unravels her hair like she can literally let her hair down now that we're planning. But then she notices I've stopped writing and picks up where she left off. "Four…"

I'm on pins and needles for this one.

"Don't, I repeat, do not talk to him until trivia night. No texts or calls." Gwyn swaps the Red Vine for a brownie, then pours herself another glass of wine. "Better yet, why don't you ask Jacques to go with you?"

I slump back against the cushions.

"This feels trivial. I don't want to play games."

Gwyn closes her eyes and exhales a breath before she eyes me intently. "Do you want your man?"

Why, yes. I do. But I don't want to trick him into wanting me.

"This doesn't exactly scream *real love*. We both know Murph isn't into commitment."

"Yet," Gwyn declares. "No man is until they're about to lose their woman. Why do you think he almost lost his shit when he saw you laughing with Jacques?" Her eyes widen like a lightbulb went off, and she grabs and bites into a brownie. "Ooh, does Jacques speak French?" I shrug but she's undeterred. "It doesn't matter. We'll have Jacques whisper something sexy like *je t'aime* or *j'adore* within earshot of Murphy. A little competition, and he will be yours in no time."

Right off the bat, I hate this.

We're strategizing like this is a game and not my heart at risk. Playing hard to get is like giving him a pop quiz on the first day of school. Do I want a real relationship with him? Yes. Is this the right strategy? I have no clue. I don't know if I want to use a strategy at all, but walking into trivia night without knowing where his head is… I might as well lay my heart at his feet.

"Okay, what else?"

Gwyn's thick brows trench. "That's it. What do you mean, what else? That's a nice even number."

"Four is not a good number." There's an entire history. It's basically a jinx. We might as well break a few mirrors and walk under a ladder in a black cat's path. No thanks. We cannot leave the fate of my one shot in the hands of a *four*.

I wave off the full explanation, instead playing to her sensibilities.

"I know you've got another one in there. Don't hold back."

She rolls her eyes like she doesn't have another one already on deck.

"Okay fine. Um…" She squints off into the distance for a sec. "Five. Don't look at him with those sappy googly eyes you always give him—all love-starved and thirsty."

Fair point.

"I'll try."

She's got it all figured out.

Just ask Jacques. *Yeah, no big deal.* We've talked about travel, financials, books. I don't even know if he's got a girlfriend. Plus, it's sort of a conflict of interest with him helping Love & Games, *isn't it?*

I flip back to the "One Shot" list, still digesting Gwyn's instructions as I drag my fingers over the page—all but three boxes checked.

Numbers don't lie.

Guess I'm taking my shot, then.

CHAPTER SIX

MURPH

Q: Dating from the 16th century, this idiom meaning "closely similar" or "almost exactly alike" first appeared in John Lyly's *Euphues* (1579).

A: Two peas in a pod

I REMOVE THE endoscope from Mrs. Bailey's nose and hand it to my assistant, Bellamy, peeling off my gloves. "Looks like we're still in good shape. Are you using the nasal spray and doing the rinses, morning and night?"

Mrs. Bailey's warm brown, velvety cheeks bunch up into a smile. "Like clockwork." She nods and tugs her purse strap up onto her shoulder as she gets to her feet. "You make sure and tell Vivian and Allen hi."

"Yes, ma'am." I nod, feeling like I'm fifteen again.

I've been seeing Mrs. Bailey as a patient for the last two years, but I've known her since I was a kid. She and Mom worked together at Carey & Acres Publishing House for as long as I could remember. Even after they retired, Mom and

Dad went on double dates and cruises with the Baileys.

As I sit back at the computer, she lingers for a bit. A faraway look in her eyes. She reminds me of Mom with her easy, bright track suits, silver curls, and buzzy energy.

She shakes her head as if losing the thought that took her away for a moment.

"Did you have any questions, Mrs. Bailey?"

She waves me off. "I was just thinking about your parents. How Philip and I had so many good times with them." She smiles to herself, but her gaze darts to my hand resting on the computer keys. My left hand. "I would give anything for one more day with my Phillip."

"Oh, I'm so sorry for your loss. I hadn't heard about Mr. Bailey." My chest tightens as I rush over to hug her.

I figured he was waiting for her in the lobby. At any minute he'd shuffle back wearing his trademark Veteran cap and short-sleeve Hawaiian shirt to take her hand. They were one of those inseparable *two peas in a pod* couples whose names you say together because one never goes anywhere without the other. Anne and Phillip.

Vivian and Allen.

A weight settles on my heart and my throat clenches.

"Now, now. None of that," Mrs. Bailey says, gazing up into my downturned eyes. "I got to spend my best years with the love of my life. I have no regrets."

I give her a small squeeze to soothe her, but the gesture does more for me.

"Don't waste your youth fighting it. Grow old with someone, sweetheart." She clears her throat and reaches up to cup my cheek before correcting herself. "Sorry, Dr. Sikes."

Laughter bubbles up inside me. Between Mom and Mrs. Bailey, they're more concerned with me finding someone than their health or loss. *What's the big deal? There are more important things in life to worry about.*

I nod and chuckle. "Okay. I want to see you again in six months."

She steps back and smooths her jacket.

"Sure thing. Hopefully you'll have some good news to share with me."

With a gentle pat to my arm, she shakes off any signs of emotion, flashes me a soft smile, and opens the exam room door to leave.

There's always something I need to do, paperwork to sign, patient files for review, but I'm rooted to this spot. All week my mind has been drifting back to Mom and Dad, to their health. I hate how I can't stop calculating, guesstimating how much time Nadia and I could have left with them. As much as I dread the grueling relationship interrogation brunches, we may not have many more to sit through.

No regrets.

My heart clenches at the tiny number I come up with. It's only ever been holidays and special occasions we get together. Never an unannounced drop-in just to say hello, how are you… *I love you.*

My head swims with all the things I've wanted to say over the years. The things I may never get to say if time runs out. I've wanted to yell at Dad, tell him to be the husband Mom deserves, the father Nadia and I miss. I want to hug again without it feeling awkward or one-sided. Just be around him, sit down and watch a movie or play a round of

Trivial Pursuit like we used to before Mom got sick. *For Chrissakes, we're all still here.*

But just once, not in a greeting card from the two of them in Mom's handwriting, I want to hear him say aloud all the things I've longed for.

I'm proud.

I'm sorry.

I love you, too.

It's never going to happen. The man is too stubborn.

Bellamy pops into the room, jolting me from my thoughts. "Your one o'clock canceled." She leans her thin frame over the keyboard to check my notes on Mrs. Bailey, but when she registers I've input nothing, she twists around, quietly studying me.

I may be a fuckup in my personal life, but I don't zone out at work. I don't stand in exam rooms with my feet cemented to the floor because I can't wrap my head around the facts of life.

This isn't me.

I've been so on edge this entire week. After brunch with my parents, then stalling with Rox at Love & Games, inviting her out for trivia night…

What was I thinking?

Everyone knows "I'll think about it" is a friendly way of letting you down easy.

"Sorry, I just, uh…I was thinking about my schedule. So, who was it that canceled?"

We've been working together so long I'm not surprised Bellamy isn't fooled. She continues to stare, her suspicious gaze searching my face. "I can do this," she says, still eyeing me, my stiff posture and scattered brain on full display. "You haven't eaten yet. Go grab a bite or just…relax for a bit."

She isn't wrong. I could use downtime to clear my head. I've got all this uneasy energy built up with nowhere to put it.

I scrape my fingers through my hair and clasp my hands behind my head, releasing a lungful of air. "Thanks, I just—"

"You don't have to explain. I've got this." Bellamy tosses me a lopsided smile. "Teamwork makes the dream work, and all that." She waves me off with a half-serious chuckle.

When I get to the lunchroom, I scour the refrigerator for the broccoli beef I had on Tuesday. My stomach growls as I push aside Declan's spaghetti container and Bellamy's teriyaki bowl. There's a rotten apple and someone's half-eaten sub in the back.

"Takeout it is," I mutter, and pull out the stack of menus we keep for nearby restaurants. I scan them absently. Going anywhere with my head all over the place, not ideal.

"Saw you had a cancellation…" Declan trails off as he ducks his head into the doorway. "Come on. Let's get some food. That sub shop down the block opened and I have coupons."

Before I have time to turn him down, because let's face it, I'm a head case (practically having a midlife crisis in an exam room), Declan pats the door and disappears into the hall.

"Be in the lobby in two minutes, Sikes," he calls out.

The promise I made to Harper floats to the top of my mind. Grabbing food might be a three birds, one stone move. I get downtime away and a decent meal, and it'll give

Dec a chance to unload whatever hang-up Harper's been picking up on.

The brisk, quiet walk to Bub's Subs takes us less than ten minutes. When we reach the cashier, Declan proudly whips out the value meal coupons and orders a foot-long tuna melt with chips and a cola before tipping his chin to me.

"What can I get started for you?" The sandwich artist's expectant brown gaze falls on me.

Despite the brief wait, I didn't pay much attention to the menu.

"Oh, I'll just go with the turkey. Everything on it."

Declan and I both fish out our wallets to pay, but he holds up his palm and inserts his debit card. Or rather, struggles to insert it.

That's when I realize not only are Declan's hands shaking, but he looks like shit. His usual bright, relaxed preppy charm and neatly combed black hair just looks worn down. His posture is rigid, and his eyes are a brittle driftwood brown.

This lunch invitation isn't about me.

Whatever Harper noticed, she was right about him being off.

"So, what's up?" I ask as we walk over near the pickup window at the end of the aisle. I zero in on how restless he is, shifting in place, constantly stretching his neck, cracking his knuckles. I haven't seen him like this since college when he was about to ask his ex, Penelope, to—*Oh shit.* When he says nothing, I try again. "Dec?"

"Hmm?" he mutters absently, rocking from foot to foot, but he doesn't look at me.

"Want to tell me what's going on? Why you were in such a rush to get out of the office? You never eat out."

Declan flits a glance at me, then shrugs. "Maybe I forgot to bring lunch today." He hikes up a challenging eyebrow.

I nod, crossing my arms over my chest.

"So yesterday wasn't spaghetti night? You're telling me that wasn't Harper's mint-green Tupperware in the refrigerator with the cute little pink I LOVE YOU note stuck to it?"

This time, he gives me a proper look. Head on, unblinking. The set of his jaw tightens against his hard expression, and a war between surprise and guilt flashes across his face. *Yeah, everyone in the office knows—and secretly reads—Harper's love messages.*

"Tuna melt value meal. Turkey with everything," a pink-haired girl calls from the window, but neither Declan nor I move.

I want to laugh. God, do I want to laugh. But I can't do that to my buddy. Not when he's clearly shitting a brick about what's on his chest.

The corners of my mouth twitch. I chew the inside of my cheek not to crumble right here in front of him, but the girl calls our order again.

Declan breaks the stare, and I pocket the small win like balm to my wounded ego.

Once we have our food, I drag my feet, lingering outside the restaurant instead of heading back. We're standing on the sidewalk, both in our royal-blue scrubs, cars rushing by and salty ocean air wafting in the breeze. Neither of us touches our food or says a word.

For a beat, I study the gnarled roots of a tree caged in by

the uneven pavement before glancing up at the sunlight beaming through its branches.

"Just say it," I blurt out. "You obviously want to talk if you chose a dry sub over Harper's home-cooking."

Declan's voice muffles under the din of traffic, but he doesn't even hesitate. "I'm going to ask her to marry me."

"I know."

A shit-eating grin spreads across his face, and he chuckles to himself. "You know?"

"I made an educated guess. How many times do I have to tell you I'm a genius?" I slap him on the shoulder.

Declan blows a breath into his fist, relief flooding his face.

"And you're sure you're not moving too fast? She's not pressing you or anything? Because it hasn't even been a year yet…" I search his eyes.

He doesn't even hesitate.

"Believe me, I've never been more certain of anything in my life. I'm so in love with this woman, it's scary. I never thought I would get another chance at love, but Harper and I have a happy, healthy relationship, and I can't wait to get started on forever together." He's got this distant look in his eyes, but his whole face lights up every time he says her name. "I swear, Harper must think something's wrong with me because of how many times a day I tell her I love her."

My gut tells me never to trust in love or notions of happily-ever-after. It feels so farfetched. But seeing my best friend drenched in it and speaking so freely about it, I've got to get on board for his sake.

I nod a few times.

"Congratulations, man. I'm happy for you." The words come out easy and casual, and I find I really am. *Happy for them.*

My best friend is going to marry the love of his life. They've got endless spaghetti nights, leftovers, and love notes to look forward to. Harper and Declan. They'll be a *two peas in a pod* couple who hold hands at doctor's appointments. Grow old together with no regrets.

A shudder courses through me at an alarming thought. *Do I want what Declan and Harper have, what the Baileys had?*

What if I get what my parents have?

The past tense, the finality of the Baileys' relationship twists my gut.

Dec clears his throat. "So, I worked myself up all week, thinking you'd be pissed, figuring how to ask you to be my best man, and you're happy for us?" Humor brightens his eyes. Well, he still looks like shit, but more alive. "You never cease to amaze me, man."

I curve my shoulders, playfully pressing my hand to my chest.

"I've never felt more honored to have my best friend think so little of me," I jest. The corners of my lips tug downward. "Yet, you ask me to be your right-hand man on the most important day of your life… I accept."

Declan wrestles me into a hug, his body sagging with relief. "That's been bothering me ever since I picked up the ring," he says, flippantly glazing over the huge admission as he rips open his sandwich and takes a bite. "Now, what was the long face about in the lunchroom?"

In the back of my mind, I assumed he was going to take his time to plan something elaborate. If he already has the…

"Wait, you already picked the ring? When are you proposing?"

"Next Saturday," he says over a mouthful. He screws off the cap of his cola and takes a long pull. "The seventeenth. Rox agreed to help me."

That's less than two weeks. "Shit."

"Yeah, I thought about doing it in Vegas, the week of the convention, since the girls will be there for Rox's birthday, but no."

My mind leaps back to Love & Games. Rox…*and Jacques.* "That's right. She mentioned it the other day when I stopped by the store. So, they'll be in Vegas the same weekend."

Declan nods, then slowly cocks his head. "What was that?"

"What?"

"You zoned out when I mentioned Rox." He snickers. "When are you going to stop fighting this? Every time her name comes up, you get all weird."

Heat creeps into my cheeks. "I asked her to meet me for trivia night. She said she'd *think about it.*"

He sips his soda. "And you think that's enough?"

"She may not even go tomorrow night," I reason, but I can't discount the way my stomach knots when I consider she might. "Plus, you know me. I'm not big on relationships. I think seeing her with that business advisor guy…I got territorial."

"Mm-hmm."

"On top of that, I've been thinking a lot about my parents. On the holiday, Nadia and I had brunch with them. It felt like it had been ten years instead of six months since I last saw them. And you know how my mother is, always asking if I've found a *special someone*. I might've gotten caught up when I saw Rox with *Jacques*." I roll my eyes.

Declan cocks his head, calling my bluff.

"Murph, come on. She's the only woman who gets you tongue-tied." He clears his throat, squaring his body to me. "Let me put it this way, what if Rox is it for you and you miss out because you're second-guessing or whatever the heck that was you were doing back in the breakroom?"

My mouth goes dry, and I can't seem to get enough air.

She deserves more.

"Do you want her?" he presses.

As much as I want to deny it, I can't ignore the dull ache in my chest. The loud drumming of my heart.

"By that pained expression you're sporting…" Dec huffs out a laugh. "I'm assuming you do. And let me tell you, the games you play with these women will not work. You need to pursue her. Take it slow. Show Rox that you care. That she's different—why you're different with her."

An elixir of fear and excitement revs up my heart. Even more as I slip my phone from my pocket and open my messages. I'm still not sure complicating things with Rox is even what I want. No matter how much my parents' marriage has hardwired me to dismiss love, Declan and Harper make me want to believe it's possible. And the thought of Rox finding love with someone else…is unbearable.

So, with shaky fingers, I tell her I'm looking forward to

seeing her tomorrow night.

The rest of the workday and into the night, I wait. No matter how much I try to distract myself with housework and video games. No matter how often I check my phone. There's no response.

CHAPTER SEVEN

ROX

Q: This Grammy-nominated song recorded by American singer Whitney Houston for her third studio album of the same name became a worldwide hit, topping charts in over fifteen countries.

A: "I'm Your Baby Tonight"

IT'S FRIDAY, WE close in two hours, and I've avoided Jacques all yesterday and most of today. All five boxes of the blue I'VE GOT A WEDGIE Trivial Pursuit–themed T-shirts I ordered with the cute little pink wedge in a wheel came in, so I've busied myself folding them. Other than that, I'm the unofficial store greeter because it's the farthest point in the store from my office—from Jacques.

I know I'm down to the wire to ask him to go with me to trivia night, but I'm not Gwyn. How am I supposed to segue my way from income statements and profit-and-loss sheets to "Hey, I don't know if you're spoken for, but wanna be my fake date to trivia night?" *Yeah, desperate much?*

"Rox."

A tap on my shoulder scares the bejesus out of me.

"Shit. Shoot. Sorry." I press my hand over my frantic heart. *Speaking of the devil.*

Jacques appears beside me, the lopsided grin kicking up the corner of his beautiful, yet still, very zero-zing mouth. *Sigh.*

"Oh, I didn't mean to startle you."

Gah, things would be so much easier if I could just ignore the dang Richter scale in my heart. Jacques is stupid gorgeous. Other women would kill to be this close to him. If I felt even a blip of a spark, I'd rush him to the back right now, keep digging for more, and forget about this crazy scheme to get Murph to acknowledge his alleged feelings for me.

But Gwyn was so sure.

What if it doesn't work? Or what if all I do is awaken my sad libido, pocket a few useless factoids, and come home to my empty house smelling like an ashtray?

I'm going to need copious amounts of alcohol to go through with this.

My heart bangs in my chest when I realize I've been standing here staring off into oblivion for who knows how long.

Right. "It's okay. I was just, um, just spacing out." I suck in a lungful of air and slowly release it on a laugh. My pulse races. "What's up?" I ask, aiming for casual and breezy, but it comes out sounding like there's a frog in my throat.

He flashes me a soft smile.

Why couldn't he just be ugly?

"I'm finished. With the business review," he stammers. "I wanted to go over the summary with you, if you have time…"

He trails off, presumably waiting for me to chime in, and since I can't do it safely without upchucking the entire trivia night debacle, I mumble a "Mm-hmm. Yeah." Which is just pathetic. Heat creeps over my neck and cheeks, and my body tenses.

It's now or never.

The few dozen feet back to my office feel like the freaking green mile. I take several deep breaths not to turn blue and faint in front of him. *Breathe*, I tell myself as I settle in my chair, swiping the back of my hand over teensy beads of sweat. *What in the actual F? If it's this hard to ask Jacques to be my moral support, what am I going to do when I'm sitting next to Murph?*

Jacques summarizes his findings diplomatically, complimenting us on increasing sales this week alone. Then, he reiterates the action plan to liquidate inventory. Heavy emphasis on the need to offload more Trivial Pursuit games at a faster pace to replace the Monopoly stock, which is "selling like hotcakes." *Who even says that anymore?* He bookends his feedback sandwich with another success. We're already seeing "measurable progress in profit" based on the pricing adjustments now that we're covering our overhead expenses.

I'm trying to pay attention. I really am, but my thoughts keep drifting to the impending question I need to ask Jacques. I can't decide whether he'll think it's a wildly inappropriate conflict of interest to even ask him to go with me to Elixir. Or if I'll flub it up and the whole thing backfires with him thinking I'm hitting on him.

Shit.

He mentions Jennifer Ling, and my ears perk up.

But then he says—*thankfully*—no one has had any follow-up requests from her, and I zone out again.

I don't know how long exactly I've been staring at the stack of bright SUMMER FUN & GAMES coupons I printed up, but Jacques is still surveying me when I meet his gaze.

"I'm sorry," I say again, hating I've had to apologize twice in the last ten minutes. "What did you say?"

He leans forward and drums his fingers on the desk. For two seconds, he narrows his eyes and studies me. "Something is bothering you. I know the store is about to close for the day and I'll be out of your hair for good, but I'm right here if you want to talk."

Note to self: Add sweet to the qualities that didn't make it on my list.

I scrunch my face, cringing inside.

Just say it. Ask him.

"Okay, this is going to seem like it's way out of left field considering we haven't gotten personal since you've been here. I mean, we mentioned a few books and travel, but nothing about our lives or the people in it. And now you're finished with your review and leaving us today—"

"Exactly!" Relief seeps into the parentheses, hugging his mouth. "It felt sort of awkward, like a conflict of interest discussing anything other than the store while I'm assessing Love & Games, but…" He covers my hand with his, and again, no zing, just full-blown panic paralyzes me. *Please don't tell me you're interested in me.* "I was hoping we could be friends?" His shaky voice rises in question.

I literally deflate against my chair, letting all the air in my lungs vacuum out of me. I give myself a couple of seconds to be ridiculously dramatic before I pop my head up to peek at him.

"I totally thought you were going to tell me you were into me." My hand clutched to my chest, I chuckle.

"Wow, I didn't realize that would be the worst-case scenario."

I shake my head, a smile stretching across my face.

"No! You're distractingly hot." I wave off his comment. "It's just...I've been trying to work up the nerve to ask you something since yesterday, but I didn't know if I should—if I *could*."

He crosses his arms across his chest, amusement sparkling in his soft green eyes as he settles back in the chair.

"Oh, now I'm intrigued. Tell me."

"This is going to sound even more weird now." I take a deep breath and then, "Do you want to be my *fake* date tonight?" I wince, squinting one eye. Jacques licks his lips and confusion braids his shapely dark eyebrows, so I feel the need to quickly elaborate. "Okay, let me explain. There's this guy—"

"Let me guess, the guy who stopped in on Monday. He looked like he wanted to pummel me."

I palm my face. "I've had a thing for him for longer than anyone should rightly admit." I sigh helplessly. "The problem is, he's a total player, commitment-phobe, who wants nothing serious. But my friend Gwyn thinks men don't commit until they're about to lose their woman. She thinks that's why he lost his shit when he saw us laughing—might've forced his hand."

When Jacques doesn't immediately chime in, I tug open my desk drawer, and pull out my emergency Red Vines. He declines my offer to share, so I stick one in my mouth, letting it hang from my lips.

"Murph texted me yesterday, and I had to resort to doing burpees not to reply. *Burpees.*" I giggle and wince at the memory of my poor abs. "It's all part of Gwyn's plan. No contact with him until trivia night."

Jacques looks at me for a beat, then lowers his chin to his chest. "She's not wrong, your friend. The part about letting him miss you..."

Uh-oh. So I'm not the only one with relationship issues. Noted.

I don't fill the silence.

"My ex is with some new guy. It's killing me, but I'm the one who broke it off. Doesn't leave much room for excuses. So, yeah, I'd say jealousy definitely clears up any confusion about whether you want to be with someone." He centers his attention on me. "Seeing the person you love find happiness without you is strangely, ruthlessly sobering."

I toss him a small smile. "It all feels so trivial, like playing games. Like, why can't we just say whether we're interested, and go from there?"

For a few minutes, we sit under our shared rain cloud. Then, I lift the cardboard tray of Red Vines to Jacques. This time, he takes one.

"These are fantastic," he says.

"I know. That's why I keep them stocked," I say over a mouthful. "For times like this."

He chuckles. "For times when the conversation veers to unrequited love and fake trivia night dates?" *Wait, who said anything about love?*

I jolt upright. "Wait, so you're in love?"

Not even an inch. He just sits there, looking crushed, wallowing in his misery as he nods. My heart aches for him.

But then my floodgates open, and a whopper of an idea hits me.

"Jacques..." I let his name hang in the air until he peers up at me from his slouched position. The wheels keep turning as I tug my hair tie from my ponytail, finger-combing curly flyways back into submission before I twist it back up into a messy bun, so I can think.

The wounded puppy look isn't what I was hoping for, but then again, I haven't shared my brilliance yet.

"We're friends, but you're gonna want to kiss me when you hear my idea. Trust me, it's beyond perfect."

BY THE TIME seven o'clock rolls around, Jacques and I are rehearsed and ready to teach Murph a few things at trivia night. One, if he's going to be my one shot, I will not go easy on him. And two, Dr. Murphy Theodore Sikes, beautiful player, has competition—even if Jacques and I are faking it until we make Murph and Bridget come to their senses.

That's her name, Bridget. The woman Jacques had to lose to *know* he loves her. *Why do men have to learn every-*

thing the hard way?

My question to Jacques verbatim as he cuts the engine in the parking lot at Elixir.

"Because we're men." He chuckles. "When have we ever gotten anything right the first time?"

Dad pops into my head, and I feel my pulse quicken. *Is it going to take Murph two, three, four times to get it right? To figure out I've been right here?*

"Nope, no getting lost in your head," Jacques admonishes me, passing me a tiny shot glass before topping it off with a dark amber liquid. "It's whiskey. Tonight, we're a team. We're going to see what a little jealousy can do for us for a change." He winks. "Murph gets a taste of what it'll be like if you're with me, and Bridget will see my post of us online."

That's the deal we made.

Make each other's love interests jealous. Let them pursue us. Or, as Jacques calls it, "clear the smoke."

But everyone knows where there's smoke, there's fire.

The instant Jacques holds the door for me to enter, I spot Murph near the bar. In the dim light, he looks like one of those cologne-ad men with the smoldering good looks and searing eye contact. No tux, but his dark-washed jeans and black T-shirt have the same drooling effect on me. His long frame is stretched over a barstool, but the typical cocky half grin is in place. Tonight, his blond hair is mussed and swept off to the side, so I get the full view of his trenched brows, which, for me, is downright pornographic.

It's like a backdraft knocking me from my feet. Warmth sizzles through me.

I release a slow sigh.

"Ready?" Jacques asks, slipping his hand in mine.

Is "no" a valid answer? I feel like I might hurl. I'm not ready. I don't think I'll ever be ready to try and fail to make Murph jealous. He's going to sniff out the lie, then laugh in my face. What on earth possessed me to do this?

Jacques drops my hand and slides his to the small of my back, inching closer to me. My back goes rigid, but I force a smile as his thick, musky scent wraps around me. He must've sprayed some on before he locked up the car. I imagine it's probably a pheromone cocktail for some women, but I'm suppressing the urge to hack out a cough the stench is so thick.

What did he do, pour on the entire bottle?

No one is going to believe this is real. I sure as hell am not buying it.

Oh God. This was a huge mistake.

Panic zips through me, but I straighten and slowly blow out another breath. This isn't the time to freak the hell out. Even though I know I'm doing the love-starved googly eyes, I suck in a cleansing breath, finding my bearings.

"You don't happen to speak French, do you?"

We're going to need everything in our fake arsenal to make this look real. Nothing can unsexify the language of love.

I hope.

CHAPTER EIGHT

MURPH

Q: What product broadcasts trivia and other games via broadband over a national network to thousands of bars and restaurants in the United States, Canada, and the Caribbean?

A: Buzztime

"YOU PLAYING TONIGHT, Murph?" Vick jerks his chin to the two untouched Gibsons I ordered fifteen minutes ago on the off chance Rox shows.

I'm usually a couple of shots and a few beers down by now, but I need a clear head.

It's rare I don't know what to expect.

"I'm headed back there in a few..." I trail off, darting my attention to the door for about the tenth time since I arrived for trivia night.

A group of twentysomething women in short, bright dresses walk into the bar. They're young, cute, stylish, and by the GOOD TIMES ONLY signs above their heads, on the hunt.

Usually, I'd sit up straighter, try to make eye contact with the boldest one. Once we've had a few drinks and ease into small talk, she'll think she's found a *diamond in the rough* doctor with no kids or recent exes who knows how to unwind and plays a mean game of trivia. Our easy conversation will edge into heated stares before our magnetic hands lead us back to her place—*never* mine.

Nothing about tonight feels usual.

I turn back to the bar in time to see the corners of Vick's mouth twist into a smirk.

He's owned this bar long enough to read between the blurred lines.

Despite its fancy name, Elixir is loud and grimy, with sports blaring from any of a dozen television screens. Trivia going on in the back near the stage. It's a cure-all escape for the workday humdrum. I come here to unwind, throw back a few drinks, and forget about my troubles.

Sometimes, I find new ones.

Of all the times I've sat in the dim light at this massive wooden bar, I've never once watched the door with bated breath.

I never once invited Rox…

It's probably for the best that she didn't respond to my text. That she didn't show up tonight. This is what I get for letting Declan get into my head yesterday at lunch. Reading too much into this whole thing… Who was I kidding? I know who I am with women. No strings, pleasure, physical needs, short-term—doesn't exactly scream fairy tale. We'd both have to be delusional to think I'm cut out for slow pursuit. I don't hold my breath for a text message reply. I'm not the guy who sits on the edge of a barstool watching the door. I'm…what did she call me? *Mr. Laid-Back, easy breezy, mellow Murph* isn't who Rox wants.

No sense trying to convince myself otherwise.

When the group of women sidle up to the bar, the brunette in a second-skin red dress tosses me a slow smile. She nips the corner of her plump lower lip and flits a glance to the two full glasses in front of me.

"Waiting for someone?"

In the back, the microphone crackles to life.

"We're going to get started here shortly, folks. We've got a little less than ten minutes, so check out the drink specials, give Paul your team names, and grab your answer sheets," the quizmaster, Sabita, announces.

After a final glance over to the door, I paste on a weak smile.

Fuck it.

I swivel on the barstool to square my body to the woman, my knees fanning out on either side of her. Before I say a word, I pick up one of the glasses and hold it up between us.

"It's about time you got here," I say.

The corner of her mouth kicks up in an alluring smile as she grabs the other drink and clinks it against mine.

"I'm Silvie. Want to get out of here?"

And Declan said the games I play with women don't work. Maybe not with Rox, but Silvie doesn't need me to take it slow and show her that she's different. Silvie is here.

"Murph." I take a long pull, popping the pickled onion garnish in my mouth. "I'll catch you later, Vick," I call over my shoulder, but as I stand, movement at the door steals my attention.

Rox.

My insides immediately flood with relief. My entire mood lifts, and it could be the mix of gin and vermouth seeping into my bloodstream, but warmth fills my chest and I'm drunk with giddiness.

I swear the air comes alive. Zipping blue and gold currents of electricity surging between us. We're heat and light, dazzling like Fourth of July sparklers in the night sky.

She came.

Rox is in simple fitted jeans and a blue Trivial Pursuit T-shirt with a pink wedge on it, which is already the picture of perfection. But she's put on makeup and let her hair down in loose waves. I let myself imagine it's all for me, the extra effort, the beaming smile, the sparkle in her heart eyes when our gazes collide.

It doesn't matter she didn't call or text. Or that I was about to let Silvie help me forget how badly I wanted Rox to show up. What matters is Rox is here, which means we're both open to the possibilities. We want two different things, but maybe we can meld a new middle.

Renewed energy fills me up and I can't stop smiling as I push to my feet.

"Your place or mine?" Silvie asks.

Damn.

"It was, uh…nice meeting you, Silvie, but…" I fish out my wallet and lay a few bills on the bar top. No harm, no foul. I'm edging away from her when I notice Jacques beside Rox with his hand in hers.

Tightness coils through my body as he stretches his arm

out to take a selfie of them. A desperate anger flares in my gut. I hate that I'm all over the place. That her presence or lack thereof can dictate my mood. In five seconds flat, I've gone from feeling like I could fly, filled with a relieved sense of joy and hope, to feeling like nothing more than a jealous fool.

My cheeks burn with humiliation as I watch them together.

Is this the guy she needs?

Rox is free to choose whomever she wants. It's clear that's not me. *So then why am I so bent out of shape?*

I try to smile, but my mouth feels tight. The muscles at the sides of my jaw harden and heat rushes over my skin. I don't know what I thought was going to happen, but this sure the hell isn't it.

"Do you know her?" Silvie asks, breaking into my thoughts. There's a territorial bite to her tone. *Same*, I think. But then I'm struck with an idea.

My next move.

I suck in a deep breath, dragging my gaze over Silvie's curve-hugging red dress down to her stilettos. The heels on those things must be at least five or six inches. She's tall, fit, gorgeous. The woman who makes other women jealous.

If she's watched even a single episode of *Jeopardy!* this just might work.

"Have you checked out the trivia nights here, Silvie?"

"I read *Grapevine* magazine…" She bounces hopefully.

A gossip rag isn't ideal, but I decide she might answer the pop culture and entertainment questions, so I flash her a reassuring smile. She whispers something to her friend on the other side of her, who peeks past her shoulder at me and giggles before Silvie gives me the all clear. I take her hand, weaving through the crowd toward the door. Toward Rox and Jacques.

"Glad you made it," I say when we reach them just in time to see Rox leaning her ear close to Jacques's mouth, traces of a laugh quirking her pillowy lips.

Her attention darts to Silvie and she swallows. "Yeah. You said it was okay to bring friends…" *I meant girlfriends, your sister, my sister.* Rox stumbles over her words, and it's just the tiny ego boost I need to make it through this night unscathed. *Well, almost unscathed.*

Silvie leans in conspiratorially. "Oh my gosh! Are you the girl from the Jennifer Ling interview, the meme? The Monopoly Queen's sister?"

Right on cue, Sabita makes a last call for trivia team sign-ups announcement, saving me from having to hold Rox back. The four of us make our way to the back. Since the crowd is larger than normal, there's only room for one more team. While none of us are sure about Silvie's ability to contribute—or Jacques's for that matter—I'm grateful not to be a third wheel on a team with only Rox and Jacques.

The table Vick reserved for me in the back is just off the left of the stage. We're able to avoid weaving through the sea of tables and we're close enough to see the chalkboard where the scores are tallied.

Once everyone is seated, the game host, Paul goes over the game rules.

There will be twenty questions total broken into six rounds of three questions each, plus a halftime and a final question. The first nine questions focus on geography, entertainment, literature. The halftime one is random. The following nine tackle sports, nature, and science—my favorite categories. Then the final question is host's choice.

When he finishes explaining the rules, Sabita clears her throat in the mic. I'm grateful my competitive spirit helps me—*almost*—forget Silvie is sitting on my left, Rox on my right. More important, that Jacques is on Rox's right.

We immediately get the first geography question about the European country that ruled Algeria for over a hundred and thirty years right, Jacques proudly remembering his country's history. Rox nails the literature one about the "T.H.U.G." acronym used on the cover of Angie Thomas's bestselling novel, *The Hate U Give*. I surprise the hell out of myself when I get Taylor Swift's successful follow-up album to *Folklore, Evermore.*

"Emmy winner Tim Gunn frequently gives what piece of advice on *Project Runway*?" Sabita dips her chin and surveys our team, aptly named The Cheese Wheels—*thanks to Rox*—before she swivels to eye the only other team who hasn't been living under a rock this past century, The Question Marks.

At their table, there's a tall, lumberjack, bearded guy with red hair, and eyes he can't seem to unsquint. It's a wonder he's playing at all since he hasn't stopped watching what we're doing. After every question, he peers over at us, then lowers his head to huddle his team together.

"Anyone know this one?" I lower my chin, but continue watching nosy Big Red.

Not that our team meshes so well, but *motley* is definitely the word I'd use for the rest of his crew. A short, bald guy who looks high as a kite and bops his head absently to some nonexistent music; an Asian girl with purple hair, fire-engine-red lips, and a trendy sense of style, who might give us a little competition on this one; and a broad-shouldered Black guy in thin-framed glasses who looks smart as heck.

Rox nips her fingernail. "Shoot. I know this one. It's on the tip of my tongue."

"The one with Tyra Banks… *American's Next Top Model*," Jacques whispers conspiratorially, like anyone is listening for his wrong answer.

"He just said it was *Project Runway*." I shake my head, but then register I'm giving my jealousy away in front of Rox. "It's Heidi Klum on this show. Tim Gunn was her cohost with the tailored suits. He went around to each designer and said—"

"Make it work!" Silvie whisper-yells. She springs up and down on the chair, her breasts bouncing as she beams from ear to ear.

"Write it down." My tone is hushed as I squint over in time to see Lavender Barbie scribbling their answer on the sheet. "Shit, I think they got it, too."

Rox gives a small head jerk. "Dammit."

The next three questions aren't even a challenge. What is *ganja* in Jamaican? Seriously? Who isn't smoking the stuff? Rox is practically ready to jump on Oprah's couch when Sabita asks who played Bret Maverick in the movie *Top Gun*.

"Have you seen the beach scene?" she purrs. I swear there's a small amount of drool glistening at the corner of her mouth. "That's when he was an absolute smoke show!"

Then Sabita keeps it coming.

Rox is on fire when the literature question veers into red room territory. "In the novel *Fifty Shades of Grey*, what was the name of Christian's helicopter?"

Rox leans in and suggestively whispers, "Charlie Tango."

Silvie joins her in a collective laugh at my expense.

I nod, letting them have their fun.

But the way Rox's sweet peachy scent bands around me, it's all I can do not to drag her away from this table and into the bathroom. Press my body flush against hers, taste her moan as I deepen the kiss...

Fuck.

"Calm down, sparky," I say, averting my attention, but I'm biting back a laugh, not to cry. *What was I thinking?* I've never seen Rox like this in her element. She's a real trivia head, but she's...stunning. She's a beacon of light in the darkness. *And I'm just a moth drawn to her flame.*

The way her lips curve when she laughs and the smile in her expressive, warm brown eyes...

I crack my neck on either side, closing my eyes.

After the halftime question, Jacques and Silvie head over to the bar for refills, leaving Rox and me alone for the first time tonight. She takes a few minutes to pass out sale flyers to the tables and leaves the stack with Paul, but then she settles back on the chair beside me.

"Thanks for inviting me. This is right up my alley, and I really think people will check out the store." Her voice is soft as she peers up at me, but she adds nothing else. Almost like she's waiting for me to say something. *But what? I'm pissed you showed up with Jacques. What would I look like saying anything with Silvie at my side? I don't know this woman from*

Eve. And now, she won't even sooth the sting of loneliness.

All I hear is Declan's voice in my head.

Do you want her?

I'd been on the fence when he asked. I thought I'd be okay knowing someone else could give Rox what she wants. I thought I was just caught up in the moment because of Jacques, but why am I fighting this? Rox isn't some girl I picked up in a bar for the night. She's more. This small glimpse of closeness tonight. The fun and laughs, feeling the heat from her body inches from mine and not being to touch her. I'm so far beyond the fence.

In my gut, I know this feeling won't pass.

I twist to face her, swallowing.

"I, uh…I spoke with Vick earlier." I toss her a glance. "Since they've had to cut trivia nights because of other events, I told him I'd ask you first, but maybe it might help Love & Games if you hosted the off weeks. They booked an event two weeks from now, so this month, they've planned trivia nights for next Friday and the last, on the thirtieth. Great way to grow the business and surround the attendees with overstock. Who better than people who already love trivia to help you offload some of your Trivial Pursuit games?"

Rox's big brown eyes widen and her lips part slightly. "Look at you, full of ideas to solve my business problems."

"I listened to you. Back at Love & Games, I heard that small tinge of worry in your tone. I know it's bothering you. If I can do even a small thing to help, I'm all in." *I care about you.*

I don't say those last words aloud, but the fact that they

go through my mind, working their way, shifting in my chest. The truth in them is as terrifying as it is thrilling.

When she doesn't fill the silence, I reach over to the table and cover her hand with mine. "If you'll let me, I want to keep helping."

She surveys me for a long beat, her bright gaze alert and searching for what I suspect is the catch. A deeper meaning. I get this tiny niggling feeling inside because I've surprised her. Shoot, I've shocked the hell out of me. Us. Like this, quiet and comfortable without saying a word. I'm burning with a new energy. All I know is, I don't want to feel this just once.

This isn't a game.

I never want to see Rox with Jacques or any other man for that matter. I want her for myself. If that means slowly pursuing her to show her I care, even though I'm not nearly good enough for her, I'll try every day. It'll go against everything I know and I'm sure I'll fuck up a dozen times, but I'm willing to try if she wants me.

I toss her a small smile and squeeze her hand.

I don't let go.

CHAPTER NINE

ROX

Q: The first diamond engagement ring is believed to have been commissioned in 1477 by what Archduke of Austria for his future wife, Mary of Burgundy.

A: Maximillian

HARPER HASN'T STOPPED talking since we parked off a side street near the shops in North Park. We're supposed to be looking for cute swimsuits and sexy party dresses for Vegas. So far, we've stopped in Vicky's for a semiannual sale and somehow ended up in the frilly, pure-as-snow, bridal nighties section. We followed that invigorating experience with a "peek" in the bookstore wedding planner nook, and now we're "just looking" at wedding gowns.

Unless Declan slipped and told Nadia by mistake, Harper still has no clue today is the day he's planning to propose.

This ought to be fun dragging her away from the FIVE dresses she's "just going to try on really quick."

"You're not excited about all this?" Harper asks from behind a ceiling-length blush-pink curtain. "I know he hasn't asked me yet, but he's obviously going to if he has the ring, so what's the big deal?"

I lean back in the coordinated pink plush round chair, checking yet another message from Declan. The big hoorah is all going down this afternoon at Love & Games at two. I've got at least a good hour, but I know it's his nerves making him frantic, so I give him a pass.

"I seem to remember a time not too long ago when you absolutely loathed weddings," I say.

There's a swooshing noise of rustling fabric as Harper releases a strained grunt. "Oh my gosh, I can't wait to show this one. It's ah-may-zing!" she singsongs. "And anyway, everyone feels like that before it's their turn."

"Excuse me, no one feels like that but you. Some of us have been dreaming about our big day since birth."

Muffled laughter bumbles through the curtain.

But then she goes silent.

A moment later, she slips out of the dressing room. She looks every bit the blissful bride. The floor-length, hand-embroidered ivory lace gown cinches her waist and trumpets out just above her knees. The strapless sweetheart bodice and nude lining sculpt her curves. And as the dutiful consultant adjusts a cascading lace veil around her shoulders and down her back, I feel all the emotions swirling inside me.

I'm so excited, happy for my sister. But just under the surface where I've swept everything out of sight, I'm also frustrated, envious, humiliated, and desperate. Ashamed to be feeling anything other than the complete elation I should.

Why can't I shake this feeling?

The corners of my eyes burn, and I blink back tears.

"You're so beautiful. Declan is going to be the luckiest man on earth."

Harper pushes out her lower lip and stretches her arms toward me. When I get to my feet, she pulls me into a bear hug, and I feel what's coming next. The same way I know when Mom is going to gently nudge an unrelated topic back around to me, I hear Harper's next words pinball around my head.

"For what it's worth, I think you could be next." She eases out her zinger, squeezing me. "I'm not talking about that fake little post of you and Jacques, either. You never told me how it's been going at the trivia nights with Murph…"

And there it is.

Deep down in the gooey part of my gut, I *knew* she'd been not-so-subtly waiting for the perfect moment to bring him up. It's been a week and a day since the first trivia night with Jacques and Murph's sexified flavor of the week. *Who in their right mind wears a clubbing dress to trivia night?* I mean, I know Elixir is also a bar, but *really?* At least she got two questions right.

That's neither here nor there, though.

Other than Murph's deep, meaningful stare as he held my hand and pledged to help me with Trivial Pursuit Nights at the store beginning at the end of the month, the thing that threw me off is the fact he didn't just leave it at that. I would've respected the lip service for the empty, if kind, gesture I figured it was. But then he texted me when I got home. After Jacques dropped me off. A sweet and thoughtful *"just making sure you made it home safe"* text.

Even now, I'm still not sure how I was supposed to respond. I kept thinking it was code for a booty call, some alternative version of Flixshow and chill. So, I just said yes.

Not to the booty call. That I'd made it home safe.

All week I got random calls and texts, which Gwyn forbade me from answering. *"How are you?" "Hope you're having a nice day." "Hitting the beach before work for some paddleboarding if you want to join me."*

Like, what the heck is that?

Then again, last night after trivia—sans Jacques and Silvie this time—he didn't make a move. Not one touch or out-of-the-blue, blood-tingling hand squeeze like last weekend. But by the time I'd made it home, locked up, turned out the lights, and changed into my pajamas, another *"make it home safe"* text. And this morning? *"Hope to see you today."*

Harper snaps her fingers next to my ear. "Hello? Anyone still in there?"

She's wearing an entirely different dress.

"Sorry." I shake my head, shoving the thought aside. "It's just, I know I said I was going to take my shot with Murph, but it's hard when I can't tell what angle he's coming from. Like, where's his head with this whole offer to help with trivia nights? And where is all of this attentiveness coming from?"

She heaves an amused sigh. Her expression is all *there, there, sweet inexperienced little sister.*

I roll my eyes. "What was that all about?"

"Maybe your little *make Murph jealous* scheme with

Jacques worked, and he really is beside himself, but you said he talked to Vick about us hosting a trivia night before you showed up at Elixir. I just think you're reading way too much into it. Love..." She holds up her palms. "And I'm not saying what you two have is *love* yet, but it isn't always about saying the words, as we well know, looking at our parents as examples. I gave Dad such a hard time about jumping in and out of marriages, but now that I'm—"

"Jumping the gun before Declan proposes," I quip.

We both laugh because she's freaking standing here in a wedding dress without a fiancé.

Shit. I flip my wrist to check my watch. Where did the time go? It's already one thirty.

I've got to wrap up this funfest.

I wind my hand in circles, urging Harper to make her point.

"What? We're not in a rush. It's our off day. I have nowhere to be." *Uh...yes, you do. You just don't know it.*

"It's not an emergency, but while you were in the dressing room, Nadia sent me a message asking to drop by the store for a few minutes. Something about a package for you..."

Harper stares at the floor unfocused, pressing a finger to her lips. "A package..." she mutters absently.

Lucky for me, that little seed seems to take root.

"Okay, I have no clue what it is, but it's entirely possible I forgot about some order with the way my brain has been overloaded this past week." She gnaws on her bottom lip, then appears to shove the thought aside. "Anyway, long story short, all I was going to say was I finally get what Dad and our moms went through. Love, marriage, relationships. It's rarely ever about the words. It's how he shows you. The little things. The *trivial* details," she says, emphasizing the word for my game-loving benefit.

"Nice play on words." I chuckle, thinking how much I love my beautiful, corny, but also wise sister.

My mind drifts to Murph. All the trouble he went through to ask Vick about letting us host games and passing out flyers. Yes, he was there with another woman, but I was there with Jacques, so I can hardly blame him. Even so, the entire night, his attention was steadfastly on me.

And the texts.

They're small gestures, definitely thoughtful. From the heart. Was checking to make sure I made it home safe Murph's way of showing me I'm important to him? Have I been missing the signs?

"The point is love and marriage are what you make of it. Friendship, romance, human connection, *intimacy*." Harper waggles her eyebrows suggestively.

At this, I pull away to sit back in my cushy chair, thinking about all the things Murph and I already share. Friendship and human connection, yes. It's the romance and intimacy I'm longing for with him.

"Go get dressed so we can go pick up your *package*," I tease.

By the time Harper changes, gets all the dress information from the consultant, and drags her feet behind me back to the car, I have exactly thirteen minutes to get us to Love & Games, where, apparently, there's a shit-ton of people waiting. According to Nadia's last frantic message, not only is Declan, Dad, the Sloane Wives' Club, and Murph there, but so is Declan's mom, and the entire Greater San Diego Hasbro Nation. Oh, and bonus, Jennifer Ling.

My nerves are freaking shot.

Somewhere in the tiny crevices of my bones, I feel this is going to be another viral Love & Games moment. Like, two are clearly not enough for our family, so the universe just keeps throwing the punches.

"Slow down," Harper says, white-knuckling the oh-shit bar.

Oh shit, is right.

I take the long way around to Love & Games and pray my expression doesn't reflect the way my heart rate ratchets up a few notches when I spot the Channel 5 Action News van *inconspicuously* parked a block from the store. As I round the corner, there's a single space available directly in front of Love & Games.

"Shit," Harper hisses, her neck craned to peer out the window.

Immediately, I zero in on our very jam-packed store. Love & Games is *never* busy on the weekends. We get a handful of stragglers throughout the day, but…*ten, fifteen, maybe even twenty people at once?*

"What…what is it?" *Wow, not suspicious at all.* "Am I about to hit the curb or something?" I ask, doing a crap job of recovering.

"Nadia should have called one of us if it was this busy."

I cut the engine and twist my body, pretending to fidget with something in the back seat when really I'm inhaling breaths not to hyperventilate.

"I'm sure it's just a brief spurt. It's probably been slow all day."

Shit, shit, shit.

Declan said to act like nothing was happening. Business as usual. Because televised—and likely soon-to-be viral—wedding proposals and Saturday afternoon spy activity are apparently the norm in our whacked-out universe.

Twisting back into my seat as Harper gets out, I do a quick double-check of my makeup in the rearview mirror.

Another fifteen minutes of fame coming up.

The bell above the door jingles announcing our entrance, but we need no introduction. I practically run into Harper's back as she abruptly stops just inside the door.

Declan is standing right next to the Trivial Pursuit table with the small navy velvet box Harper found in his drawer. And she was right. He did well. I'm mesmerized and blinded by all three carats and obsessed with the swirly design of the pavé diamonds along the white-gold band.

This is really happening. My sister is getting married.

I won't lie, knowing Harper is about to take her shot, it gets to me. I can't help thinking about Gwyn's "Get My Man" list. As I look past Declan's shoulder to Murph, I'm reminded again of my jealousy game with Jacques and my undying need to define, outline, quantify, and overanalyze the data to test actual love. They will not change the fact the numbers keep pointing to Murph.

He gives me a small wave.

Maybe I've been so narrow-minded about his relationship avoidance. I never once wondered why. If I'm taking my shot, I need to focus on the little things. The details, I remind myself. Which means spending time really getting to know Murph up close and all in my personal space.

I'm about to walk over to him when out of the corner of my eye, movement snags my attention. Jennifer Ling weaves through the crowd, making room for her cameraman to get the best shot of Declan and Harper.

"The instant I saw you in sweats, flip-flops, and your favorite red trench coat about to attack a barista over a cup of coffee, I knew I had to meet you." A collective wave of laughter washes over the room as Declan takes a step closer to Harper. "When you challenged my Monopoly skills, you were a beautiful pain in my ass. Most days, you still are," Declan mumbles, but a wide smile grows on his face as he stares endearingly at her.

"Hey, that's my daughter you're talking about," Dad jests, only half-serious.

Declan palms the air, gesturing for Dad to hold off for him to get to the good part.

"When you ended up helping breathe new life into Pop's little bungalow, our home, I got a small glimpse of your heart. From that day forward, I tried to fight this feeling growing inside. But when I finally got out of my head, I knew I wanted to be with you. Love you, with every inch of my heart."

My eyes water as I watch them together. Pressing my hand to my heart, I'm listening. To the snapshot moments of their relationship. To the tiny details that might sound trivial to anyone else, but to them, they're the magic that makes up a relationship. Love. It doesn't feel like the makings of a marriage merry-go-round like Dad or a one-and-done like our moms. Harper isn't wasting her shot or jumping the gun. She's found a third option.

One I want so badly.

"So, I brought us back to where it all started," Declan continues. "Because I want to keep loving you and playing games with you for the rest of my life," he says as he kneels. "Marry me Harper Sloane and live happily-ever-after with me."

Harper nods a million times. Her face is flush and tears stream down her cheeks, but she's beaming and beautiful as she rushes in to kiss Declan.

Joy wells in my heart.

The crowd, which now includes an outdoor audience, erupts in whistles and cheers. Jennifer Ling plasters on a smile as she reports "You heard it here, first" despite the sea of phones aimed at Harper and Declan.

Soon, food and drinks flow, and Nadia turns on the music. It's loud and wild, and a *proper* celebration. Everyone is here, so I make the rounds with the newly engaged couple and the parentals before checking in with Micah, who owns Booked Up, Jacques—with a redhead I'm hoping is Bridget—and a few of the store regulars. Declan's mom starts a hug fest, passing me along to Rita, Jade, and finally Everly, who are all—surprisingly—getting along.

I think I get to every person in the place, slipping past Jennifer Ling before bumping into the only other person I've been dreading talking to. Well, not dreading so much as building up my nerve.

"Hey, Murph." I flash him a small smile, and I'm greeted with his trademark lopsided grin.

"Hey, sparky," he says so softly. It comes out like a tiny breath, but he says nothing more. His blue gaze skates across my skin, sending chills thrumming through my veins. My entire body comes to attention.

I would give my left arm to know what he's thinking right now, but I'm too scared to move—to lose this moment.

The music changes and the slow, soulful beat of "Nothing Even Matters" electrifies the air. I'm caught up in the lyrics as Lauryn Hill and D'Angelo confess the world could fall apart around them, but nothing would matter more than the love they share.

"Dance with me?" His voice is faint but rough around the edges, the usual carefree, playful side of him absent in his expression.

Everything around us fades away. In this quiet moment, my universe tilts on its axis. My cheeks heat and my breath hitches in my throat as he takes my hand, tugging me flush to his body. I'm a bundle of nerves as we sway with the easy tinkling piano notes. Every millimeter of me craves this man, throbs in places it has no business throbbing in a room full of people. But I can't ignore the slow heat curling down my spine as he places his hand on the small of my back. The same whisper of longing I feel is reflected at me in his stare.

Does he feel it, too?

All my lists and relationship books, they've made a mockery of me. I know they'll never be able to convey what it feels like to dance this obscenely close. Our heartbeats in sync, his familiar freshwater scent enveloping me, desire radiating between us. This is my love language. I figured acts of service or words of affirmation, but now I'm one thousand percent sure I'm physical touch. *Murph's touch.*

My heart skitters.

Back at the bridal shop, I couldn't see past my swirling emotions, but now I get it. I've always wanted to find what Harper and Declan share, but I've never felt so close. No wonder I'm frustrated and envious, desperate and afraid to find a love that didn't look like my parents'. But the one person who I could actually have a fighting chance at finding it with, I've been holding at a distance.

I never let Murph in.

"Glad I got to see you today," I say as I rest my head against his chest. The faint rhythm of his heartbeat lulls me, and I decide the world could fall apart around us—nothing else matters.

CHAPTER TEN

MURPH

Q: Name the song written by composer Alan Menken and lyricist Glenn Slater for Walt Disney Pictures' 50th animated feature film, *Tangled*.

A: "Mother Knows Best"

YESTERDAY, I DANCED with Rox Sloane. She rested her head on my chest and I don't think I've ever felt closer to her. Our bodies, the way we moved, our steps in time with each other's. It was almost like we were communicating on a cellular level, yet we barely said a word.

The quiet made me think of my parents.

Maybe I've been so focused on the big picture, the meaning of marriage and relationships, I missed the silent stares and small touches between them. Maybe I've been blind to what it means to be so comfortable with another person, words aren't necessary.

Jerking my key fob over my shoulder to arm my car, I take easy strides up the paved walkway to my parents' house.

It's early Sunday morning, so I find the familiar gold house key and let myself inside.

"It's just me," I call out, making my way through the living room to the kitchen at the back of the house.

Mom is in her usual spot at the small bay window facing the backyard. In one hand, she holds the #1 MOM mug I made in eighth grade pottery class, and in the other, from what I can tell by the bold, menacing red letters on the dark book cover, her latest mystery suspense read. She's had the same morning ritual since I could remember. But I'm reminded time hasn't stopped ticking when I round the counter and see her oxygen tank off the edge of the chair.

"Oh, Teddy, isn't this a pleasant surprise," she says, setting her mug and book down, and preparing to grip the table.

"Don't get up, Mom." I lean down and kiss her velvety cheek like I've done a million times before. "I'm just stopping by for a few minutes to check on you and Dad. Is he here?"

A soft smile colors the cherries of her cheeks.

She sips her half-empty cup of coffee before she answers. "He went to the hardware store. Still trying to fix that old barbecue grill. Got his mind set that it's the connector fittings or hose this time, so I figure we'll be getting a new grill in a month or so." Her smile widens.

"Oh boy." I laugh.

Dad is one of the smartest men I know, but he is downright destructive when he fixes anything other than a plate of food.

Absently, I run my fingers along the shattered yellow and

orange mosaic tiles set on the surface of the table. I haven't seen Mom and Dad since the Fourth of July. Deep down, I know I've been putting it off, dreading the sight of them fragile, dependent on oxygen, *aging.*

Mom reaches across, gently rubbing my hand. "He'll be so happy to see you, Teddy."

It's been a long time since I've asked about Dad, and I know the chance of her men finally getting along warms Mom's heart.

Yesterday at Love & Games, seeing Declan's mom and Harper's and Rox's parents, I longed for that kind of closeness. The relationships where, despite all the changing family dynamics—celebrations and storms alike—they're present for each other. For me to ever have that with my family, I'm going to have to let go of my hang-ups about my parents' marriage, *eventually.*

It won't happen overnight, but maybe Mom can shed some light on the tiny details I missed. That's why I'm here. I didn't want to wait to see them until after I get back from Vegas next weekend.

Somehow, being here, it feels urgent.

When I think about strong family bonds, Nadia and I have one as siblings, and Mom and I have a great mother-son relationship, but I want unconditional love and strength with my family as a unit…*if I'm ever going to have a family of my own—a marriage of my own.*

The realization is too much to take in at first.

That I'm even thinking about a future with someone, it feels meaningful. Like a shift. An irreversible change. My heart pounds against my chest, long-seeded panic twisting my gut. It's the familiar unease I always get when I think about committing to a woman when I can't be certain I won't turn into my father.

Rubbing the back of my neck, I glance over at Mom, considering the questions I need to ask her without Dad.

I texted Rox this morning to see how her day was going, but I couldn't get the image of that selfie of her and Jacques out of my head. The way they were huddled close, their heads pressed together like they'd done it a million times. The familiarity swirls around in the pit of my stomach, acidic and unsettling, coming up like bile in my throat.

"Do you love Dad?"

Is being lonely better than being alone? That's what I'm really asking, but I don't have the nerve to put it in those terms.

Mom seems put off by the question at first. Not mad but unnerved by my blunt delivery. But then she smiles endearingly at me, the wrinkles at the corners of her eyes twisting as she flashes me her trademark smile.

"Next week, you'll be married forty years. That's four years longer than I've been alive. I'm just trying to understand what makes you and Dad tick, what makes you stay."

She takes another sip of coffee, probably cold by now.

"I will always love your father." There isn't even an inkling of doubt in her tone. "If you're asking if I've ever thought about divorce, the answer is yes."

I gasp because she's hit the nail on the head. Other kids want their parents to stay together forever. I always wondered why she never left. Based on what I thought I knew about their marriage, I almost would've preferred they separate.

The weight of her words steadies me.

"But..." Mom's sparkling blue gaze settles on me. "I suspect anyone who has ever been married or committed to another human with flaws and hang-ups and baggage of their own will tell you it sort of goes with the territory. It's a choice, though, Teddy," she says, like it's a caveat. "One we make every single day. Do I want to be alone and have a clean house with a working barbecue grill?" She laughs. "Or do I want to be with someone who knows me and loves me, and also knows every one of my buttons to push?"

I pinch the bridge of my nose, considering this angle of Mom's words against the first eighteen years of my life. They didn't yell and fight even though I'd always thought if they had, it would've been proof they were at least passionate enough about each other.

"Teddy, I've always known how you've viewed your dad's and my marriage, but there are many versions of love. Dad shows me in so many small ways. It's a gift not to have to grow old alone." She drums her delicate hands on the table, but the corner of her mouth kicks up in a smile.

I tilt my head, wondering what she could find funny about this conversation when I'm floundering, trying to figure out what to do with all these feelings. I need to know if all relationships lead to dead ends, whether a person leaves or stays.

"Oh, I wondered if this day would come," she coos, looking right at me, but I sense her mind is far away.

"And what day is that Mom?" I counter.

She refocuses, searching my face like the truth is scrawled

across my forehead. "My handsome Teddy is finally looking at life through a different lens. Not only has someone special caught your eye, but from what I can tell, she—or he—seems to have snagged a piece of your heart."

I don't know what to say to that.

As long as I've known Rox, she's had both my attention and a small piece of my heart. The problem is, lately, without my knowledge or consent, she seems to have taken more pieces. *And then there's the matter of Jacques.*

My phone pings with a message notification and I slip it from my back pocket, swiping away the photo of Rox and Jacques huddled together. It's her.

> *"I am having a great morning. Thanks for asking. If you're not sick of seeing me with trivia nights and wedding proposals, want to hang at the beach today? I'm just going to lie out with a book, but I wouldn't mind the company. Let me know."*

Jacques who?

I try—*unsuccessfully*—to bite back the smile stretching my mouth as I reply that I'll meet her in a couple of hours. But Mom detects my mood change and zeros in on it.

"Like I was saying, love comes in as many shapes and forms as do the ways people show it, Teddy. It could be something as dramatic as publicly professing it in one of those viral videos or on the news, like your friend Declan. Or something as simple as a quick message to ask how your day is going." Mom shifts in her chair to look at me head-on. "It doesn't always look on the outside like it feels on the inside. If you decide you want to try your hand at love, I want you to remember one thing. Your version doesn't have to look like what Dad and I have—that's the beauty of it. It's yours to choose."

I nod, still considering Mom's words.

It's a choice. I don't have to choose their version of love.

This thing I've got for Rox, it's not love, but it's not nothing, either.

I'm not sure how to define it. Or how to make sense of what I'm feeling. But there's no one I'd rather have help me discover my choice.

Mom and I talk and play a short round of Trivial Pursuit over cold cut sandwiches. When Dad calls to tell her he'll be another hour or so, I take off to meet Rox at Mission Beach, making a quick pit stop by the house to pick up my wetsuit and paddleboard. Packing enough snacks for two, it occurs to me while I haven't seen Rox with Jacques since the first trivia night, he was at Love & Games yesterday. *What if Rox invited him to the beach, too?*

I try not to let the thought of being a third wheel dull my excitement during the drive over and as I walk along the boardwalk searching for Rox.

A few minutes later, I find her lying on a neon pink beach towel just off the water.

Alone.

"There you are," I say.

Rox squints up at me from under a bright yellow book with a hot pink script title that reads, *The Blame Game.* "Hey, stranger. Long time no see." She smiles.

I set my board and bag down, then roll out my towel beside hers before plopping down on my side to face her. For a second, I really look at her. I'm mesmerized, memorizing the small flecks of gold in her sparkling brown eyes. I don't know that I've ever noticed, but there's a thin spattering of tiny freckles dusted over the bridge of her button nose and slightly flushed pink cheeks. Her loose honey-streaked curls are piled on top of her head and she's in a pale blue bikini tied off in bows at the curves of her hips. I'm lost in the way the sun casts a warm bronze glow to the long, taut lines of her lean body down to her brightly painted pink toenails stretched over the length of the towel.

She lightly clears her throat and bites back a grin, the corners of her mouth twitching.

"Like what you see?"

I lower my chin to my chest, heat creeping into my cheeks. "You know you're beautiful. I'm just admiring the view."

It's her turn to blush now.

A shiver trembles down my spine at how breathtaking she really is, and for a beat, I'm at a loss for words, basking in the quiet. On the drive here, I thought of a million things I wanted to talk about to avoid the awkward silences. Trivia, Vegas, what she wants for her birthday, the store. This is the first time Rox and I don't have family or friends around to fill in the lulls in conversation. We're not in a loud bar with dim shadows and a quizmaster at the center of the spotlight.

But now that I'm here, I don't mind the silence.

Rox tips her chin. "What's in the bag?"

I flit a glance at my duffel, then back at her. "Just your standard stuff. Wallet, phone, sunscreen, trivia cards. Water and snacks."

Amusement brightens her eyes. “What kind of snacks are we talking about here exactly?”

The corner of my mouth tugs up. “Chips, apples, a couple of granola bars. Red Vines.”

She shoots me a full-teeth grin, dropping her book to wiggle her fingers. “Gimme, gimme.” She laughs.

I chuckle and hand her the bag. “Have at it.”

She goes right for the Ziploc of Red Vines, fishing out a couple, and biting into a vine. “Ah. This is the life.” She moans her approval. “Sun, surf, candy, and good company…”

“I aim to please.”

It’s the strangest thing. She’s in nothing more than waterproof underwear. We haven’t touched or kissed or slept together. But this playful, fun-loving side of her. This turns me on. *All the way on.*

Desire flickers to life inside me. My entire body sizzles, heat curling down my spine. I’m overheated from the inside out, so I drag the wetsuit zipper down and peel the sleeves off, letting the top hang around my waist. The warm breeze cools my skin.

When I turn back to Rox, I’m blindsided by the heat pooling in her eyes as her gaze scrapes over my chest.

Fuck.

I want to say something. Let her know the feeling is distractingly mutual, but I still can’t get past the barriers in my head. That I’m not nearly good enough for her. That I’m not her choice. She may belong to someone else.

The selfie Jacques tagged her in haunts me.

Tugging free a Red Vine, I toss her a glance. “How are

things with, um…Jake, was it?" It's fishing, but I need to know where her head is.

She draws in a long breath, then blows out her cheeks. "We're… *Jacques* and I are just friends. That's all."

I nod, both loving her answer and hating how the question dims the light in her eyes.

"Not going to lie, I'm not sad about it."

Rox releases a disbelieving laugh, her lips parting. "Well, what about Sophie, or Silvia, or whatever her name was? How are *things* with you two? It looked like you had a budding romance on your hands."

The same way I know Jacques's name isn't Jake, Rox remembers Silvie's name. But the tinge of jealousy in her tone does wonders for my ego.

"She's fine," I say, watching as Rox nods.

It's wrong to milk the moment, but I rake my fingers through my hair and close my eyes, lifting my chin skyward. I suck in a lungful of air, fighting the smile threatening at my lips. When I can't hold it a second longer, I say, "I mean, I guess. I haven't talked to her since the first trivia night, but she was a great fourth for The Cheese Wheels."

When I chance a look at Rox, I adore the return of light in her eyes.

"You asshole!"

"In all honesty," I say, laughing, "I'd just met her at the bar that night, but when I saw you with Jacques…" I scratch my nose, willing myself to take another step—show Rox how I feel about her. "I hated seeing you two together, but I wasn't exactly in a place to say anything with her around."

Rox pushes up onto her knees and squares her body to

face me. She surveys me with curious eyes, her full pout parted with newfound realization.

"Let me get this straight. Are you saying you were jealous, Dr. Murphy Theodore Sikes?" Her lighthearted tone is like a caffeine buzz, lifting my mood.

With downcast eyes and a smile kicking up the corner of my mouth, I nod. "Yes. I was jealous as fucking hell."

"Holy shit!" She shakes her head, speechless before she claps a hand over her mouth, her big brown eyes beaming at me. "I totally thought you were going to deny it!"

I shake my head, letting the moment settle between us.

But then she folds her arms over her chest. "Would it surprise you to know that was the desired result? That I might have had a hand in ensuring you were?"

Wait, what?

This whole time, I've been… Now that I think about it, when I walked into Love & Games and spotted Rox and Jacques laughing, there wasn't a romantic undertone to their interaction. Even at trivia night, beyond the photo, they didn't touch or share lingering stares. In fact, yesterday at Love & Games, I didn't see them together at all. And wasn't he with someone else?

"So, you were trying to make me jealous?" It's my turn to stare open-mouthed, but I can't discount the rush of heat surging through me that she went through the trouble. I pick up a Red Vine, take a bite, and boop her nose with it before standing and taking off toward the water.

The playfulness between us sets the tone.

The rest of the day is comfortable, quiet, and easy laughs. We talk about her love of brightly colored romance novels and Algoberto's tacos, my obsession with trying new beers wherever I go, and how she wants to challenge me to a game of *Blue December*.

My heart knocks around in my chest as we swim, and I teach her to paddleboard. With every touch I feel us inching closer, the inkling of this—us—that we might work. It grows stronger by the minute.

By the time we crawl back onto our sandy towels, a new quiet energy settles between us. Rox reads from her book aloud to me, and as the characters fight the urge to be together, my ache to touch Rox escalates to combustible desperation. I inch my hand across the invisible barrier between our towels, and our fingers touch in the sand. When she slips her hand in mine without missing a beat, I know without a doubt Mom is right.

I'm finally looking at life through a different lens, and Rox is at the center of my focus.

CHAPTER ELEVEN

ROX

Q: Name the original singer of the 1983 hit song "Total Eclipse of the Heart."

A: Bonnie Tyler

"WHAT DAY IS it?" Gwyn's voice booms into my car on Bluetooth.

Lord, give me the strength.

"Hi." I heave an exhausted sigh because it's only Tuesday and I need a Friday in the worst way. Between the truckload of new Monopoly stock coming in, entering it manually after the computers went down, and setting up a makeshift *selfie-station* for Harper to sign game boxes and do photo ops, I'm over this week. In fact, it should be against the law for a week to be this shitty when it started out so well.

How did a sunny Sunday at the beach turn into this?

"Answer the question."

I flip on my blinker and veer into the left turning lane at the red light before I take a deep breath. I know exactly where this conversation is headed. Gwyn didn't stop by either trivia night, per my request. Literally, no one needed her staring Murph down with exhausted, disappointed eyes.

But I might've forgotten to bring her up to speed on how the "Get My Man" list has played out.

"Oh my goodness, *please*. It's Tuesday. And no, I didn't get around to calling you, in case that was going to be your next question." I blow out my cheeks. I don't have the patience to deal with her good cop/bad cop routine after today. I am starving, it's raining, and I am tired. "I was planning to call you."

"Mm-hmm."

"I *was*. I promise. But then things got sort of out of pocket with Harper and Declan's engagement. As you might have guessed—or seen—spoiler alert: their public engagement went viral over the weekend. If everything they do is going to go viral, I just can't." I release another big sigh. "But before that, nothing really happened."

For a moment, I let myself get lost in the memory of Murph's tropical blue eyes. The contoured ridges of his long, lean, and tan torso—

There's loud smacking and slurping as Gwyn eats and talks. "Nothing?"

"Nope."

My misophonia kicks in, making me want to cringe and cover my ears to muffle the sound. *A little trivia obsession bonus: having a wealth of little-known knowledge about things like irritable reactions to repetitive—and sometimes gross—sounds.* I try to focus on the wet city streets at night. They're a swirly neon watercolor painting in front of me.

But it doesn't work.

Unlike Gwyn's noisy chewing, her tone is dry and filled with skepticism.

"So, you're telling me between that first Friday when you met him at Elixir for trivia and today, a whole week and three days later, not one lingering stare? No phone calls or texts? You didn't see him?" Disbelief smudges all rank and rancid through her tone.

Technically, a hand squeeze upgraded to a handhold and a bit of harmless grab-assing in the water. The rough feel of his large, firm hands on my thighs and back…

Rightfully, I should tell Gwyn about everything that's happened with Murph. She strategized and came up with the list. But there's a small part of me that wants to keep the moments Murph and I shared for myself.

Gwyn sucks her teeth when I don't respond, calling my bluff.

"Okay, *fine*." I drag the word out on a whine. "At the first trivia night, he had a date, and I had Jacques, so I thought it was no big deal. He worked it out with the bar owner to have Love & Games host trivia nights on their off weeks, though. So that was nice…"

Behind me, a horn beeps, letting me know the light changed. As I ease off the brake and turn, my mind keeps spiraling, turning over the events of the past week and a half. The texts, the bolt of lightning surging through my body when he'd covered my hand with his on the table. Our dance at Harper and Declan's proposal. Our day at the beach.

And yes, he'd worked things out with Vick without me having to ask, but—

"And then?" Gwyn prods.

And then there was frolicking in the water at the beach because that's just what you do when the sun is out and casting glorious shadows over a gorgeous man's square jaw. That's what you do when the murky water is jealous that the sun glints in his sparkly blue eyes. When he does that unbelievably sexy knitted brow thing that sends flares low and tight in my belly because he looked like he wanted to ravage me…

"And then…what?" I shrug even though she can't see me.

"What was the point?"

That's my point. You frolic, dammit! And make the most of the day until he sends you the next check-in text that stirs up all the memories of the heat blazing over my aching skin.

"There really wasn't much else…" I trail off.

"Not even a tiny spark or a touch? He didn't do or say anything that made you feel like the feeling was mutual?"

Good God, the woman is relentless.

I mean, yes, he brought Red Vines, and he didn't make fun of my romance novel…and he asked me to read to him… I'm pretty sure most women who haven't had sex in as long as I have… They would look at this staggeringly beautiful golden boy with his sun-bleached blond hair and chiseled body, and they'd pray the zipper on that wetsuit malfunctioned, too.

Surely.

"What about at the second trivia night? Nothing? I know he was at Declan's proposal. Did you talk to him there?"

"Oh my goodness. Are you serious? I swear, nothing's

happened. It's all been very platonic." The words eke out of me, squeaky without the least bit of conviction. I can practically see Gwyn shaking her head, her red lips screwed in sheer disappointment.

"Excuse me, but why are you holding out on me, Roxanne Sloane?"

Because I still don't know what any of it means. Because I may or may not be starting to like spending time with a man whose history is proof he doesn't do relationships. Because I'm afraid this is all one-sided and I'll look like more of a fool than I already feel…

But I don't say any of that.

Gwyn's advice is questionable, and she isn't a fan of Murphy because all she knows are the stories I told her about him before we drifted apart. But she means well. She wants me to be happy. She wants my heart to be whole. For things to work out with Murph so we can go on spectacular double dates to Disneyland—okay, I'm the one who wants to go to Disneyland—and grimy bars where we'll drunk-dance to nineties pop songs. I know this because I want it, too.

So *badly*.

But what if I'm reading too much into this thing with Murph? We've done nothing, really.

"Your silence is louder than the traffic buzzing by you, so spill," she demands.

I groan. But then it all comes out like a thorough timeline recap.

"Yes, okay. He touched my hand once. At the first trivia night. He sweetly calls and texts daily to see how I'm doing or if I've made it home safe. We danced with my head resting on his chest at the proposal, and I may have swooned. A little." I roll my eyes because this is mortifying. "Sunday, I invited him to the beach, and we played in the water. He gave me a hands-on lesson in paddleboarding. And then I read to him while we ate Red Vines and held hands under the sun. And—"

"You read what to him?"

Butterflies send my stomach fluttering as I bite back a smile, and sheepishly say, "Romance. An angsty friends-to-lovers rom-com…" I chew the inside of my cheek, waiting.

For a second, the line is unnervingly quiet, but then Gwyn bursts out laughing. "This is some good shit. You cannot make this stuff up. It's too good."

"Right?!"

"Girl… I knew you all had chemistry, but I'm over here getting geeked up about this. If you two keep this up, we could be couples' vacationing in the Maldives by next year," she muses.

All the humor drains from my face as I turn into my driveway and let the engine run.

My chest tightens with worry, my heart rate syncing with the rapid staccato of the crickets chirping outside.

"See, I can't think like that. Murph is doing all the right things, but what if I'm setting myself up for a huge letdown? It doesn't matter how easily I can see myself falling for him—that's not a question." *It's too dangerous.*

"I know."

"Exactly. I can go deeper, but can he?" I huff out a sigh, anxiety swirling in the pit of my stomach. "Gwyn, this is Murph. I won't be able to turn my feelings off. I feel like this is a point of no return. Like I need to turn back now, or I'll end up throwing away my only shot."

"Slow down. You're the one who gets to decide if you want to go deeper with him," she reasons. "This is going to sound bananas coming from me, but I kind of think you should give him a chance."

"Wait, what?"

All the air vacuums from my chest.

I did not see this coming.

"You probably thought I was going to be against it, but if Murph is doing all the little things you say he's doing, then this might be his way of showing you that he cares."

Shit.

"I don't know," I say, cutting the ignition and getting out of the car.

As I unlock my front door and kick off my shoes, Gwyn tells me to pay attention to the way he proves himself. I put her on speaker and set my phone on the white marbled island as she drones on about letting his actions guide me. I'm still listening as I drag my tired bones into the kitchen where I stare blankly into the refrigerator.

I zone out looking at all the chicken breasts and vegetables I planned to make tonight, thinking about how much time—and energy I don't have now—to take to make a meal when my phone pings super loud.

"Did you hear what I said?" Gwyn asks.

"Yeah, I just..." My words die on the tip of my tongue as I pick up the phone. There's a text from Murph. And not just a regular *"how was work"* text.

"Have you eaten yet? I was in the neighborhood, and I

picked up some Algoberto's. I'm not too far from your house. I can be there in five if you're up for it."

I read every single word twice.

A small gasp spills from my lips. "Oh, shit."

"What, you think it's a bad idea to invite him to lunch?"

"No. Yes, well, maybe… I don't know. He wants to stop by." The words rush out of my mouth in a jumbled mess of nerves. "Like, now. He picked up tacos and asked if I'd eaten yet. What should I do?"

Like I'm not over here short-circuiting, Gwyn calmly asks, "Well, did you eat yet?"

"That's not the point. I'm starving and Algoberto's tacos sound like heaven, but if Murph comes here, I might as well hand him my heart on a freaking Styrofoam platter," I say as I make my way into the living room. "This isn't good."

Lightly nudging aside the front window curtain facing the street, I peek through the crack. Relief washes over me when there's nothing to see but darkness and trees dancing in the breeze. I drop the edge of the thin fabric and the silk sways back and forth until it's as still as I am.

The sinking feeling in my stomach pins me in place, and a tidal wave of panic washes over me.

"It could be *really* good." There's a smile in Gwyn's tone. "If my calculations are correct, it's been a little over a year since you've had an orgasm not induced by battery-operated devices. I say let the man prove his affections, eat delicious tacos, then see if he lives up to your steamy romance novel fantasies."

I wouldn't want to be rude. Let all that good food go to

waste…

As if on cue, my stomach croaks, rebuking any notion I had of declining. Screw it. A girl's got to eat, right?

Before I overthink it, I tap out a quick message.

> *"Nope, you caught me just in time. I was about to whip something up, but tacos sound amazing. See you in a few."*

CHAPTER TWELVE

ROX

Q: In what Broadway musical does a large plant called Audrey II demand, "Feed me, Seymour"?

A: *Little Shop of Horrors*

I'M A MESS. My heart is in my throat and my stomach is in knots. Murph will be here in two shakes of a little lamb's tail, and I look like who did it and why. I've got to do something with my hair.

Once I get Gwyn off the phone with the promise to call her the instant he leaves my house—*no matter the hour*—I rush over to the foyer mirror to work a little magic on myself.

By the time I hear his car door shut outside, I have barely enough time to pinch my cheeks and finger-comb my hair up into a loose ponytail.

He rings the doorbell, and even though I'm literally waiting on the other side of the door, I take a few breaths to steady my nerves before I open it.

"Hey..." It comes out awkward and not at all breezy like

I'd planned. Partly because I'm a nervous wreck about him being here, and partly because he's in royal-blue scrubs looking like a snack. In general, I'm a sucker for a man in uniform. But what his body does for wrinkle-resistant polyester cotton could fund the entire adult film industry.

His face lights up, affection glowing in his eyes as he takes me in. "Hey, sparky…"

Okay, so I should not love this little nickname—it's a dog's name, for goodness' sake—but on Murph's lips, he makes it sound downright pornographic.

My mind goes straight to the gutter. Images of us on the beach, but it's night and fiery sparks shoot off our bodies as he flattens me on my back, his weight hovering deliciously above me—

"You're a sight for sore eyes."

My whole middle melts.

Not going to lie, it's a damn struggle to stand upright with him looking at me like he had a sneak peek of the dangerously tempting and filthy reel running through my head.

"You, too."

His hands are full of food bags, beer, and his duffel, but he leans in for a hug, wrapping me in his scent—mint and winter fresh soap and Murph.

"After I talked to you, I figured you had a long day and might not feel like cooking."

Right, so earlier I *might* have unloaded on him about how horrible it was going at the store with the computers crashing and all the new Monopoly stock…monopolizing the stock room.

My cheeks heat. "Thank you. This is so nice of you."

"It's no problem. I wanted to see you, too."

Don't swoon out loud.

I inhale softly, sinking my teeth into my lower lip. Moisture gathers in my mouth. I can't take my eyes off him. I expect texts and small displays of interest now, but the words…

His gaze skates over my skin and a shiver trembles down my spine. Every inch of my body throbs under the heat of his stare like electricity racing through my veins. I'm hyper-aware of his proximity to me, and my stomach does a giant somersault.

"Me, too. I mean, I wanted to see you, too."

Murph shifts his attention to my lips, then meets my eyes again before he sucks in a breath. He does the sexy knitted brows thing, and I nearly come undone.

"Uh, where should I put these?" His voice is gruff as he studies me a second longer, then schools his features to a calm.

Before long, he fills up our plates while I uncap the beer, grab the utensils, and set us up on the couch in front of the television. When I flip it on, Jennifer Ling is on Channel 5 Action News, reporting about vacation rental scams. Happily, I change the channel to the Game Show Network where *America Says* is playing.

Between bites of his gigantic carne asada burrito and my shredded chicken tacos, Murph and I call out rapid-fire guesses to the top fill-in-the-blank survey questions.

"So, what's on the agenda for Vegas?" he asks over a mouthful. He traces his tongue over his lower lip, plopping back against the couch when the show cuts to commercial. "Any requests for your birthday?"

Would it be totally out of pocket to say Nadia's hot bad-boy brother? No? Too much?

I feel a bit woozy.

The way he's sitting with his knees hanging open, our thighs touch and it sends all kinds of magical fantasies about what I want to do swirling in my head. I'm on the edge of the couch, my back ramrod straight, and I'm afraid to move an inch for fear I might do something stupid like straddle him. But I also don't want him to think I mind his touch.

"Uh, other than some club on the Strip Friday night, I don't really know what else Harper and Nadia have planned," I say, hating the way my voice shakes.

He leans forward to take a long pull of his beer before sitting back again. But this time, he's closer. Our thighs flush against each other.

My breaths shallow and I'm stiff as a board.

"Hopefully I'll get to see you. I'm headed out tomorrow morning. I'll be there until Sunday morning."

I twist awkwardly to meet his eyes, a smile pulling at the corners of my mouth. "Oh yeah? What are your big plans?"

"Nothing as wild as a Dirty-Thirty Party..." A smile dances on his lips. "I'm being honored this year at the Academy of Otolaryngology Conference."

"That's amazing, Murph. Congratulations."

A flush grows on his cheeks and his lips quirk into a small smile.

I don't know how, but modest Murph is probably my favorite of all. He's adorably boyish as he waves off my praise, but I sense a tinge of sadness from my usually carefree crush.

Grabbing the throw pillow behind me, I scoot against the arm of the couch, and pull my knee to my chest, undeterred by his attempt to wave this off.

"Seriously, this is *huge*," I say. "Nadia's going to be in Vegas for my party, but is she flying up early? Are your parents going?"

He bows his head and gives me a small shake, then shrugs. "No…it's really…it's not a big thing. Just endless workshops, research panels, and a bunch of medical professionals tooting their own horns…" He tries again to laugh it off, but I know what it's like to put on a good face—always celebrating everyone else's wins.

Inwardly, I wince.

A weight settles on my heart for him. He's built this amazing career and clinic in the Greater San Diego area. Professionally, he's respected and trusted by his community, and no one is going to be there to celebrate him or his hard work?

It hurts my heart to think of him standing on a stage, receiving this award commemorating his accomplishments, alone. Not a soul who he cares about will be in the audience to congratulate him or tell him how inspiring and special he is.

A gasp pushes past my lips.

"How are you downplaying this? This is amazing and I'm so freaking proud of you. It's not okay you're going to be alone to celebrate."

He sighs, his head still bowed to his chest. He covers his

forehead with his hand, kneading his temples with his middle finger and thumb.

"Thank you, but Dec will be there." For a quick sec, I think that's all he's going to say, but then he lifts his tropical blue gaze to meet mine. "We don't have that type of bond as a family. Nadia and I talk all the time and we look out for each other, but I'm not tight with my parents like you are... Well, not my dad."

I huff out a laugh.

"That's just it. I'm close with Harper. I have separate relationships with Mom and Dad, and I get along with his exes, but..." I shrug, and I feel my shoulders loosening slightly. "We're so blended, it's almost watered down. It makes me afraid of the family I'll end up with."

Murph nods and I can tell he gets what I'm saying. It feels so good to go deeper, talk about this with someone who might understand firsthand.

"Dad's on his *fourth* marriage and Mom isn't going to try again. Sloane women are one-and-done in relationships, so I feel like, one way or the other, I'm doomed to repeat history. That's why I make lists."

Murph's eyes brighten with curiosity.

"Oh, yeah." I press my palms against the air. "There's an entire book of them."

We both laugh because that's basically who I am. A list-making, trivia-loving, understand-it-at-its-roots kind of person. I'm logic, statistics, and percentages because numbers don't lie. The "Get My Man" list pops up like an air bubble in my head, reminding me the man who all my numbers point to is sitting less than an inch away from me.

Apparently, besides an actuarial addict, I'm a masochist.

I cannot believe what I'm about to say to Murph, but I've got the verbal runs and it's now or never.

"That's also why I haven't really dated." The words do a slow tumble from my lips like dice on a game board and I'm just waiting to learn what the little dots have done to my odds. "I've got one shot at happiness—at real, lasting love—and I don't want to screw it up on just anyone, if you know what I mean."

I cringe, hating how I've just put all my cards out on the table for Murph to call a misdeal and reshuffle the deck. *Sorry, remember me? Not a relationship guy, barking up the wrong tree here, sparky.*

Fuck. What did I just do?

With the air conditioning whirring to life around us and the goddamn crickets chirping outside for the thirty-six seconds I count in my head, I feel like I'm about to burst. But then, to my complete and utter shock, Murph doesn't push off the couch and run for the hills.

"About the time I was a junior in high school, Mom got sick with pneumonia. She was bedridden and fighting for her life…"

I press my fingers to my lips and scoot forward to gently touch Murph's shoulder.

He's got a faraway look in his eyes, his eyebrows knitted like they always are when he's stuck in his head. Then, the cords in his neck tighten. "Do you know where my dad was when they released her to come home? Gone to the store or golfing—everywhere but home, taking care of his wife, or for once telling her how much he loved her. He left his children by her bedside where he should have been standing all along."

"I'm so sorry."

Murph shakes his head, but he's still there, wherever he's gone.

"I was so mad at him, determined to never be like him, but I was scared I was made of the same cloth, like you said, and therefore destined to repeat history." He blinks rapidly, the edge of his teeth grazing his lower lip. "I figured if I never had relationships, I'd never have to worry about being like him. I'd never neglect my girlfriend or wife, like him—there'd be no one to disappoint."

My mouth falls open.

Of all the reasons I assumed Murph never stuck around, it never occurred to me it wasn't about emotional avoidance. Or plain being a player who wanted to bed as many women as possible. But this…

My heart wrenches. He's afraid to open up—to let any-one down.

He won't let anyone love him.

"Oh my goodness, Murph…"

"Dad and I haven't really seen eye to eye for years. But on the holiday, I saw him and Mom…" He huffs a mirthless laugh. "We've become that *get together only for big occasions* family—strictly birthdays, holidays, anniversaries—no unannounced drop-ins or texts just because. But then I see them, and she's on oxygen and he's barely making it. It gutted me because they're like walking proof of how long I've been holding this grudge." The muscles at the sides of his jaw tighten and he swallows hard. "It feels childish when

I think how I could lose them any day..." His voice breaks off.

I'm so overcome with sadness for him. I toss the pillow aside and lean in, wrapping my arms around him.

"It's okay. But you can't be morbid about it. They're still young, and the funeral home is a ways off. There's still time to build that bond with your dad—with your family."

It was supposed to be a warm, sympathetic hug. You know, between friends—just to sooth him a bit, reassure him. But somewhere in the middle of all these emotions pinballing around us, an electric current passes between us and my ungrounded resolve short-circuits.

His eyes darken and every frayed nerve in my body overloads. Sparks fly as I pretzel my body to be closer still. We're pressed together, our mouths only a whisper apart, and I feel the heat emanating from his body.

His gaze darts to my mouth, then up to my eyes.

Before I can stop myself, I lightly brush my lips over his.

It's the sort of kiss that starts out slow and languid with tentative sweeps and tiny licks as the taste rolls around on my tongue. But then the spicy heat of it sends SOS signals like fireworks flaring in my belly.

The circuit board in my brain malfunctions as I realize that *Holy shit, I'm kissing Murphy Theodore Sikes.*

I've only had a crush on this man for a little more than a decade, and now his delicious, soft lips are touching mine. Then my thoughts spiral, and I wonder, what if this is the only time I get to kiss him? What if I screw it up and I never get to touch him like this again?

A breath hitches in my throat as I weave my fingers up

into his soft blond curls and inhale.

I release a moan. "You smell *fantastic.*"

He smiles into the kiss, alternating between tender nips and sweet pecks. A low rumble of a laugh vibrates through the thin fabric of his shirt, and I just want to fist it in my hands.

"Aw shucks, sparky, you're going to make me blush."

"Is this okay? I mean, I did sort of throw myself in your lap and maul your mouth. It's a nice mouth, though."

Murph kisses me with his whole body, his fingers crawling to flex around my hips as he lifts me on top of him. His mouth curves deliciously as he teases my tongue with his, tasting, exploring, learning me. Every sensation in my body heightens, hums with anticipation as the length of his hardness centers beneath me. My pulse thunders as fire licks through me, my breathing growing ragged.

Together we're this combustible, heady, urgent mixture of electric pulses, desperate licks, groans, and moans as he answers by deepening the kiss.

This is more than okay, and for all intents and purposes, I'm one hundred percent certain there's no turning back.

I'm in so much trouble.

CHAPTER THIRTEEN

MURPH

Q: What did Dwayne Johnson, who originally gave the smackdown as Flex Kavana, change his wrestling name to?

A: The Rock

I'M HALF LISTENING as the recipient of the Women of Science Award beams with gratitude. She's thanked her entire department, her staff, and a fellow ENT who nominated her based on her in-depth analysis and research. But then she turns toward the right of the hotel ballroom stage where there's a man looking up at her endearingly with his hand covering his heart.

She's petite with big dark brown curls and thin-rimmed glasses, barely visible above the podium, but her tears glint off the bright overhead lights.

"Last, I want to thank my kids and my amazing husband, who's a hero in his own right. Thank you so much for supporting me while managing your own practice. Thank you for understanding when we're at dinner and I'm stuck in my head, or we've had leftovers three nights in a row. When the laundry doesn't get done right away. And by right away I mean until it turns into a mountain—"

Laughter rolls in waves over the audience, but all I can focus on is the way she's staring at him. Like there isn't another person in the room. He is her rock. She's able to balance a home and a family without disappointing them because they support each other.

After an early flight and hotel check-in, I spent the better part of my day lost in my thoughts. I should have been eagerly listening during groundbreaking discussions of advances in the medical field, but I can't stop thinking about last night. About Rox. How she wanted to be there for me—how she consoled me without judgment. Almost like she was my rock.

And then there was the kiss.

It was soft and tender, but I chased it with a hunger I didn't expect. It left me blindsided by the way my throbbing body came to life as it never has. Sensory overload for my aching flesh as she weaved her fingers through my hair, sending heat curling down my spine. I was almost dizzy at the weight of her body pressed against mine, her legs straddling me, my pulse and heart racing.

It felt too good. Almost addicting to finally be able to touch her, have her look at me like I was worthy of every second of her attention. Like she couldn't tear her eyes away. Like I'd stepped out of her romance novels…

My heart swelled at the idea, but I couldn't risk this amazing feeling by going too fast, so I had to slow us down. Begrudgingly go against the static in my bloodstream and pull back.

Immediately, guilt tormented me as heat crept into her cheeks.

But now, watching and listening to this woman looking at her husband, it reminds me how Rox had looked at me last night before I broke the kiss and I want that look back. I want to deserve the many versions of love Mom talked about. It won't be the way her parents or mine expressed their feelings, but it'll be ours. A new version that fits us.

I want to be her rock.

Declan taps my elbow from behind. He's seated on the inside curve of the round ten-seater white-clothed table, so I twist to meet his gaze as he leans in.

"Ready? You're up next, buddy."

I'm still reeling from the realization about my feelings for Rox as I glance up to the stage where the woman descends the stage steps, taking hurried strides toward her husband.

When I turn back to Declan, Barry Kostner gives me a small wave to get my attention. I jerk my chin to him, listening.

But the microphone crackles to life.

"Our last award of the evening is the Paul G. Arnold Foundation Award for Humanism in Medicine," the director of the academy says with a proud smile stretching the lines of his dewy face. "This practicing otolaryngologist is not only an excellent physician, but he also exemplifies compassion in patient-centered care..."

Kostner taps the table to draw my attention again, and I tilt my ear toward him.

I've known him for years. His practice is also in San Diego, and while he's a good ENT, he's sort of a tool. Over-the-top personality, sleazy toward his female staff, and he only comes to these conferences to get drunk off free drinks while betting the minimum at the roulette table. I made the mistake of letting him tag along with a group of friends at a conference a few years back and I've never regretted a decision more.

Figures he'd choose the moment right before my award to pull my ear.

"Sikes, I'm glad to see you here this year, my man. What do you say? We partying tonight?" He waggles his thick, scraggy eyebrows, a grin twisting his pockmarked cheeks.

I turn my attention back to the stage but he's still talking.

"You can be my wingman…" He guffaws even though he uses the same corny joke every time I see him. "I say we load up on drinks at the casino for a bit, then hit up a few bars, get some strippers, have ourselves an epic night…"

Behind me, Declan snickers as I pretend I can't understand him over the collective round of applause when the director calls my name.

My heart drums against my chest as I push to my feet and make my way to the stage.

Not only do I have zero desire—with or without Kostner—to have a wild, alcohol-fueled Vegas night, but I don't want to go to bars or clubs and bring a string of women back to my suite. I never want to again.

As I ascend the steps, my nerves kick into overdrive.

"Thank you so much, sir. It's an honor." I shake the director's hand and accept a framed certificate of achievement before turning to the podium prepared to give a brief address.

I tell myself not to think about Rox, or the urgent need to confess my feelings to her. Just breathe and keep my focus on the doors at the back of the room. *Don't make eye contact.*

Taking a deep breath, I plaster on a smile, set the award down, and grip both sides of the podium before I speak. "I'm thrilled and honored to accept this award. Thank you to my fellow nominees. Thank you to the Association of Medical Specialty Societies, the Paul G. Arnold Foundation, and the Academy of Otolaryngology. Thank you to my best friend, colleague, and partner in my practice, Dr. Declan Wilde, for nominating me for this award…" I begin, ignoring the lump in my throat.

My attention sweeps over the back corners by the ballroom entrance. I imagine how nice it might've been having my family in the audience. Mom's and Dad's faces brightly staring up at me with pride, knowing their son is not only successful in his field, but that they had a hand in making me the man I am.

"I would also like to give thanks to my parents and my sister, who couldn't be here today…" Movement in the darkened corner against the back wall grips me.

Is it…?

Am I?

"I'm sorry, I…" I stutter, squinting my eyes, blinking a few times to be sure. Then she gives a small thumbs-up.

Rox.

She's here. In Vegas two days early.

I can't stop staring, and I realize I'm on stage in front of a few hundred people. They've had to sit through speech after speech, likely bored out of their minds, and they can't wait for this to be over. But my heart skitters. I'm overwhelmed, something like hope and unbridled joy bubbling up inside me, and I don't think I've ever been this happy.

"And finally, I'd like to thank someone special to me. You know who you are, but thank you for believing in me, supporting me when I didn't realize how much I needed someone in my corner. So thanks, sparky."

From all the way up on the stage, I see the tiny hinges at the corners of her mouth lift as she presses a hand to her heart, and it's all I need to know. I thank the academy once more as I grab my award, descend the steps, and take long, wide strides on the verge of sprinting toward Rox.

"Congratulations, bud—" Concern twists the lines of Declan's face as he watches me curiously. But I don't have time to bring him up to speed.

I pass him my award without taking my eyes off Rox and keep walking.

My heart is beating a million miles a minute, my pulse skyrockets, I've got a desperate adrenaline rush, and probably a shit-eating grin plastered across my face. I'm still not sure what I'm going to do once I reach her, but I keep moving, restlessly wringing my fingers. The need to touch her grows urgent as the distance between us narrows.

Taking in her rolling suitcase, the tennis shoes, black yoga pants, and white T-shirt she must've worn on the plane, I'm giddy. It feels like a dream, and I don't want to wake up.

I have no clue how to be who she needs me to be, but I'm going to give everything I've got.

"Surprise." Rox shrugs sheepishly when I reach her. "Congratulations."

"Hey, sparky." It comes out as a hushed whisper. I'm breathless and I can't stop smiling. All I want to do is tug her into my arms. Feel her soft, pliant body flush against mine, electricity racing through my veins as she clasps her fingers behind my neck. "Decided to fly in early?"

We search each other's faces. Her cheeks heat and her breaths come fast and shallow. She gives me a tiny nod.

"It was either that or a three-hundred-and-thirty-two-mile drive..." She smiles, and her expression is soft and hopeful.

"Just for me?"

"Only for you." Rox tucks her lush lower lip between her teeth, desire darkening her warm brown irises. "I've only got one shot. I'm taking my chances on you."

Warmth floods my insides, and my mind is bombarded with all the things I want to say. I want to tell her how she was the last person I thought about before I went to sleep, and the first when I woke up. *I missed you. I can't stop thinking about you. I think I'm falling for you...*

But none of it feels like enough.

She makes me want to be the guy who deserves her only shot.

I drag the pad of my thumb along the curve of her jaw, settling my hand at her nape, as she tips her chin up. She sucks in a stark breath, and a wave of pleasure courses through me. There's a shift inside my chest, almost like something's been knocked loose. *Or free.*

"That's good because I'm taking chances on you." I dip

my chin and cover her lips with mine, letting the intensity grow. For once, letting myself feel every breath, every touch, every whisper of longing I've never allowed myself to feel. And because this is Rox, I let myself fall.

WHEN ROX AND I leave the hotel, the plan is to grab a quick bite and drop off her bags at her hotel. Then spend the rest of the night aimlessly walking around the Strip, holding hands, and staring into each other's starry eyes while I've got her all to myself. That's my plan, anyway.

We find a walk-up pizza place two hotels down, and I order a couple slices and waters before I run it by Rox.

"So," I say over a mouthful of pepperoni. "I was thinking about how happy I am to have you all to myself..."

Her mouth twitches as she surveys me. "Oh, yeah?"

We're both leaning against the small metal bar top, facing each other, so I get to see the amusement sparkling in her neon-lit eyes and how the faint breeze dances through her wispy, loose hairs. How her warm brown skin glows a metallic bronze under the lights. I don't know when it happened, but I've memorized the soft curve of her cheek, the slight turn-up of her button nose, and fullness of her lush Cupid's bow lips.

"Mm-hmm. We've only got until Friday before my sister and Harper show up to whisk you away from me, so we have to make the most of tonight."

"And tomorrow, but..." She squints her eyes, nodding as she chews, before grabbing a napkin to dab at the corners of her mouth. "I see what you mean. Time's ticking, so—"

"So, we better take a few more bites then drop your bags off at your hotel."

Rox winces. "Well…about that…"

"Which part?" I ask, failing to see where the flaw is in my plan. I haven't even mentioned the hand-holding and starry eyes.

"Technically, I don't have a room yet." Rox squeezes her eyes shut then peeks one eye open. "Not until Friday at three."

I clear my throat of the laugh bubbling up inside me. "Let me get this straight. You left work early to fly to Las Vegas—a whole other state—without securing a hotel reservation during convention season or really knowing whether you'd find me?" I flit a glance at her plate, shaking my head. "And you're a crust waster?"

She rolls her eyes, her thick fringe of lashes fluttering as she heaves an amused sigh. "When you put it that way…"

"It sounds crazy?"

"I don't know, I just thought…" She releases a warm, musical laugh and shrugs. "I figured it was so easy to switch my plane ticket, maybe I could book another night and check in early at the hotel, too. If not, this is Vegas, it's literally the city with the most hotels per capita. I'm sure I can find a room."

At this, I tilt my head side to side, understanding her logic, but I shove her abandoned crust into my mouth, anyway.

"Or maybe your plan was to come here and tell me this, knowing I'd be inclined to let you stay with me." I scratch my temple, struggling to feign seriousness as she bursts out laughing. “Tell me the truth, Rox, because I’m looking at you a lot different now. After you threw yourself in my lap last night and mauled my mouth, was your grand plan to come here and seduce me? Might be working, but not the point.”

This earns me a playful slap on my chest, but I catch her hand and pull her into my arms, loving how comfortable things are between us. I can’t stop smiling as I cup her face with both hands and press kisses all over her cheeks, eyelids, neck, beautiful greasy pizza lips.

“You should be ashamed of yourself, trying to take advantage of a vulnerable man. I’ll have you know I’m more than just a devastatingly good-looking doctor who loves Red Vines and Trivial Pursuit. I have a heart and feelings, sparky,” I say with a chuckle.

She clasps her hands low and tight around my waist as I deepen the kiss, stroking her tongue with mine, tasting her salty sweetness, teasing, loving how good we feel together. She sucks my lips and my tongue. My body tightens and hardens, blood rushing to my muscles.

Well, mostly one “love muscle.”

I pivot, turning us so her back is pressed against the side of the building. As she thrusts her pelvis into me and scrapes her fingers down my back, I grunt my approval.

Fuck.

“What are you doing to me?” My voice is low and rough as I pin my hips against hers. “I want you so fucking bad.”

A horn blares from the street. “Get a room!” someone yells.

“I’m working on it,” Rox mumbles through a laugh as

she grabs handfuls of my ass.

We both laugh into the kiss, pushing off the wall.

I step back, breathless, and completely turned on, as I pinch my thumb and forefinger at the corners of my mouth. We're both quiet for a beat as I toss out our trash, pull up her suitcase handle, and slip her hand in mine.

Turning back toward my hotel, I shake my head at her.

"For the record, sparky..." She beams up at me, her starry eyes glinting off the menagerie of neon signs. "I have to say, your grand plan was masterful."

CHAPTER FOURTEEN

ROX

Q: What was the name of the first hotel casino located on what became known as the Las Vegas Strip?

A: El Rancho

ON THE WAY to Murph's hotel, I call mine. On principle. Which turns out to be a mistake since it is indeed convention season and they neither have a forty-eight-hour early check-in policy nor any available rooms.

"Really, I'm flattered that you would go to this limit to seduce me," Murph says as we exit the elevator on the twentieth floor. "You can drop the innocent act now. I'm onto you."

We walk the short distance to his room, and he swipes his key card, laughing the entire way, but I am not.

Shit.

When we enter the cool, elegant suite, there's the mainstay mix of beige and gold accents. Plush carpets and curtains and the standard stately wooden furniture with the desk tucked in the corner. But my feet are cemented at the foot of the massive king-size bed.

Everyone I know books the double bed for the cheaper rate and the option to sleep near the window beneath the air-conditioning vent or close to the bathroom. Not Murphy Theodore Sikes, though. He's spared no expense to treat his tall, lean body to extra legroom.

Then again, he didn't exactly plan on me crashing his five-star room.

He plops down on the bed, sending the thick navy duvet and crisp off-white sheets flouncing in the air. Turning on his side, he pushes up onto his elbow and props his head on his hand to look at me before patting the space in front of him.

"It's going to be tight, but I think we can make it work." He flashes me his trademark lopsided grin, all bright white teeth and cocky confidence.

The thing is, when I came up with this big idea of showing up here for him, somehow, I gave far too little consideration to anything beyond the conference. It was spontaneous and free-spirited; me throwing caution to the wind. I didn't even make a list about it. I just left work early, fueled by that kiss on my couch and the chance to make a heartfelt gesture. *Okay, and maybe moving the fun and games along.* It seemed harmless.

Kissing is one thing. Having sex with the man I've given unlimited access to my heart is...a completely different board game.

What the heck was I thinking I'd do once I got past my big move?

In romance novels, the grand gesture always happens right before the end. I know this. But Murph and I are just getting started. I've only just acknowledged—*to him*—that I like him. Our first kiss was yesterday. I just got so invested in being here to cheer him on during his award acceptance. And now I've gone and told him about my one shot…

Shit, shit, shit.

Mentally, I'm facepalming myself.

I want to freak out, but Murph is still staring at me, waiting for me to join him on the bed, so I roll my suitcase to the corner of the room near the window. Laying it flat on its side, I unzip it, and shove aside three novels and my *Book of Lists* to thumb through my clothes.

"I'm going to get out these clothes."

"Good idea," he says suggestively, still watching.

What in the actual F is wrong with me?

Today, I hop on a plane, practically profess my undying love, and publicly grind on him at a pizza joint in front of the entire Las Vegas Strip? *And grab his cute ass…*

My stomach tightens and heat crawls up from my neck to my cheeks. This is humiliating on so many levels. What am I doing, jumping right into happily-ever-after territory? *Amateur move.*

Next thing you know, I'll be throwing in the L-word.

Sure, I know how I feel about him. The chemistry between us is combustible, but Murph hasn't exactly confessed his feelings for me.

Gah, I need to slow this only-one-bed, hot-mess express down.

I pop my head up over the top of the bed. "What do you

think about grabbing some drinks and hitting the casino for a bit?"

Needing no convincing, Murph springs off the bed, cheesing. "Let me let Declan know I'm headed out, then I'm ready. There's a bar downstairs, and the word on the street is…"

I hike up a curious brow.

"Trivia," he announces with a far-too-excited fist pump.

"Say. No. More."

I am amped. I halfway expected we'd be those button-pushing slot hoarders, hogging machines, too afraid to get up and let someone else win after we've fed all our money to the machine. My head is right with him on this one, though. Drinks, trivia, my new boo beside me whispering sweet nothings and correct answers.

That's my idea of a good time.

But then he holds up a hand and twists his wrist to check the time before he cocks his head to me. "Thousand-dollar jackpot."

We both nod, totally in sync.

I shower quickly and we both change clothes. We're out the room with our game faces in place looking like a pair of badass fanny-pack-wearing tourists ready to see what Vegas is bringing to the trivia table.

Downstairs, the casino is in full swing.

The glitz and glam atmosphere is alive. Loud, pinging slot machines, servers in little more than swimwear, and pit bosses with their eyes on all of it. I'm talking wall-to-wall swarms of table games and people begging to give away their money in the name of horrible odds.

"This way, sparky."

Murph takes my hand as we step off the elevator to the right and weave through the crowd to the far back. Up ahead, I spot a board-game-themed bar that makes me feel right at home. Giant stacked classics. Monopoly, Clue, Sorry!, Scrabble, and my sweet spot in dusky blue with golden lines, Trivial Pursuit.

"I'm in heaven."

Murph squeezes my hand, smiling.

Immediately, I note the hanging question marks and jumbo game pieces strung from the ceiling. Enlarged and framed game cards line the back wall. There are brightly colored Trivial Pursuit wedges and pie hubs. My game-loving mind is blown as I take in the full panoramic view of humongous game board murals.

I feel like I'm back at Love & Games but on steroids.

"Do you like it?" Murph asks, snapping me out of my revelry.

"What kind of question is that? Do you know me at all? Heck yes I like it. I *love* it." I'm grinning from ear to ear as I whip out my phone and take pictures of everything that draws my eyes. "If we have time, I've got to bring Harper and Nadia back to this place."

A few seconds tick by as I snap a load of shots. But then Murph's words in the room come barreling back to me.

The word on the street is...

Jolting around to face him, I see the recognition on his face.

He shrugs, his blue eyes sparkling with affection. "I may have searched for anything board game related before you got here. I was hopeful you'd let me tag along, but I wasn't sure you'd want me around."

Here you go. Just take my heart. All of it.

Where has this version of Murph been hiding all my life? These past few weeks, he's gone way out of his way to prove how much he cares. He's sweet and thoughtful, and I don't have a doubt in the world he's it for me.

Slipping my phone back in my pocket, I tip up onto my toes to kiss him.

"I don't know if you're ready to hear this, or if you feel the same way, but I'm falling hard and fast for you, Murphy Theodore Sikes."

He says nothing because I don't give him the chance. Right here against the blue-spoked wheel wall of the game that brought us together, I kiss him with my entire body. Electric pulses rev through me, my heart knocks against my chest, and an entire bar full of trivia heads whistle and cheer us on.

I cringe when I hear someone call out, "It's the Monopoly Queen's sister." Like, really loud.

"All is fair in love and board games, ladies and gentlemen," the blue-haired quizmaster says, leaning into the mic as she curls her fingers into a heart shape.

"Heck, yeah. Vegas!" someone screams, which sends the rest of the bar off the fanatical edge.

There're hoots and hollers and even a little impromptu beatboxing on the mic as we slink hand-in-hand into a pair of seats at a table in the middle of the room. The quizmaster throws her hands in the air, telling us to wave 'em like we just don't care.

She raps the old McDonald's commercial jingle Mom and I used to sing about Big Macs and Filet-o-Fishes.

Because this is "Vegas, baby, *yeah*," I take my cue from her, getting to my feet to help her out.

And then the entire crowd joins in. "At McDonald's."

Game Face is literally the liveliest bar I've ever been to and I'm certain it has ruined me for all bars going forward. I need more handholding in game-board-themed bars with beatboxing trivia night fast-food rap collabs in my life.

I tell Murph as much, but he's still staring at me with stars in his eyes and an ear-to-ear smile on his gorgeous face that makes my heart flutter.

"What?" I ask, settling back on the chair.

He scoots it so close to him our thighs touch and he puts his arm around my shoulders. "After that performance, I'm a hundred percent certain I'll be beating them off with a stick."

We laugh as he hugs me into his chest, pressing his lips to my hair.

"Welcome to the lovely couple who just joined us. Special shout-out to the badass woman in the pink jumper who knows addictive commercial jingles and raps with oomph."

Don't even get me started with Golden Girls *or* Fresh Prince…

The quizmaster jabs her finger in the air toward me, so I do my obligatory wave to the crowd to the tune of more applause.

"All right, all right, all right. Now that we have everyone hyped up, let's get down to some Trivial Pursuit. I'm Raine, your badass quizmaster from the boogie down Bronx. Alicia is walking around with your controllers for your virtual game markers, and don't forget DJ Jazzy Geoffrey coming straight at you from Sussex holding down the Ketel Ones and Dos Equis at the bar. Remember, no lip, just tip. Let's go."

She hits a button, and I might be dreaming, but a wall-length screen with digital Trivial Pursuit board descends from the ceiling.

Hello, beautiful…

There are no words to describe the glory in knowing if it was on the ground, I could literally walk on a Trivial Pursuit board.

It takes me a good minute to calm my nerves, but then we get our little handheld clicker and it's on. Team Sparky Sikes (yellow) against the best Vegas offers.

Right off the bat. We. Are. On. FIRE!

We get the pink entertainment and brown literature wedges *easily* getting no questions wrong—Forrest Gump's best friend's name and Jane Austen's second book about making hasty judgments…

Come on. You're going to have to try harder than that to take us down.

Also, it's worth mentioning my normal two-cocktail rule is out the window. I'm at least three in. *Or is it five now?*

Lost count, but oh well. Either way, it's still our turn.

Murph hits the roll button, and our virtual die does its little spinning tumble, landing on a six. He knocks sports out of the way, so we move back to the orange cheese wedge.

"How many seconds must a cowboy stay aboard a rodeo bronc?"

Immediately, people squirm, praying we get this wrong,

so they have time to steal.

I lower my chin, tilting my ear to Murph, figuring he's got this one. But he gnaws his bottom lip. "I'm about ninety-nine-point-nine percent sure it's six seconds." He nods, pleased with his answer, but I'm not feeling it.

Not that I'm the expert on rodeo, but for some reason, it feels like he's low-balling it.

For a beat, I drum my fingers on the table, racking my brain for any rodeo movies I've seen. There's *Urban Cowboy*, classic. *Dallas Buyers Club* with scarily skinny Matthew McConaughey. Ooh, *The Longest Ride* with sexy Scott Eastwood. *What was that Luke Wilson movie? No, Luke Perry from that old school* 90210*?*

"Time is running out. We're going to need to hear your answer," quizmaster Raine says.

"Eight seconds. It's eight seconds," I whisper-yell, cupping Murph's ear, reverting to childhood.

I suspect I'm right, too, because a collective groan sounds from the next table.

He surveys me with the direst expression like this is life or death and not just our reputation in front of people we'll likely never see again. "Are you sure?"

"Ten seconds," Raine calls out.

"Absolutely."

I think that's the end, but then he drags his tongue into the corner of his mouth. "Willing to make a wager on that? Say, if you're right, we stay and play. I'm right, we go up to the room right now and you stop torturing me."

My body prickles with awareness at the gruff tone of his voice.

Holy sexpot.

"Five seconds," Raine counts down.

I don't have time to overanalyze what I'm doing to torture him, and by the knitted brows making their first appearance of the night while I'm horny and hyped up on brainpower, I know I'm going to want to torture him some more.

"You're on," I say to Murph, then call out, "Eight seconds," without taking my eyes off him.

We get the orange wedge, but now I can't get my mind off tortured Murph. Deliciously sexy, tormented Murph, who I decide I do want to do many bad, bad things to me on that king-size bed. And then there's the wager.

Why did I have to be right?

My take is he's doing it on purpose, but as Murph slouches in his seat, letting his knees hang open, my gaze catches on the tented denim of his jeans. And stays there because I'm a saucy little trivia minx.

I'm determined to get the last three wedges, collect my bragging rights, and then—if torture is code for what I think it's code for—I will be in my birthday suit in Murph's bed two days before my birthday.

Note to self: Calm down and play the game.

Whipping the clicker from Murph's hand, I roll the die and move our marker three spaces, landing on blue, geography. It's not for a wedge, but I've got to get this show on the road *before* I get arrested for public indecency when I rip off Murph's clothes and straddle him right here.

"What's the largest Japanese island?"

Oh, quizmaster Raine. Inwardly, I'm puffing out my

chest. I only know this answer because I have an obsessive tendency to study Trivial Pursuit cards. Because my libido is raging against my incessantly throbbing machine, I don't even consult Murph before I answer.

"Honshu."

The next two rolls, I answer like a common knowledge Jedi, whipping around the virtual board. Murph and I aren't even a team anymore. This is the Rox, newly crowned Trivial Pursuit Queen, show—this woman has royally pressing matters to tend to.

"Hydronium," I call out for the green science and nature wedge.

Everyone else in the bar gets the picture. Drinks are flowing and all chairs are turned to face me. I don't even care it's likely no fun for anyone else. I'm horny, we're in Vegas, and I'm a hundred percent sure by the *I want you so bad* expression on Murph's face right now we won't even wait until we're properly in the room before we rip at each other's clothes.

Let's go. Mama needs a new pair of sexy lace panties for Murph to bite off with his teeth.

Two more wedges.

Geography and history.

Not my strongest subjects, but that's what studying cards is for.

A few more rolls and correct answers earn me more applause. Then finally, I land on yellow. History. Admittedly, I've only got an eighty-twenty shot of getting this right, but history has nothing on a woman in—

"We might have a record for fastest trivia domination

here, folks," Raine says, pulling the next card. But then she blows out her cheeks and slowly releases a breath. "Whoa… Let's see what this amazing lady does with this one."

Well, that's not a response I'm used to hearing.

"How old is the world's oldest sex toy?"

I dart my eyes over to Murph as the corner of his mouth hitches up and his brows dip obscenely. My stomach muscles are clenched far too tight to be embarrassed now.

"Thirty thousand years," I say straight-faced with my head held high.

Damn right I get the wedge, and the crowd chants, "Trivial Pursuit Queen, Trivial Pursuit Queen."

But after that question, with the images flooding my head, there is no way in hell I'm staying a second longer.

Forget the thousand bucks. I stand, grab Murph's hand, and before anyone can ask me what's happening or why I'm walking out on the game when I'm one wedge away from a grand and serious bragging rights—that won't produce a mind-blowing orgasm, mind you—I announce, "It has been a pleasure, but my birthday is two days away and I don't want to wait that long to get laid."

Murph's open mouth is priceless.

And maddeningly sexy.

If I was in my sister's shadow or the laughingstock of memeville before, I'm pretty sure the cheers behind me will change that up real fast.

The elevator ride is an exercise in personal willpower. Of course we have to go up twenty floors with easy listening music grating on my nerves, but when the ping sounds and the doors glide open, it is a literal race to his door.

"Hurry," I say when he fumbles with the key card.

The lights aren't even on as we toe off our shoes, connected by our mouths in a messy, urgent kiss. He slides the straps of my romper over the curve of my shoulders. My greedy fingers tug him free of his black T-shirt before I unzip his pants, my pulse thundering, fire surging through me.

But I pull back for a second to drink in sight of him sans scrubs and wetsuit. This is just Murph in his regular rumpled clothes but…

Oh God.

Wide, muscular chest. Angular lines of his V-shaped obliques dipping appetizingly into his jeans…

Gah, I want to just lick him.

"Just so you know, I still can't believe you told the entire bar you wanted to get laid." His tone is laced with laughter as he tucks a flyaway hair behind my ear. It's the tiniest touch of his fingers, but it sends flames blazing through me.

"What, like it's a secret? I really, *really* do." I'm barely suppressing a groan as I drag my fingers over the hard ridges of his abs and shudder. "Lord have mercy, it's been too long."

And you're so freaking hot.

Golden-blond hair, full lips, tan skin, a whisper of smoke in his seaside-blue eyes—and he's all mine. And moving excruciatingly slow. I'm two seconds from telling him to move it along. He doesn't have to carry on tormenting—or rather, torturing—me, as I am currently a bag of throbbing flesh and hormones.

He tugs my romper down, taking my panties with it, and I try not to be self-conscious as his half-lidded blue eyes sweep over my body.

A ghost of a smile plays on his lips, but his expression turns intense.

"You're so beautiful."

The way he breathes the word, it's a wonder I don't come undone right here. My heart is a metronome incessantly ticking, edging me closer, and Murph has barely even touched me. Heat blooms in my belly as he walks me backward to the bed. When he yanks the duvet off, I wilt onto the cool sheets.

He rummages around in his suitcase at the side of the bed and comes up with a foil wrapper. I'm salivating as he frees himself from his pants and sheaths his hard length.

But for real. Like, is this normal? To be this horny.

I know it's been nearly a year—maybe more—but are people usually champing at the bit like this? Because I am. *I so am.*

I take a deep breath, trying to be cool as he climbs onto the bed and scrutinizes every inch of my body.

"What's that face about?" he asks sweetly.

"If you must know, I'm giving myself a mental pep talk about the merits of taking this painstakingly slow and grappling with the determination not to physically drag you down on top of me so I can ravage you." This is said with the straightest of faces.

The corners of his eyes crinkle.

"Why are you in such a rush? The faster we move, the faster it'll be over, and I can't bear the thought. I'm committing you to memory because I never want to *not* know what this moment feels like."

My poor, poor little heart.

"For the record, being adorably sexy *and* sweet is not helping my situation. *At all.*" I tug him down on top of me, my nipples hardening as he settles between my legs.

He chuckles. "Fine. Have it your way, but we're going to need to do this more than once so we can take it slow."

"Deal," I say, lifting to kiss his beautiful full lips. "Only after I've been sufficiently sated, there will be another round."

Murph holds his weight over me, lingering. All the humor of seconds ago drains from his face as he presses his blunt head between my aching thighs.

"Is this okay?"

Hallelujah!

I nod because words don't cover the range of emotions and magical sensations overwhelming me now. I don't remember sex ever—*ever*—feeling like this. He moves in deep, long strokes, electrifying, smooth, and powerful. His mouth on my ear, then my neck, down to my breasts, licking, sucking, winding me up. Every nerve ending on every inch of my body zings to life, fire searing my skin as I tighten my ankles behind his back, letting my nails bite into his skin.

"Oh my God." A mix between a whimper and a moan spills from my lips, but that's all I can manage.

Words are not important. The only thing that matters in this moment, in life, is Murph and me moving in time to this steady, urgent rhythm.

It's like there's this invisible thread inside of me. As he goes deeper, harder, faster, he pulls it until I'm almost unraveled. *No, I don't think the thread is it at all.* More like my body is one of those small champagne-bottle-shaped party poppers you pull until celebratory confetti and streamers explode into the air. Yes, except with Murph the confetti is deliriously happy, toe-curling orgasms shouted into the cool hotel air conditioning.

Yes. That's it.

A storm rages in Murph's eyes as I thread my fingers through his soft blond hair. He leans in to taste the moan he's pulled from me.

I arch my back, my throat bared to him as an orgasm swells inside me. As fireworks ripple through me, my body quaking with pleasure, I'm heady with emotions and the fullness of my heart.

Just as my party popper explodes, I lose all control of my body and apparently my mouth because the words spill from my lips before I can catch them.

"I love you."

Oh no.

CHAPTER FIFTEEN

ROX

Q: Though the SMS concept was first developed in 1984 by Friedhelm Hillebrand and Bernard Ghillebaert, what technological advancement was officially sent on December 3, 1992?

A: A text message

Ladies Group Chat

Thursday July 22

Rox Sloane 6:43 A.M.
911

Harper Sloane 6:45 A.M.
What happened? Are you okay?

Nadia Sikes 6:45 A.M.
What?

Rox Sloane 6:46 A.M.
I did something stupid and now I'm

freaking the hell out. I don't know what to do.

Nadia Sikes 6:48 A.M.
Uh-oh… How many margaritas did you have?

Harper Sloane 6:49 A.M.
If you want advice, it might help if you tell us what you did.

Rox Sloane 6:51 A.M.
Okay, I'm sorry if this is awkward for you, Nadia, but…Murph and I had mind-blowing, ugly-cry sex. It was amazing. Like, soooooo good. The way I lost all control. I don't know what came over me. But I got emotional because this is Murph, you know?

Nadia Sikes 6:51 A.M.
Ew. You do realize this is my brother, right? I'm happy for you and all, and this is going to be weird coming from me, but DO NOT go into details.

Rox Sloane 6:52 A.M.
He's sleeping right now. I know he's probably going to run, but I sorta slipped and told him I loved him. While we were having sex.

Harper Sloane 6:52 A.M.
Oh God. Did he say it back?

Rox Sloane 6:52 A.M.
Ugh, no. He sort of stared blankly at me for a sec like he was going to but then I didn't want him to say it just because I did, so I stopped him. Then I kissed him to avoid the awkwardness.

Nadia Sikes 6:53 A.M.
Whoa! A little fast, considering you've been a thing as of this weekend, but at least one of you finally got the nerve to say it.

Rox Sloane 6:54 A.M.
Wait, what? What do you mean we finally got the nerve? Did he say something to you?

Nadia Sikes 6:55 A.M.
Newsflash: Not New News

Harper Sloane 6:55 A.M.
That's true. Declan and I have known for a while.

Rox Sloane 6:56 A.M.
Well, shit. And no one thought to tell us? Great, how am I supposed to act around him now?

Nadia Sikes 6:56 A.M.
Say something, Harper. I'm happy for you, Rox, but I cannot cheer on my brother's sex life.

Harper Sloane 6:57 A.M.
First of all, don't freak out and ruin the weekend. Tomorrow is your birthday. For now, try to just enjoy each other's company and don't make a big deal about it. Nadi's right, if it was me, I wouldn't be on a group chat overanalyzing it when you could be giving him a nice wake-up call.

Rox Sloane 6:58 A.M.
Shoot! He's awake. Thanks, guys. Call me when you land tomorrow. Pretending nothing happened from here on out.

Nadia Sikes 7:00 A.M.
Harper, she's clearly talking to you. You know me and flying. Unless you change your mind and decide to drive, I will be emptying those tiny liquor bottles down my throat.

Friday July 23

Harper Sloane 8:02 A.M.
Happy birthday!!! We are in Vegas! About to turn it up! #dirtythirty

Nadia Sikes 8:03 A.M.
Happy birthday, Rox. The exclamations and excitement will come after coffee and a few hours' sleep. #notawakeyet

Rox Sloane 8:03 A.M.
Thank you! Dirty-Thirty Party tonight! Murph and I are headed to the pool in a couple hours if you all want to join us. But first... #birthdaysuit #dirtiestthirty #sexhappensinvegas #itsmybirthday #stillpretending

Nadia Sikes 8:06 A.M.
I'm pretending this is all a nightmare and you're not talking about my cornball brother. #ew #covering myears #coveringmyeyes #enough withthehashtags #itstooearlyfor allthis

Harper Sloane 8:08 A.M.
What's on the agenda today besides orgasms, birthday girl?

Rox Sloane 8:09 A.M.
Check out the Linq, shopping, eat, make a few slots donations. Dinner isn't until 6:00 pm so we've got all day to do whatever before the 7:00 pm showing of "O" at the Bellagio. It runs about an hour and a half, so I'm thinking we'll hit up the club at like 9:00 pm.

Harper Sloane 8:11 A.M.
Okay, I'll let Declan know, but you're sure you're good with the guys joining us tonight?

Rox Sloane 8:11 A.M.
Three words: Little Yellow Dress. I want him to see me in it, then promptly remove it.

Nadia Sikes 8:12 A.M.
I know you all are enjoying torturing me…

CHAPTER SIXTEEN

MURPH

Q: Name the 1991 movie for which Julia Roberts was a Golden Globe winner for best actress.

A: *Pretty Woman*

"I'M SORRY. WHAT did you say?"

I scoot to the edge of the black velvet couch in our booth and bend my ear toward the server. The music is insanely loud and reading lips…not the best with all the flashing lights.

She blinks a few times, looking mildly irritated that I'm making her yell over the music when this is her third time checking on our table.

"Can I bring you another bottle?" she repeats loudly, raising another sparkling gold bottle of rum into the air. It's hard not to be intimidated by her when she's wearing a cheetah-print leotard with knee-high black boots and looks like she could give me a swift Lara Croft action kick to the groin.

Her dark eyes dart impatiently to the untouched array of

fruit juices and garnishes sitting on the table in front of me.

I get it. This is how she makes the bulk of her money. Bottle service equals large tips from sloshed tourists hell-bent on re-creating *The Hangover* movie experience. Except our table is one of just over a dozen in the main room at La Vie en Rose, Las Vegas's hottest new club at Le Coeur Hotel & Casino. I'm talking laser beams and falling confetti synchronized to the latest techno anthem played by the best DJ. What self-respecting Dirty-Thirty honoree sits down long enough to drink?

Not Roxanne Sloane.

She's busy having the time of her life.

"Uh, yeah, we're good for now," I say, flashing the server an apologetic smile.

She gives me a nod then flips her long jet-black hair over her shoulder and slips into the curve of the crowd just as Nadia walks up. Her chest rises and falls, and her hair is stuck to her sweat-dampened face from dancing, but she's smiling from ear to ear.

"Taking a breather?" I ask.

"Keeping those purses safe?" She snickers as she leans over the table, pouring herself a rum and pineapple juice cocktail. She swirls her finger around the edges of the glass to mix it. "Wouldn't want you to slip up and actually have a good time dancing with a beautiful woman who cares about you…"

"Relax, big head. I'm fine right here."

She nods then takes a long sip as she turns to face Rox, dancing with Harper and Declan.

"Yeah, I guess you're right," my sister says, and it's in her small pause that I hear the sarcasm barreling toward me. "I'm sure she wore that skimpy little yellow dress—that barely covers her thighs—for her sister and her *fiancé* because no Dirty-Thirty Party is complete unless you get to be a third wheel."

She whips her gaze to me with an impatient tilt of her head. I'm assuming it's meant to guilt me into joining Rox on the dance floor.

"Look, Nadi, Rox and I are taking things slow."

"So slow, you're practically moving backward."

"Whatever... Besides, this is supposed to be your girls' night out. Dec and I shouldn't even be here for a freaking Dirty-Thirty Party..." I huff out a laugh, but even as I say the words, I know it has nothing to do with my reservations about being here tonight with Rox.

If anything, it's an excuse.

A cop-out.

There's no other place I want to be. For damn sure, no other woman I want to be with. But this weekend has turned my entire universe on its axis. Rox showing up for my award dinner, celebrating her birthday under the backdrop of neon lights, us sleeping together... Then she tells me she loves me.

She *loves* me.

We were caught up in the moment and she stole my breath. It was a slip of the tongue, but those words felt like I'd always been waiting to hear them from *her*. The purest form of delight had washed over me. Unbridled joy, triumph, happiness. This stunning, brilliant woman who glows like the sun loved me. Her words felt like something to celebrate. Like clarity.

For a split second, I felt like I'd always been waiting on her. All the dates, dissecting my parents' marriage, the fear of relationships and disappointing women. The years leading up to this weekend. They were all preparing me for this woman.

I wanted to reward her faith in me.

But before I could get my footing to process my response—fully grasp that those amazing words could pass her beautiful lips—she shut it down.

"Don't say it," she'd said, pressing her fingers to my lips. Again, three words. But these made me question whether her trepidation stemmed from nerves or regret. Did she think I wouldn't rise to the occasion? That I wouldn't want to? That she felt she needed to err on the side of caution…

I felt let down.

Almost like it was in slow motion, I got a glimpse of the blinding panic that flashed in Rox's eyes.

Then, like nothing happened, like I wasn't on the edge of uttering words I'd never used in a romantic relationship, Rox kissed me quiet.

With every nip of my lips and graze of her fingertips over my skin, I tried not to focus on the feeling that somehow she was trying to erase the words. Take them back. We spent Thursday together, playing slots and being lazy in the room before we caught up with Declan, and I couldn't find the right moment to ask her. No matter how many times I looked at her in passing this weekend, attempting to broach the subject, or how many times I searched her face, hoping for a hint that she didn't want to unsay the words. Rox averted her gaze. She ran ahead with Harper and Nadia, or dipped into another room, another store, another conversation...

Just like that, the moment was lost in a blur of sightseeing, shopping, gambling, and world-shattering sex. We've gone from zero to sixty in two seconds, and now... How am I supposed to downshift that fast?

"Hello?" Nadia snaps her fingers next to my ear, jolting me out of my thoughts, her plastic penis-shaped DIRTY-THIRTY AF necklace dangling in front of my eyes.

"Murph, the time to zone out is not when the competition is stealing your spotlight."

I stare at her, confused for a beat before she fans out her hand toward the dance floor.

The tightness in my chest throbs with the incessant drum beat of the music as I glance past Nadia to where Rox stands. She's smiling at a tall guy with dark hair, ugly shoes, and two drinks in his hands.

My pulse quickens.

Without a second thought, I push to my feet, ready to rush over to Rox, double down on us despite the odds stacked against me.

"Whoa there." Nadia halts me with her outstretched arm across my chest. "Take a deep breath. Give it a sec before you go fumbling over there and ruin everything," she warns.

My heart is in my throat, my breaths coming coarser and faster, my mouth running dry. But I do as my sister instructs, and suck in a lungful of air. Then, I stand back and watch the scene play out in front of me.

The guy leans in close to her ear.

From where we're standing, it's impossible to read their

lips, but Rox steps back, smiling politely. She doesn't reach for the drink. Neon lasers pierce the air, flooding her in a spotlight as she falls back in sync with the wild melody. I can't fault him, though. For trying to dance with her. For wanting to be near her.

Like a moth to her flame, I'm mesmerized by her smooth bronze skin cast in a rainbow of sparkling golds and electric blues. She's vibrant and beautiful, and anyone would be lucky to simply be in her presence.

I'm the only idiot here willing to leave her out there by herself.

I take a step closer, suddenly needing to be near her, but Nadia holds firm. "Seriously, let's see what she does."

I'd say she's enjoying it, but it feels like a test for both Rox and me. Are we willing to truly give this a try?

"Yeah, okay," I say reluctantly.

Again, the guy stretches the glass toward Rox and fury flares in my gut.

Heat flushes my body as I clasp my fists, holding my elbows wide, chest out.

"Yeah, I'm not really interested in standing here while this corny dude takes his shot and forces a drink in her hand."

"Yeah, why is that? You wouldn't happen to have deep, protective, *emotional* feelings for Rox, now, would you?"

Fuck.

I claw my fingers through my hair, clutching fistfuls as I begrudgingly turn back toward Rox. *Yeah, I have feelings for Rox, but what good is it if I can't put a name to them?*

See this…sharing feelings, relationships, labels, hopping

on planes on a whim just to be there for another person… It's romantic. But this gut-wrenching jealousy. The urge to do bodily harm to some guy who offered Rox a drink and a dance… I don't know how to navigate these new waters.

"He is kind of cute." Nadi tilts her head to the side like she's envisioning them together. "I guess in a slimy club hookup sort of way."

"Shut up right now."

She giggles.

The muscles at my jaw turn to steel. I swallow hard and jerk my gaze away back to Rox, shoving aside the tormenting image of them hooking up in a dark corner. Nadia's taunting me, trying to get under my skin.

Fuck if it's not working.

Nadia pats my chest sympathetically. "Jeez, give her some credit." Her chuckle bubbles into a full-on laugh, the rumbling of her shoulders vibrating against my arm. "Rox is not stupid enough to accept a drink from a rando wearing a leather jacket in a hot-ass club. Talk about *roofie alert.*"

"You're right. She wouldn't."

But Nadi's laugh fizzles out and I sense the serious shift in her posture. She drops her hand. We both watch Rox's attention flit between the drink and the guy before she shakes her head again.

"Murph, I'm going to need you to step up in a big way." Nadi is still staring ahead as she stands taller. "Now. Not tomorrow or when we get back to San Diego. All Rox wanted was to celebrate with the people she loves. She deserves someone who's not going to sit back and watch while she spends her birthday turning down every guy who asks her to dance because you've got your head up your—"

"I get it," I bite out.

Point made.

I scrape a hand through my hair and blow out a breath. I take a few steps forward, bracing myself for everything Rox makes me feel—everything that scares me.

I stop at the edge of the crowd and pivot to face my sister. "Hey—"

"Don't worry. I've got purse-duty covered." She rolls her eyes playfully and tosses me a soft smile. "Go, ding dong!"

I nod a few times before I mouth *Thank you*, feeling grateful for the extra shove in the right direction.

Nadia points her index and ring fingers playfully at her eyes before turning them on me. It's her sisterly, nonverbal *you owe me.*

And I do.

Big-time.

When I reach the dance floor and weave through the crowd behind Rox, when I slide my hands into the curve of her waist, and she twists in my arms, sinking into me without a glance backward at the guy, I feel lucky. Like I'm on cloud nine and nothing and no one can bring me down. She smiles, and just for tonight, I don't want to think about labels, whether I could love her, or she regrets telling me she loves me at all. I don't want to think about what I should've said in the moment or how much more she deserves and whether I can give it to her. All that matters is now. This untainted moment, and the overwhelming feeling that somehow we can find a way to make this, us, work.

Warmth sweeps through me, sending flames buzzing

over my skin.

"Hey there, sparky," I say, cupping my hand to the curve of her cheek.

All around us, people sway and bend with the beat, but I can't take my eyes, or my hands, off her. I let my fingers dip into her wild curls and trace my thumb over the swell of her lower lip. How is it possible that I can still miss this woman when I'm holding her?

"You're here," she says, blinking up at me. Amazement flashes in her sparkly brown eyes. But then something passes across her face that I can't quite place. "I thought you didn't want to be here…with me."

With me.

The pain in her eyes guts me and I feel like an asshole for being stuck in my head. For letting her think I'd want to be anywhere else besides here, with my body molded to hers, letting our heartbeats, our breaths, us, fall in sync.

My heart wrenches because no matter how much I wish I wasn't, I'm still stuck on my parents. On settling down or settling. On the words Dad didn't say.

"I…" *Love* clings to the tip of my tongue but it won't pass. *Don't say it.* "I missed you," I say instead.

"You really missed me?" she whispers.

Heat courses through my veins, my body aching with need as she scrapes her fingernails teasingly along my spine through the starched fabric.

"Mm-hmm. So much," I say, leaning down and slanting my lips over hers, tasting sweet rum and Rox.

Oh God, I'm drunk on her lips and the soft moans as she opens for me. Always open for me. I take full advantage, deepening the kiss with exploring licks and hungry nips. My pulse races as I band my arms around her waist, pulling her body taut against me as I lean back.

"And I love this dress…and your phallic necklace, birthday girl." I chuckle.

She tucks her bottom lip between her teeth, eyeing me sheepishly. "I missed you, too."

"Good, because I just want to be with you. I thought that meant sitting on the sidelines, giving you space to be with our sisters. But not if that means letting someone else take my place."

"There's no one else."

"I need you to know that I want to give us a chance, Rox. If that means spending this weekend shopping until I drop or taking a helicopter tour over Hoover Dam, I'm in. Neon Museum, Mob Museum, trivia in board game bars, eating your discarded pizza crusts." She smiles and it all feels worth it. "I want to do all of it, any of it, everything. Here and back in San Diego. As long as it's with you."

"I want to be with you, too. So bad."

I release a relieved sigh because I couldn't get enough of Roxanne Sloane even if I tried.

So, I don't even try.

Not when the main DJ hits the stage at one in the morning and the pandemonium rises to the soaring tempo. Not when our group squishes together for dozens of Nadia's selfies to mark the occasion. Not when Declan declares he needs "quality time" with his fiancée, and dips out of the club with Harper, leaving us and Nadia, who seems to have found her own tattooed knight in shining armor.

No, Rox and I barely register time passing.

She drags her teeth over my lower lip, kissing along my jaw until she reaches my ear. I think she's going to say something sweet. Tell me how happy she is that I'm here in Vegas with her. Maybe say the words again. But she traces her tongue over my ear, swirling until the wet heat fills the inside, sending chills spiraling down my spine, and leaving me unsteady on my feet.

I melt into her, my fingers flexed at her hips. "Christ, woman, what are you doing to me?" I growl.

"Showing you how much you were missed," she whispers.

My chest rises and falls as she slips her hand under my shirt and over the waistband of my jeans and boxer briefs, blazing a fiery trail as she takes fistfuls of my ass.

The rest of the night we don't leave each other's sides. We can't keep our hands off each other. We kiss hungry, desperate kisses like she hasn't occupied my mind for years. She lets her hands wander free over my chest and thighs, getting lost in the fit and feel of us together like there aren't hundreds of people around.

With every passing minute, my body responds under her touch, throbbing and hardening to a near breaking point. The way her soft curves press into me… I don't know how much longer I can wait to feel her writhing underneath me.

"Let's go to bed," Rox says.

"Oof, you read my mind."

She smiles into the kiss and my entire world turns on its axis. It's like I've stepped on the gas instead of the brakes, but I don't care anymore. I'm just lucky to enjoy the ride and see what happens next.

CHAPTER SEVENTEEN

ROX

Q: Name the *Dynasty* star and *Hollywood Wives* novelist who were famed sisters.

A: Jackie and Joan Collins

Ladies Group Chat

Saturday July 24

Harper Sloane 10:11 A.M.
Bottomless mimosas in an hour. Is it weird that I'm excited to see the Mob Museum and Fremont Street?

Nadia Sikes 10:15 A.M.
Girl, usually I'm like, why do you all insist on waking up so early? But today… Your girl is ready to see Bugsy and Capone.

Rox Sloane 10:16 A.M.
Do you all want to do a helicopter tour of Hoover Dam?

Nadia Sikes 10:16 A.M.
Nope. You know I can barely do airplanes.

Harper Sloane 10:17 A.M.
Someone send me pictures from last night. I need to update my profile picture on IG.

Rox Sloane 10:18 A.M.
Nadia, send them to me too.

Nadia Sikes 10:18 A.M.
Sent.

Harper Sloane 10:23 A.M.
Thanks, I got them. Nadia, what happened with that guy last night?

Rox Sloane 10:24 A.M.
Ooh yeah. My sources say she found herself a tall, dark, and tattooed bed warmer…

Nadia Sikes 10:27 A.M.
Luckily, since you two abandoned me.

Rox Sloane 10:28 A.M.
Don't even try it. Tell me when the last time was I was getting regular sex.

Harper Sloane 10:30 A.M.
Fair point. It's working too. I have never seen you beaming and glowing, all giggling and holding hands. I'm not mad at all.

Nadia Sikes 10:31 A.M.
But it's my brother.

Rox Sloane 10:32 A.M.
Your brother who is a delicious, sculpted stick of hotness. Good lord, I can't keep my hands off him. If it wasn't for you all, I don't think I would leave this room. Vegas will be there when I come up for air. Phew! I'm getting horny just talking about him. I may be late for mimosas.

Harper Sloane 10:33 A.M.
Me too. You're getting me all hot and bothered. Declan may get a second round this morning.

Nadia Sikes 10:33 A.M.
Again, ew.

Nadia Sikes 10:33 A.M.
I said what I said.

Harper Sloane 10:35 A.M.
Let's do that rollercoaster at New York, New York, and the Neon Museum later.

Nadia Sikes 10:37 A.M.
I'm down. I'm trying to milk this little weekend for everything it's worth. This is the first time since we opened Love & Games that we've closed the store for a non-holiday weekend.

Harper Sloane 10:38 A.M.
I know. We should do this at least two times a year. Or consider hiring seasonal staff to give ourselves periodic breaks.

Nadia Sikes 10:45 A.M.
Agreed. Any word from Jennifer Ling?

Rox Sloane 10:51 A.M.
DO NOT say her name. I can't believe she had the audacity to show up at Harper's engagement.

Nadia Sikes 10:52 A.M.
I'm pretty sure she wants to be besties with the Monopoly Queen.

Harper Sloane 10:57 A.M.
Actually, I got an email from her late in the workday yesterday. She wants to do a follow-up interview after our BusinessFunder investigation is completed next week. I think we're getting all the money back. Even the stuff from Love & Games Shop on University Lane.

Nadia Sikes 11:01 A.M.
Damn right.

Rox Sloane 11:02 A.M.
Thank God. But also, I'm still going ahead with the trivia nights even when we get all the money back. Like Jacques said, the stuff with the

Monopoly buzz and the viral videos gave us a nice bump, but it's not sustainable. We need to always be thinking of ways to grow the store, anyway. We need more events and reasons to draw people in off the street.

Harper Sloane 11:03 A.M.
I definitely think you're right.

Rox Sloane 11:02 A.M.
Around the holidays, if we're in a good place, I think we should talk to the landlord about expanding to the pad next door. Nadia, you could do something Clue related since that's your jam.

Nadia Sikes 11:04 A.M.
I love that idea.

Rox Sloane 11:06 A.M.
Did you see that board-game-themed bar at Murph and Declan's hotel? I took a ton of pictures and made a list of things I want to implement. Sooner rather than later. I think with the first trivia night coming up next weekend, I'm going to turn them into the virtual Trivial Pursuit nights.

Nadia Sikes 11:08 A.M.
Yesss! Queen! Even if it's sex with my brother, I'm loving how love

looks on you. Go have your pre-mimosa sex! You too, Harper. I'm fully planning to get myself a morning quickie before I kick this guy out. Lol.

Harper Sloane 11:08 A.M.
On it! See you in a few. Bye.

Rox Sloane 11:09 A.M.
Nadia, are you going to your parents' anniversary dinner tomorrow night? Murph invited me and I'm trying not to get too geeked up about meeting your parents, but it might help if you're there.

Nadia Sikes 11:10 A.M.
Yup.

Rox Sloane 11:11 A.M.
Ok cool. All jokes aside, you're good with Murph and me doing…whatever this is we're doing?

Nadia Sikes 11:13 A.M.
To be clear, the two of you were fooling no one with your little trivia nights and fake excuses to get together. TBH I'm beyond thrilled we'll officially be sisters.

CHAPTER EIGHTEEN

MURPH

Q: What 2013 romantic comedy film starring Aubrey Plaza and Bill Hader centers on a recent high school graduate who catalogs the intimate experiences she wants to have before she starts college?

A: *The To-Do List*

"SURE YOU DON'T want me to join you, sparky?" I let my gaze sweep over the curves of Rox's sudsy warm brown skin. "I'm pretty handy to have around. I think you missed a spot on your back."

She giggles, shaking her head at me.

"While I'd love to go a third round, our flight is in two and a half hours, and I don't want to be late." She glides her washcloth over her breasts, and my dick twitches. "You definitely can't miss the flight if you want to get home in time for your parents' anniversary dinner."

I heave a disappointed sigh, letting my head sag against the doorframe.

She's right, I don't want to be late.

This weekend has been a whirlwind in the best way possible, and I can't wait for Rox to meet Mom and Dad. Mom watches Jennifer Ling religiously, and I can already see her and Rox talking about the interview. Or some book they've both read. Dad may be stoic and tight-lipped with us, but he has a knack for making others feel like they have his utmost respect and undivided attention.

My phone vibrates against my thigh, and I slip it from my pocket, pivoting back into the room to look at the screen. It's Dec.

"Stopping by your room to grab my wallet."

Right. Last night at the New York, New York Hotel & Casino, Declan asked me to hold his wallet on the rollercoaster before the women came back from the casino. I shut the bathroom door, grab his wallet off the nightstand, and make my way to the room door before he knocks.

"Hey, here you go."

"I see you got a late checkout, too. What time is your flight?" Declan asks, but I sense a bit of hesitation in his tone as he tucks his wallet away.

His shoulders look tense, too.

"Yeah. Rox is just in the shower now. We'll be out in another half hour." I fold my arms across my chest. "You doing all right?"

"Yeah, yeah. Yes." His response is too rushed, high-pitched to feel natural.

"That the story you're sticking with?" I stifle a laugh.

The flick of his eyes in the bathroom's direction gives me a hint of what this is about. I pat my pocket to feel for the plastic key card and step into the hallway, letting the door shut behind me.

"Shoot," I say.

Declan blows out his cheeks then slowly releases a breath. "Man, what are you doing?"

"As far as I know, standing in this hallway waiting for you to stop beating around the bush. What exactly are we talking about here?"

"I'm talking about the fact Harper said Rox told you she loves you. You know she's had a crush on you forever. She hopped on a plane to be here for you. And I know you've got a thing for her, too, but you need to figure your shit out. If it's not love, you can't play with her emotions like this." He pinches the bridge of his nose, releasing a lungful of air. "She's *in* love with you and it's growing stronger every second you spend together this weekend."

I scrub a hand over my face. "I know."

"You know? Then what the fuck are you doing? Harper tells me everything and I shouldn't be telling you this, but you're my boy, so I am. Harper, Rox, and Nadia have been in a group chat every single day this weekend talking about you two. She's worried about Rox getting her heart broken, and honestly, so am I."

I toss a glance over my shoulder at the door, lowering my voice. "I mean, I *know*. We've had a blast. I'm more me when we're together than I've ever been with a woman. I'm not going to break her heart."

"Yeah, and?"

"And"—I crack my neck on either side—"yes, I feel myself falling, and I don't want it to end."

"Did you tell *her* that?" Declan cocks his head, leaning in for a half hug and a heavy slap on the back. "Look, I know you've never said the words to a woman, so this is a big step for you, but make sure she knows that you're getting there." He shoots me a stern glance as he steps back. "Don't wait."

"All right. I've got it." I nod, *but do I?*

I slip back into the room, letting the door snick closed behind me.

"Who was at the door?" Rox calls out from the shower.

"Uh, yeah. That was just Dec. He stopped by to pick up his wallet."

I have a few minutes to get my thoughts in order. I pack up my toiletries, roll up my phone charger, and tuck them in the corner of my suitcase, scanning the room for anything else I might've forgotten.

Just in case, I shake out the sheets and pull up the pillows, but something flies out and lands with a thwack on Rox's side of the bed.

Rounding the foot of the bed, I spot an open notebook on the floor. A two-page-long checklist stares up at me. I smile to myself, bending to pick it up as I toss a glance toward the bathroom door. I'm just about to close it and set it on top of Rox's bag when I read the title and curiosity gets the best of me.

It's not really snooping if it fell open on its own, is it?

ONE SHOT LIST

- *Zing* ✔ ✔ ✔
- *Loves Trivial Pursuit* ✔ ✔
- *Wants a lasting, loving relationship* ✔
- *Family is important to him* ✔
- *Taller than me* ✔
- *Enjoys movies and books* ✔
- *Knows how to have fun* ✔
- *Passionate about his work* ✔
- *We have amazing sex* ✔ ✔
- ~~*Tells me he loves me*~~

The list must be at least thirty or forty items long. From the title, it's hard to tell, but I gather from the list items they're Rox's must-haves or deal breakers for the man she wants.

I have no clue what "zing" is or why Trivial Pursuit is so high on the list, but I get stuck around the tenth item.

Tells me he loves me.

It's crossed out, and I'm just a little confused here.

She tells me not to say the words, then takes them off the table completely? Here I've been turning it over in my head figuring how the words will change us. Should I say the words? How should I go about it? I'd figured maybe we were both just scared and didn't know how to talk about us.

Below *we have amazing sex* on the page, I drag the pad of my thumb over the lined-through words. They feel like a wake-up call. A reminder that while we've had a blast this weekend, maybe we're only playing roles.

Even after everything I said in the club, maybe she still doesn't believe I'm ready. Or that I'll ever be.

I've only got one shot.

Is she going to keep removing things when I don't do them on her timeline? I didn't realize there were goals I was supposed to fulfill, and a ticking clock to meet them.

I didn't think I'd ever want a relationship, but the idea of spending my days and nights playing games, talking and testing each other, waking up with our bodies curved to each other's…nothing about settling down with her feels like settling for me.

But what if, for her, being with me is settling?

I don't say much as she packs her bag, and we check out of the hotel. On the ride to the airport, she asks me for the third or fourth time if anything is wrong. I smile and tell her everything is fine.

And it is fine. On the plane as she sleeps softly on my shoulder, our hands clasped in my lap. It's still fine when we land back in San Diego, and I offer to drop her home instead of letting her call a rideshare.

But then she kisses me on her doorstep and lingers like she wants to say more. Like she wants *me* to say more.

Except, deep down, I'm not fine with her list, her words, the fact that taking love off the table means it would always feel like she's settling for me. As much as I care about Rox. As much as I love being with her and can't stand the thought of her being with anyone else, what if being together isn't enough?

I squeeze her hand, press a soft kiss to her forehead, and tell her I'll be back in a couple hours.

I'm still pondering what it all means on the way back to my place, picturing the rest of the night with Rox meeting my parents and even next weekend with her first trivia night at Love & Games. I slowly pursued her, and it worked. We made plans and she ditched her room with the girls to live with me for a weekend, but is it enough? Am I enough?

Can I check all the boxes on her list?

Later, when I pick her up for dinner, she's beaming and beautiful in a short black dress with full makeup and her loose waves spilling over her warm bronze shoulders. There's a shifting in my chest. I've seen her every waking minute this weekend and still I'm mesmerized and speechless.

"Please tell me what's bothering you." She turns in her seat to face me, her pointed stare pinned on me. "Ever since we left the hotel, you've barely said two words to me. Did I do something wrong?"

"No." The word slingshots out of me and I need to look at her, let her know I'm still in this. The fact of the matter is, I may never be enough, but I've got to try. *We've just got to make it through tonight.* I focus back on the road. "I'm fine. *We're* fine."

Even as I say it, I'm reminded of our conversation after the Channel 5 interview. The reason I stopped at Love & Games in the first place was because I knew she was *not* fine.

We both know how inadequate that word is, yet here I am using it the same way she did to sweep my problems under the proverbial rug.

Rox quietly surveys me.

"Let's just say, I'm working through a personal problem. I'm *making do.*" I smile.

She seems to register her words and gives me the benefit of the doubt, flashing me a warm smile.

"How about you? You hanging in there? Was your Dirty-Thirty birthday weekend everything you hoped it would be?"

With a small headshake, she grazes her lower lip with her teeth. "Better. So much better because you were there."

Fuck.

For the rest of the drive to La Dinette, I keep my replies to a minimum, nodding when appropriate. Mostly, I'm stuck in my head using the spaghetti method, throwing all my hang-ups at the wall, and waiting to see what sticks. Am I still clinging to my resentment toward Dad? Is my view of my parents' marriage hindering me from having a loving relationship of my own? *Can I give her what she needs in a relationship?*

I take Rox's small hand, leading us to the restaurant entrance.

"Welcome to La Dinette. May I have the name under your reservation, sir?"

I blink out of my trance down at the petite brunette hostess. "Uh, yes," I stammer. "It should be under Allen and Vivian Sikes."

She drags her finger over the computer screen, scrolling through names before she comes to a stop about midway. "Here we are." Grabbing a handful of menus, she passes them off to a server before she offers us a small smile. "It looks like you're the first to arrive, Mr. and Mrs. Sikes. Allow me to be the first to wish you a happy anniversary."

I force a tight smile in response. My heart slows to a heavy thud, a wave of panic washing over me. "It's actually my parents' fortieth anniversary. We're here to celebrate with them."

How am I going to make it through this night?

"My apologies for the error. Please pass on the sentiment to your parents for me."

The busy mixture of silverware clanking and idle chatter muffles my thoughts as we trail the server at a slow pace, weaving through rounders of white-linen-clothed tables.

"Are you sure you're okay?" Rox asks, but all I can muster is a small nod. She waits until we're seated to press further. "I know you said you're just working through a personal problem, but it feels like you're clamming up. Did Declan say something when he stopped by the room before we checked out of the hotel? I need you to make me believe this isn't about us, Murph. *Please.*"

She gently drags the pads of her fingers over the light stubble of my jaw and my heart raps against my ribs, my pulse quickening.

"Is it about me telling you I love you? Because if it is, you don't have to worry." She's undeterred. "I care about *you.* I don't expect you to say it after a weekend together."

It's the perfect opening and I take it.

"So then why ask me not to say it back?" I flatten my hands on the table, still grabbling with her words.

"Murph, baby, I stopped you that night because it doesn't matter what words we use. I don't regret telling you that I love you. Say it when you're ready. If that's in one week or one year, I don't care."

I hold my breath, letting my chin rest on my chest. It feels like all the air in the room seeps out and I'm suffocating, our future sealed in a single moment.

"Do you know I've never told a woman I love her?"

Realization smears over her face and it feels like the restaurant walls are closing in on me.

"So, all day, it has been about me."

She lowers her head, but I tip her chin up to look at me. "I don't want to hurt you, and I know it worries you I haven't said the words, but when you stopped me, it threw me for a loop. I didn't know if was nerves or regret. And you're right, it has been bothering me since the hotel. I saw your list. I saw you crossed out the line about your one-shot guy telling you he loves you—"

She draws her shoulders back.

"You went through my things?"

"No. Well, yes, but…" I go for her hands, but she pulls them out of reach. "You were in the shower and—"

Rox's eyes widen, and she's shaking her head.

"And you just thought it was okay to snoop. Just flip through the pages of my book." She releases a disbelieving laugh. "The funny part is, I'm not even mad you saw the list. That list is *you*, Murph. You're everything I've ever wanted in a man, and I crossed that line off because I realized it didn't matter if you said the words. You made me realize that it doesn't matter what words we use because your actions—until now—they proved you cared about me…" Her voice breaks.

"Sparky—"

Rox holds up her palm against the air, her gaze darting

self-consciously at the other restaurant patrons.

Her eyes pool with unshed tears, her lower lip quivering as she whispers, "I wouldn't have cared, you know?" She chews the inside of her cheek, nodding. "We could've talked about all of it. Instead of telling me, though, you take my words and a stupid list, and twist them into some warped conclusion. Then you give me the silent treatment, internalizing it for an entire day."

"You have to know it wasn't like that. I've been racking my brain—"

"But we didn't *talk*, Murph." Her voice lands hard and accusatory.

In my periphery, I catch a glimpse of Mom, Dad, and Nadia entering the restaurant and approaching the hostess.

"They're here. Can we just get through tonight, then we'll go somewhere? We'll talk about all of it?"

"Actually, I've lost my appetite." She swipes at a tear trailing the curve of her cheek and fear claws through me. All this time I berated my parents because they didn't communicate. Now I'm doing the same thing.

Rox loops her purse strap over her shoulder.

"What are you doing?"

She straightens and forces a shaky smile at me. "I'm sorry, I can't do this right now. I don't want them to see me like this."

Before I can get a word in edgewise, she's up off her chair. She swipes and taps her phone screen, then lifts it to her ear. "I need a ride. Don't ask questions yet. I'm at La Dinette."

"Rox, *please*, don't leave."

I reach for her hand, but she moves it out of reach and walks away, zigzagging through the tables toward the entrance. I watch as she smiles apologetically as she passes my family without a backward glance. Then she's gone.

I'm standing here as they reach the table with my fingers clasped behind my head, wondering whether I should go after Rox or if it'll only make things worse.

"What the hell did you do?" Nadia asks. Her face is red, and she's fuming. "We've literally been back from Vegas a few hours and you've managed to fuck it up somehow?"

Just great.

I take Mom's hand and help her get settled in her chair.

"I presume that was your someone special…" Mom's expression is sympathetic as she tilts her head for me to kiss her cheek. "Do you want to talk about it, sweetheart?"

Talking about it is the last thing I want to do with my family.

Dad tips his chin up and I can feel the weight of his piercing blue gaze on me. Scrutinizing, judging, disappointed as usual.

I shake my head. "Let's not take the focus off the reason we're here tonight. We're here to celebrate you and Dad and forty years of marriage."

Nadia huffs out a laugh.

"Here we go. Classic Murph. Let's ignore the fact you've screwed up with the only woman who ever made you a better man." Her tone drips with sarcasm. "Yeah, let's just pretend that didn't happen because you can't get over something Dad did almost two decades ago… Like get over it already." She shrugs when I glare at her. "Please tell me where the lie is…"

"This is *not* the time, Nadia." My voice is sharp and curt, but my sister is apparently fed up and unfazed by my irritation.

"Really? When is a good time? When Mom and Dad are long gone, and you've finally talked it through with a shrink instead of talking to your own father face-to-face—"

"That's enough." Dad's thunderous voice strikes right through our sibling bickering. The muscles at the sides of his jaw harden and jut out, but he doesn't look at us. Not that I expect him to. He steeples his large, calloused fingers on the table and blows out an even breath. "Now, what we're going to do is enjoy a nice dinner together as a family. If you can't act civilized with each other, you're welcome to leave."

And that's the end of it.

Right. Because that's what we do. We don't talk things through as a family or work out our problems. Never let 'em see you sweat, right, Dad?

I guess I learned from the best.

CHAPTER NINETEEN

ROX

Q: What can be broken but never held?

A: A promise

THE GREEN TEAM clicks the button and the virtual die tumbles across the projector screen, landing on a four.

My least favorite number.

For most people, they think of four-leaf clovers, staying at the Four Seasons luxury hotels, four wind directions, the music of the Four Tops, the Fantastic Four superheroes. Even a fourth time's the charm marriage. But again, I study Trivial Pursuit cards like some people study tarot or oracle cards. All I can think of is how unlucky the number four is in Chinese culture, even if it's just because it's pronounced the same as the Mandarin word that means *death*.

I don't know why, but watching those four tiny dots on the screen, it feels like an omen.

After the team captain moves the game marker to a blue geography space, I pluck out the next card from the deck and read the last question of the round.

"St. Croix, St. John, and St. Thomas are part of what US territory?"

While the team deliberates, I flip the card over to confirm I'm right about my guess of the Virgin Islands, then I continue studying the rest of the questions and answers.

"The Virgin Islands," the redhead on the What the Hex team calls out.

With a thumbs-up, I confirm her response and a blue wedge appears in their green pie. I inform everyone it's time for a break and remind them to look around. In so many words, pointing out not only is Monopoly on sale—*and not the only game on the face of the planet*—but Trivial Pursuit is our featured game for the Summer Fun & Games sale.

What's it going to take to sell some games tonight?

Disappointment flares in my gut as a few stragglers walk over to check out the Trivial Pursuit display. Then only one person picks up a game box to take it to the register.

"It's only the first night." Harper appears at my side. She gives me a quick shoulder squeeze, knowing how obsessed I've been about growing the business and selling off some of our inventory. Even with all the frozen funds from both donation accounts released back to us when the Business-Funder investigation closed, I've been focused on sustainability.

"I know." I toss her a small smile.

"Seriously, give people a chance to look around and fall in love with the game..."

Fall in love.

I let my chin drop to my chest with a defeated sigh.

"Sorry. Bad choice of words." Harper pulls me in for a

full-body hug. "I hate seeing you like this—throwing yourself back into work all week, not having any fun. Have you talked to him?"

My heart wrenches, twisting, wringing dry in my chest.

I shake my head, fighting the sadness that's been tearing through me since I stormed out of La Dinette on Sunday. It's almost been a full week and I haven't so much as received a *"how was your day"* text from Murph.

Is it really over between us?

"Thanks for coming to get me that night. I just needed to go. I didn't want to face his parents not knowing where we stood, you know?"

"Of course. I love you. I'll always be here for you."

She hugs me tighter, and I struggle not to cry.

I miss him so much it hurts down to my bones. My entire body aches to be with him. No matter how much I know not seeing him this week was probably for the best.

For both of us.

I needed to get my head on straight—see clearly through the haze of being so close to Murph.

Every reservation I had about him avoiding relationships was basically confirmed. His choice might not be about him being a player, but his family dynamics have made him apprehensive with me.

I know now I shouldn't have told him I loved him, then stopped him from possibly saying it back. I shouldn't have let him know I was using my one shot on him. Especially with a long weekend together. I'm sure it was a lot of pressure, but haven't we been slowly inching toward this for years?

Am I pushing him into something he clearly isn't ready for?

"Listen. I know you and Nadia want to help, but honestly, I think Murph and I both know it's over. We had a great weekend celebrating his award and my birthday. We enjoyed each other's company, and I had fantastic sex. But I think that's as much as he can give. And I want more." I shrug off the sorrow thickening my throat. "I blame *you* and Declan. And my damn romance novels. I just can't settle knowing my happily-ever-after is still out there."

"And you shouldn't have to." Harper presses her lips to my hair. "It'll all work itself out. I promise."

But aren't promises meant to be broken?

We share a melancholy laugh. I know my sister's heart is in the right place and she just wants me to be happy, but I'm not even sure what Murph and I thought would happen.

"Are you two at least going to talk it out?"

I blink away the familiar tears stinging at the corners of my eyes. "Maybe. It'll have to be when we run into each other..."

"Is now a good time?" Harper whispers, and I follow her gaze to where Murph is standing off to the side of the entrance, watching us.

I'm struck with a mix of joy and fear. A flush of adrenaline tingles through my body. All my thoughts go fuzzy, and I've lost the ability to think straight. I'm practically euphoric and dizzy at the sight of him.

He's in dark-washed jeans and a cool blue shirt that I'm sure up close makes his eyes a vivid watercolor dream. His hair is mussed and a little wilder than usual, but he's still beautiful in the most boyishly adorable way.

I chew the inside of my cheek to bite back my tears. I can barely breathe because I don't know what any of it means—that he's here.

Sure, Murph was the one who planned with Vick for us to host trivia nights, but he didn't need to attend tonight knowing Love & Games is my place of business. He doesn't need to slink into the shadows. He certainly doesn't need to remind me in a battle against my brain, my heart always wins.

"Go talk to him." Harper slips her hand into mine and squeezes, snapping me back to reality.

"Doesn't look like I have a choice."

"He's here," Harp says simply, and my thoughts echo her words. The fact he's shown up, didn't run away and hide, it gives me hope.

A dull ache echoes in the hollow of my chest as I watch him try to fade into the background when he's the light.

It's like one of those teen movies when they're at a school dance and all the house lights go down save for the two spotlights on them. I don't see or hear anyone else. The room feels like it's shrinking and I'm hyperaware of my heart thumping in my chest.

It's just us.

The question is, when we meet in the middle, which direction will we turn?

He's either here to talk things through and find an alternative path together, or he's just tying off loose ends.

Flipping my wrist, I check the time. We're going to need more than five minutes for what still needs saying between Murph and me.

"Will you take over on the next round for me?" I ask Harper as I meet Murph's gaze across the room and jerk my head toward the register where the main door to my office and the stockroom is just off to the side. "Here goes nothing."

"You've got this."

I suck in a few breaths. It can't be over twenty feet to the door, but it feels like the dang green mile all over again for the way my heart jackhammers against my chest. I don't see when Murph turns up behind me, but I sense his presence as I enter my office. I toss him a tentative smile, closing the door behind us.

"Hey."

The tiny fissures in my heart spread a little further when he responds with only "Hey" in return. The absence of his usual endearing *sparky* nickname leaves a void I can't discount.

Do not cry. Do. Not. Cry.

"I didn't think you'd show up…"

The vein at his temple pulses.

"I gave you my word I'd be here." He shrugs, but his tone is strained, measured. He stands taller, lifting his chin and baring his throat without meeting my gaze. "Look, I just came to congratulate you. I'll get out of your hair."

I should just say thanks and let him go on his way. But neither my heart nor my brain can draw a line in the sand that fast.

At least, not a straight one.

Murph turns toward the door, and when he reaches for the handle, the urge to scream sears through me.

"So that's it?" My voice rises. I back over to my desk and sit on the edge, crossing my legs at the ankle, arms folded across my chest. My foot bounces as I do my best to steady my breathing.

When he turns around, his eyes are a steely glacial blue.

"What more do you want me to say, Rox? I care about you, but I think we both know we've reached a fork in the road."

Screw it.

"And which way are you going, Murph? Whatever direction I don't? You said you wanted to explain, well, have at it." I throw my hands up. "You've got the floor now."

Murph rakes his hands through his warm blond hair. He sucks in a lungful of air and blows out a frustrated breath. "First, your book was under the pillows and blankets in the hotel. It flew out when I was checking to see if we forgot anything, and I saw what was on the page when I picked—"

"I don't care about the book or the list, Murph."

"Yeah, but for the record, I don't know *any* guy who wants to be reduced to a list of boxes to be checked."

Even as he says it, I know this is what's really bothering him.

"I mean, I knew on some level you were methodical about dating, that you made lists for everything. But, seeing it with my own eyes…and the fact you crossed off an item already…"

There it is.

I discounted his ability to love.

He cups his fingers to his temples and explodes them out in a mind-blown gesture. "I know I'm not exactly an expert, but did it ever occur to you it may take more than a weekend to build a relationship?"

"Yes, it did. It slipped out, and that's why I didn't make a big deal. I'm upset because you didn't talk to me about what you were feeling. You just shut down on me—without giving me the opportunity to weigh in on any of it."

Murph nods, but I sense he's still working his way around to the crux of his issue. I want to tell him I don't need to hear the words if he keeps showing me how much he loves me.

But his expression is resigned.

"I'll give you that, and I'm sorry, but…maybe I don't want to be corralled into literal boxes, requirements I wasn't made aware I needed to fulfill. Neither of us has had the greatest examples at home. I'm still trying to understand what version of love and relationships I want to have and you're already writing me off—walking away from me."

"Babe. I love you so much and I don't care if you never say the words—"

"That's just it. *I* do." His voice thunders. "I care about saying those words for the first time and meaning them. My father never said them. Do you think I want to end up like him, in a relationship where I never say how much I love you? Where I walk away when things get hard? I don't want to be set up to fall into that box. And you shouldn't be forced to stay in that box with me."

His eyes water and he swallows hard.

"This is us," I say.

His voice falls barely above a whisper. "Don't you get it? I don't want to be like him, and the fact is, when you walked out of the restaurant, it felt like you'd raised a mirror to my face. We didn't talk. I shut down on you just like he did with my mom. I'm not going to do that to you."

I shake my head.

"But I love you and I don't want anyone else…"

"And I care about you." Murph scrubs his hands over his face, groaning into his palms. "*Fuck*, I'm screwing this up."

My chest tightens and my body floods with a manic energy. Panic assails me and I need to do something, say something to change his mind. Reason with him. *Please don't end everything when we just got started. Give us more time. I know you'll learn to love me. I'll add every line back to the list. I'll burn the entire book.*

I'll do anything, but just don't give up.

Just be with me.

He takes to pacing the short length of the space, shaking his head the whole way. Then he stands directly in front of me.

I'm holding my breath, waiting for the other shoe to drop.

He lays a hand across his breastbone, his expression pleading. "Are you always going to walk away like you did at the restaurant? Keep crossing lines out on your checklist every time I don't meet your requirements?"

I blow out a breath.

"What's *really* eating at you, Murph? Because I just can't accept that this is all about my list or walking out of La Dinette. If you're scared of love, then just say it. I'm scared, too. God, I wish I could just take it back—"

I gasp.

A flash of sadness plays in his pained expression, and I'm flooded with regret.

"I'm sorry. I didn't mean it like that. You've got to believe me. I just meant that I wish we could—"

"It's okay." He swallows and stands taller, and I know it's not okay. The hurt in his eyes feels irrevocable. "I just..."

He doesn't finish his thought, but my body is weighed down, sinking in agony.

I let my chin rest on my chest.

"Please don't do this." Tears stream down my cheeks, trailing to my neck, and I don't move to wipe them away.

He scrapes a hand through his hair and erases the distance between us. He blows a soft breath over my eyes, soothing the sting. "I don't know how to do this. I need to work on me—be better for you."

I tip up my chin to meet his gaze, but it hurts too much.

How can we spend these amazing few weeks, building toward something that feels so right, and have it end just like that? Over. If he can so flippantly dismiss what we have, were we as happy as I thought we were?

"It's just so easy for you to change your mind like nothing happened?" I blink back more tears.

"No. These past few weeks have meant *everything* to me. And I'm not changing my mind. I think we just need to take a step back."

I want to yell, hit something, bargain with him. Find some reserve of strength. I was this close to my dream of love and now it's slipping away—crumbling right in front of me. And I know I won't ever have another shot because I'll never feel about anyone else like I do about Murph.

As I close my eyes, I pray he'll lean in and lightly press his lips to mine. But he doesn't touch me. He simply whispers good-bye and walks away, and I'm gutted.

CHAPTER TWENTY

MURPH

Q: The 1987 film *The Secret of My Success* features Michael J. Fox juggling a funny lampoon of corporate business life to what chart-topping Katrina and the Waves song?

A: "Walking on Sunshine"

IT'S BEEN SUNNY for the past two and a half weeks. Warm, not a cloud for miles. It's the perfect weather to be outside, for paddleboarding, a good run or hike, reading in the park. But as days go, this one is just another in a string of reminders there's nowhere I want to go.

No place I haven't wanted to share with Rox that doesn't remind me how good I had it—thought I had it.

I wish I could take it back.

I stare at the window at the vivid blue sky, my mind far away. Ever reeling over the past month. Back at the beach, listening to her read as the surf crashed against the shore. In Vegas, the rush of joy I felt seeing her at my awards dinner, then the easy quiet poolside, and the pure exhilaration lighting up her face at the board game bar. Dancing at the club on her birthday, and just being near her at the Mob and Neon Museums and on Fremont Street.

And always, *always*, at Love & Games that first day.

Every muscle in my body aches to be with Rox.

I miss her. And I fear, although I know I did the right thing for her, I need Rox.

In the reflection in the window, my office door opens with a creak, and I don't have to turn toward the faint footsteps to know it's Declan. He's been calling and texting, checking in on me between breaks.

"Did you have lunch yet?" He closes the door behind him. "We can go grab some Thai food up the block if you want..."

It's Thursday. Even from across the room, I smell the warm spices from Harper's leftovers from spaghetti night.

I swivel around in my chair. "Nah, I'm good. I grabbed a granola bar from the vending machine downstairs, but thanks for asking."

Declan scratches his head. He's doing the lingering thing again, and I sense I'm about to be on the receiving end of another one of his pep talks.

"So, you're good, then?" he probes.

"Yup. I'm *fine*."

My gaze snags on a spattering of bright, shimmery dust particles dancing in the air.

Declan chews his bottom lip, nodding as he scrutinizes me.

I know I look like shit. I feel like shit. It sort of goes with the whole sadistic fuckup vibe I'm going for. No haircut, same rotation of dingy blue scrubs. I've shaved, but it was a half-ass, shoddy effort, and I'll get a haircut at the same time I decide to go grocery shopping, which is about never.

I'm living off food deliveries and video games. I keep dying over and again on the screen, too, but at least it's quick—none of the slow torture. None of the memories, regrets, uncertainty replaying in my head on a loop.

I couldn't even touch her.

I crack my neck on both sides, closing my eyes. "Was there something you wanted?" I say dryly when Declan stalls.

He folds his arms over his chest and then the other shoe drops.

"Yes, I have a complete list." His tone is clipped. "You look like shit. You smell. Our staff and patients are looking at you sideways, wondering what the hell is going on with Dr. Raincloud, and—for all intents and purposes—you've been a shitty friend."

Wow. Don't hold back on my account.

Clasping my hands on my desk, I shift to face him. I'm not surprised. Lately, I seem to let everything fall through the cracks. Might as well add being a crap friend to the list.

Lists.

I pinch the bridge of my nose between my thumb and forefinger, kneading small circles.

"Anything else you need to get off your chest?"

Declan is restless. He curls his arms behind his neck and blows out a frustrated breath as he takes short paces, stopping midstride to let out an impatient snort before throwing his hands up.

"We've got to figure something out here." He scrubs a

hand over his face. "You can't keep going at this rate. And I know you don't want to hear it, but Harper's stressed out about Rox. On top of wedding planning. Yeah, she wants to do a New Year's wedding, which I can't even dedicate any brain space to right now because I'm stressed out—worrying about her, you, Rox, and now my mom has all these ideas for the wedding that Harper hates."

"Sounds like nightmare fuel."

"You're fucking telling me… And guess what?" Declan storms my desk and splays his fingers on the grainy wooden surface. His eyes are wide and overbright. "I have no one to vent to because my best friend has his head up his ass."

I recline my chair, letting it bounce, strangely buoyed by the prospect of something to focus on other than the multitude of ways to wallow in self-pity.

"Listen. I know I've been in an awful place these last few weeks, but I want to be here for you. What do you need me to do?" I ask. "Weddings aren't really my thing, but I can help with vendors or locations. I know the owner of a bakery not too far from here."

He searches my face, seeming to weigh what he wants to say next before he pushes off my desk with a smile tugging the corners of his mouth.

"You think I want your help with wedding planning? No, I want you to stop staring out the fucking window, replaying montages of this past month with Rox. Forget about your ego and stop being an idiot."

I let my head rest back on the chair and close my eyes.

This isn't how it's supposed to be. We moved so fast. I figured I'd hang in the shadows, give her space. Then we'd find our way back to taking our time learning and exploring each other. Take time to let go of my hang-ups about my parents. A reset, so when we returned to each other, it would be with clear heads and certain hearts untainted by our fears, our sensitivities.

But somehow, a few days, a few steps back, turned into a few weeks, and now I don't know how to find my way back—if she even wants me back.

"What do you want me to say?" I swivel to face him.

"Let me make myself clear." Declan closes his eyes, and when he opens them again, his expression is hard and serious. "When I told you that morning in the hotel to figure your shit out, I assumed you knew it was love you and Rox shared. But clearly, based on what you pulled at the trivia night almost three weeks ago, it's not sinking in. So, let me make this plainer." Declan stands taller, chin high, throat bared, like he's only going to say this once.

And I'm listening. Hanging on to this last shred of hope like it's life.

"You're falling apart because *you're in love* and you're *fighting it.*" He emphasizes the words, slowing them down like we speak different languages.

"She wanted to take it back and I messed it up." I shrug, holding my hands out, trying to get this through Declan's head. "I got stuck on the words, on her walking away. I didn't know I wanted love until Rox. I wasn't prepared."

I open my mouth to speak, but he holds up a hand.

"No offense, but you're not doing *the right thing* here if that's somehow the way you've rationalized it in your warped mind. You don't need to be the martyr. That you are wallowing at rock bottom and she's working herself to the bone to keep her mind off you… Neither of you is better off without the other. Plain and simple. And you may not get it, but I want to stress that you *chose* rock bottom over being with Rox." He slices the air, drawing a line in the sand. "Love is always a choice."

The weight of his words crashes down on me. My chest tightens and my stomach churns.

Did I do this to myself? Was it always my choice?

Love.

What Rox and I shared, was it love?

I think of my parents. Their quiet marriage. The walls all around them, letting no one in. A business arrangement. A contract between two people who share last names, addresses, and offspring. But never the fun, loud laughter, hand holding, and passionate desperation. They don't argue or yell or get under each other's skin.

Forty years and still, they're growing old together with no regrets.

Mom's soft smile flashes in my mind. *It's a choice, though, Teddy. One you must make every single day.*

Why am I so hung up on their version of love? Maybe Mom is right, and love comes in as many shapes and forms as do the ways people show it. The Baileys were a two peas in a pod couple who held hands at doctor's appointments and wore corny matching Hawaiian shirts. That's how they showed their love. Before Declan proposed to Harper, his face lit up just saying her name. He freely talked about professing his love for her every day.

I twist my watch.

Sure, Rox and I have our own flaws and hang-ups and baggage, but isn't the chance of making our own version of love worth it? *Isn't it her choice whether I'm good enough?*

Declan snaps his fingers near my ear. "Are you hearing anything I'm saying? Like, is it sinking in?"

I sit up taller and take a deep breath, rubbing the back of my neck. "I've just been thinking about my parents. Forty years…"

There's no way it's been loveless.

Just because I never heard them say the words doesn't mean they don't prove it to each other every day.

"I'm going to take that as a yes. Look, I know people are always hung up on what their parents shared, but you've got to remember, we're not our parents. And forty years… That's what happens when you love someone on the deepest level, flaws and all—with or without the words. You're a team and you go through shit together. The question is, are you going to choose to go through it with Rox or keep being a stubborn ass?"

I shift my focus from Declan back to the window where the vivid blue sky beams back at me like a wink. The most beautiful, sunny day outside.

There is someplace I want to be.

I slide all the files on my desk into a pile and tap them against the desk until they're a neat stack. Shoving them in my drawer, I feel the first ray of light piercing the raincloud I've been living under these past few weeks. I push to my feet, beaming, my chair scraping the floor. In one fluid movement, I pull Declan into a full-on hug. It's a silent thank-you. No words needed.

He answers with a loud slap on my back.

We've always been friends. With any luck, we'll be brothers, too.

"What are you going to do, and do you need my help?" he asks, visibly pumped. He seems half excited for me, and half confused by my sudden burst of energy. "Please tell me you're going to see Rox..."

My heart hammers against my chest.

"I will," I say to both questions, patting my pockets for my wallet and car keys. Not finding them, I bend down beneath my desk and shove my hand inside my duffel bag. A smile creeps over my face as my fingertips graze over sand, a stray Red Vine, and the banded stack of Trivial Pursuit cards I took to the beach when I met up with Rox.

"When?"

Fishing out my keys, I hike my duffel up my arm onto my shoulder and blow out a breath. I'm bubbling over with nervous energy. "I have something I need to do first, but do me a favor and have the front clear the rest of my calendar. Tell them it's a family emergency."

Turns out I've been making the wrong choices for a long time. If I don't want to live a life full of regrets, I need to course correct immediately.

CHAPTER TWENTY-ONE

ROX

Q: What American television series on the A&E network follows one to two participants who are dependent on or addicted to drugs and/or alcohol?

A: *Intervention*

I MAKE IT to Nadia's apartment without getting a ticket or heaving up the comfort food contents of my stomach. I don't even have time to knock before she yanks me inside by the arm, sending my tote bag dangling down to my wrist.

"Holy shit!" I let out an ear-piercing yelp and clutch my heart.

Nadia and Harper are in full charcoal face masks, and it scares the bejesus out of me. "You could've warned me."

I laugh despite the hollow urge to cry flaring in the pit of my stomach.

Nadia's already in her flannel pajamas, Harper in a red cotton short set. They've got tissue weaved between their brightly colored toes. The wine is open, and three glasses are on the coffee table beside a batch of freshly baked chocolate chip cookies.

I didn't realize how much I needed a calm night like this.

These women were born ready for bonding and much-needed girls' nights. As of late, though, Nadia's sheepish expression around me says she's still weary of being guilty by bloodline. That what's transpired between Murph and me has changed my relationship with her.

"I hate how distant we've been lately. I want us to be *us* again." She skips all the small talk, champing at the bit to get right to the crux of things. "Even if my brother's an idiot, we're still sisters from different misters."

My sentiments exactly.

I pull her into a hug, and Harper joins in. Because I don't want to think about Murph or how close we all were to being family. I lean into their embrace, letting my heavy body sag into their familiar warmth.

"It's too bad Declan doesn't have a brother, otherwise we would be golden," Harper adds, and we burst into laughter because…*if only, right?*

If only I wasn't so anal that I make lists about everything. Or jump on planes to make grand gestures. Or tell the man I've always wanted I love him and want him to be my version of one-and-done.

Yeah. If only…

"I love you all," I say, giving another squeeze, needing to get out of this head space. I step back, jerking my chin to the television. "So, what's on the playlist tonight? I was thinking, *Sinister* or *The Conjuring…*"

They both stare at me, shock smoothing the lines of their

faces when I flash them a pleading grin.

"What's wrong with the movies I suggested?" I ask.

Nadia grabs the remote and clicks a button, wincing. "Not exactly on brand with what I planned, would you say?"

A whole extravaganza grid of my favorite rom-coms fills the screen. Each cover with smiling couples standing back-to-back. Some with the woman on the right, others on the left, or with her back leaned to his chest because, of course, she's petite and he towers over her protectively. Or my favorite, in some pretzel twist of a hug with curious looks on their faces.

All of them in bright, cheery colors keeping with their promise of upbeat hijinks on the way to happily-ever-after.

I stare at them, knowing too well whether in a movie or a book, the love will be earned in the end, wrapped up cheerfully with a bow.

Harper groans.

"I had my heart set on *Never Been Kissed*. You know how I feel about that movie, Rox," she whines, and I know she's referring to Declan's public profession of love at the Monopoly tournament a few months ago. She's been obsessed with it since.

I get lost thinking about what nineties rom-com movie would fit Murph and me. My heart sinks when I clunkily tuck us into a few of the upbeat plots. I'm a list-making Trivial Pursuit fanatic and game store owner. He's a commitment-phobe otolaryngologist who I can't imagine caving to make a grand gesture. I'd be a fool not to realize some love stories just end in tragedy.

Not everyone gets four tries, sometimes it's one-and-done.

"Actually…" I wave off my reservation with a smile, hoping it reaches my eyes. "Put on whatever you want. I'm ready to maximize this girls' night for everything it's worth."

It's almost been three weeks since I saw Murph. With Harper planning a wedding and Nadia still sneaking around with Micah from the bookstore around the corner, Booked Up, I need to get used to being around blissfully happy couples.

I need to move on.

Which is why I came tonight, despite wanting to slink beneath my covers and cry. This is me coming to terms with reality, making peace with the past. I haven't had the heart to read any of my novels or dating handbooks recently—definitely *not* my *Book of Lists*—but it's sort of ingrained in my brain. The list for moving on when you still love your ex.

If I can even call him that…

Step One: Cut off contact. Check. *Even if it's not my choice.*

Step Two: Let go of the fantasy. *It sort of let go of me, so check on that one, too.*

Step Three: Make peace with the past.

I'm still working on this one, but I know it's going to be a process. I don't harbor any ill-will or anger toward Murph. He was just doing what he believes is right.

Then there's Step Four: It's okay to still love him.

This one I struggle with the most. While love is never wrong and I got the gift of experiencing it in its truest form, it doesn't change how much it hurts to know love wasn't enough to keep us together.

Especially not one-sided.

So, that leaves me at Step Five: Love myself more.

That requires sisters, haunting psychological thriller movies (or rom-coms, because tough love), wine, chocolate chip cookies, even scarier singing, and my secret stash of Red Vines.

Harper is still making her case for *Never Been Kissed* or *Love & Basketball* when Nadia shoots me a meaningful glance. It says, *I've got your back. Murder over magical romance tonight.* My heart wrenches as empathy softens her delicate features.

I'm the lucky one here tonight.

Instead of letting my broken heart and this movie battle dampen the mood, Nadia scrolls through her phone, finds a happy playlist she calls "No Take-Backs." Would I expect anything less than a curated mix featuring a bunch of breakup and revenge-fueled songs? Not one bit.

As bass and bouncing notes fill the air, it feels like glue putting my heart back together.

On cue, Nadia and Harper both break out into wild gyrating dances, arms up, stealthily swaying to the beat, careful not to smudge their toes.

This is what I need all my Thursday nights to be like. *TGI Thursday!*

I'm already stripping out of my leggings and T-shirt and digging out my pajamas, ready to get on the same page. I need to relax as I sing along with the music—doing my best not to let my thoughts linger on Murph.

Once I'm in my PJs, Harper swipes through Nadia's music app on her phone, finds "Girls Just Want to Have Fun" by Cyndi Lauper, and blasts it.

I belt the chorus out into a rolled-up magazine and bump Nadi's hip on my right before switching it up to Harper on my left. They grab the wine bottles and use them as makeshift microphones, howling boisterously and off-key at the top of their lungs. I love them so much.

We're like this—screaming and jumping around like teenagers—for at least an hour before the high dissipates. We crumple to the floor and sprawl our lifeless bodies out on Nadia's pale pink shag rug. We're sweaty and gasping for air. But as soon as the euphoria wears off, so does the haze.

Nadi reaches for my hand. "Are you thinking about him?"

"Uh-huh," I murmur.

If I say more, they'll hear the emotion thick in my throat.

Nadia pops up first, checking her watch before Harper follows suit. They make their way over to the couch and plop down on opposite ends.

"Come on over. Let's get nice and comfy," Nadia says.

Harper pats the couch cushion, signaling for me to sit in the middle, which seems sort of sweet of them to be literally at my sides in my time of need.

"Right here. Snug as a bug in a rug," she says.

Something about the way my sister smiles throws me off, though. I drag my gaze between the other two-thirds of this tripod, taking in their extra smiley faces and stiff posture. When I settle in between them, I wonder if my downer mood makes them feel like they need to walk on eggshells around me.

Maybe tonight wasn't such a good idea.

"So, what movie did we settle on?" I slap my hands down

on my thighs, pressing them forward restlessly.

Just as Nadia points the remote control, the doorbell rings, and I flinch.

"Probably just the food," she says, jolting to her feet.

But she doesn't grab her wallet, so I'm not the least bit surprised when Nadia returns without a bag of steamy deliciousness, and instead trails behind Gwyn, the mystery guest of the evening.

I mean, I'm both happy to see her and confused why none of them—my friend included—thought to let me know she was coming.

Tilting my head to eye each one of these coconspirators, I ask, "Who wants to fill me in on what's happening? I know for a fact Christian doesn't let Gwyn out on weekdays—not even for emergency girls' night sleepovers, so…"

She waves me off, bending to hug each one of us, saving me for last. Then she sets her purse down and shrugs off her leopard sweater, revealing a set of fabulous purple satin pajamas, before she sprawls out on Nadia's plush pink area rug in front of the coffee table.

Noticing only three glasses on the table, Nadia gets up and walks to the kitchen to grab another one from the cupboard.

Gwyn waits for her to settle back in her place on the couch before she speaks. "Look, I didn't get to do Vegas." She takes a long swig of wine. "At least this is local, so I can be a part of it."

"And by it, you mean movie night, right?"

The three coconspirators share a coded stare before their attention crashes down on me.

"Allow me..." Harper holds up a hand. I shoot her a sidelong glance, my brows lifted in anticipation. She pauses for a beat before she tips her chin up, twisting to square her body to mine. "This isn't just a girls' night..."

Well, no shit.

I lower my chin painstakingly slow, waiting for the silent *but.*

Except it doesn't come.

"This is an intervention," they say in stereo surround sound.

Each one of them eyes me nervously, seemingly anticipating my reaction, but I'm all out of steam on this. When I slouch back, kicking my feet up on the table, the tension in their shoulders drains. I think I even notice Nadia exhale.

I sip from my glass, then reconsider, gulping the rest down.

"Okay, we don't want you to feel ganged up on or anything, so if you're feeling any sort of negative vibes about this, let us know now." Gwyn nods absently, her lips pursed in concentration. "We love you."

"Totally," Nadia adds.

Harper squeezes my hand. "We're all here for you."

I can't close my mouth. My eyes are wide, confusion lacing a mirthless laugh. "This is all really dramatic. The man was quite clear he wanted nothing further to do with me. What exactly are you all proposing I do, chain him down to a chair and force him to love me back?" Nadia's expression turns pensive, like she's considering this option. "To be clear, there will be no chaining Murph to a chair."

She shrugs and quietly pulls her knee to her chest.

"Yeah, while I certainly appreciate all the sugar, wine, and sappy movies you went through all the trouble of gathering, *really*, I'm..." *Not fine.* "I'm going to focus on me."

There's a long pause that feels like a collective sigh.

Again, they share a meaningful look, their attention pinballing between the three of them like they're weighing if this is a satisfactory course of action.

"That's all fine and good, but we've got to get you out of this funk you've been in, and we need a plan to do it," Harper says. *I guess not.* "What about making him jealous? I know a guy at the Thai place who's pretty cute. That might get Murph's butt in gear."

Gwyn shakes her head as she absently scrolls through her phone. "Nope. Been there, done that with your little business guy, Jacques."

Harper and Nadia shoot me a death glare from both sides.

"What? I needed someone to go with me to the first trivia night. He was an excellent stand-in." I shrug, then reach for my wineglass. "Besides, it clearly didn't work out to my benefit."

"What if we tell him you're leaving?" Nadia waggles her eyebrows like this is the clear winner. "Like moving away to another state or something?"

"But I'm not..." I trail off, hoping she'll see the error in her logic. I release a guttural groan, swiping my hands through the air to clean the slate. "What if we accept reality and let this be?" I tilt my head hopefully. "Seriously, I'm okay with things the way they are. I'm working on learning to love myself. Period."

It's an instant mood killer.

I'm met with an actual group sigh coupled with eye rolls for "taking the fun out of everything." *How selfish of me for throwing a wrench in their evil matchmaking intervention scheme.*

"Aren't you willing to do anything for love?" Harper's tone is laced with desperation, and I get it. She's found it and she's going through the phase where she wants everyone else to experience the same blissful magic. "This has been your dream, and I really, *really* don't want you to give up on it because of Dad and our moms' track records. It's still possible but you have to fight tooth and nail for it."

But that's the thing.

Before Murph, finding a real true love felt Disney epiphany urgent. Like I needed to consider kissing frogs and living in castles with grumpy beasts before I'd find my prince. But these past few weeks have helped me realize I'm not going to, poof, turn into a spinster. I have so much life to live, fun to have—once my heart pieces itself back together…

There are lists I haven't even started yet. Who knows? I could be at a Trivial Pursuit championship, and he could be waiting for me.

The point is, I'm still here.

A little more broken and bruised, but at least I got to experience love. No matter how short-lived it was. And it goes against the lie I've been telling myself, but I finally get why the Sloane Wives' Club exists. Why they never tried again.

If Murph was my one shot, I'm okay with it.

"Hear me out." I sit up taller, feeling a renewed energy

despite the hollow ache in my heart. "I promise, I'm going to be all right. *Eventually*. I have this 'Moving on When You Still Love Your Ex' list. I'm already working my way through step—"

I'm thrown off when the pointed stares begin again and Nadia, Harper, and Gwyn jolt to their feet.

"We *really* hoped it wouldn't have to come to this," they say in a scarily unified robotic drone. Honestly, if hot drunk women in pajamas were a thing, they could totally persuade people to join their cult.

That's the left-field thought spiraling through my head when Gwyn power blasts the coffee table away from the couch with one arm, sending our empty wine glasses and game boxes crashing to the floor.

Shit.

"Told you we'd need her for this." Harper flashes Nadia the most wicked smile I've ever seen.

"Guys…" My voice shakes as I get to my feet, too, scanning possible cracks to slip through. Now I'm really regretting the choice to sit in the middle. *But was it really a choice?* I'm surrounded by the Bobbsey Twins at my sides and my best friend who looks like she's ready to rush me. "What is happening?"

Gwyn cracks her neck on both sides and rolls her shoulders.

I don't have a chance to ask for a second time. Before I can even get my bearings, Gwyn tackles me to the couch and Nadia runs interference, holding my legs.

"We're doing this for your own good," Harper says.

I crane my neck to see her running for my weekender

tote. She hurriedly unzips it like they've done a timed practice of this underhanded heist before.

"This is premeditated criminal activity," I yell at the top of my lungs. Wiggling to get free proves useless because I'm banded into the couch cushions by my alleged friends. The funny thing is, to look at them, anyone would think, *Oh, I can take a crimson-lipped bombshell brunette and a sweet-faced leggy blonde easily.*

Well, they'd have clearly been wrong.

"Let me up." I struggle, twisting, turning, and kicking to break free. "This isn't right."

"Resisting is futile." Gwyn smiles. "You brought this on yourself. It's time to live without bullet points."

Wait, what?

My eyes widen, and I feel the horror contorting the lines of my face. "No." It's a desperate plea that falls on three pairs of deaf ears.

I watch in sheer panic as Harper retrieves my sacred *Book of Lists* from my bag, victoriously wielding it above her head like the holy grail. "I've got it," she announces, her eyes glittering.

The bullet points and beautifully curated washi tape and stickers. My proof of life. My plans in gorgeous, expensive ink. They flash down at me in splintering glimpses.

My stomach turns as fear twists my gut.

"What are you going to do with it?"

"That depends on you..." Nadia chimes in.

Another wave of panic tugs me into its undertow as I think about all the things I've done, still want to do, beautifully listed inside my journal. My brain space inscribed on a page. At my own risk, I chance a question.

"Are you going to burn it?"

Gwyn centers her focus on me. "Babe, we all love you. We wouldn't do that to you." Her expression softens. "All we're saying is, we want you to try living without a roadmap for a bit. No lists or bullet points guiding your decisions. Just you, your heart, and your brain."

"And no self-help or dating books, either," Nadia adds.

"Romance novels?" I ask hopefully, regretting abandoning them during my mope. I don't know that I'll make it living outside of the comfort of my pages.

Harper cocks her head. "Fine," she concedes. "But you also need to come to terms with the fact book boyfriends are all perfect and swoony and hot and everything… Real men don't measure up. Period."

This is her best point yet.

Murph isn't perfect. *He was just perfect for me.*

I'm flooded with the warm, fuzzy relief that at least I'll have the company of old and new fictional lovers to patch up my heart.

"Okay," I bend begrudgingly. "No more lists."

Harper leans over the back of the couch so her face is directly above mine. "And to be clear, we're watching *Never Been Kissed.*"

Whether I want to admit it, tough love works.

CHAPTER TWENTY-TWO

MURPH

Q: Name the dark retro horror video game set in a comic-book-style world inspired by the novels of H. P. Lovecraft.

A: *Forgive Me Father*

THE NIGHT SKY is one of those almost ominous cobalt-blue smudges against the back light of the moon. I've got a mind to turn around and get back in my car, but Mom opens the door before I get the chance. She pulls me into a warm hug, squeezing her arms around my waist. We both know this talk with Dad is too long overdue.

I can't move forward until I check this off my list.

"He shouldn't be long, I hope." Mom pulls back, laughing. "You know how he is. He's back at the hardware store again. Like a kid in a candy shop." She shakes her head and walks through the foyer back to the kitchen. "Have you eaten, Teddy? I've got some pasta and chicken warming in the oven if you're hungry," she calls over her shoulder.

As if I can eat at a time like this.

I flex my fingers, feeling restless as I trail behind her.

"No thanks. I'm good for now—"

But it's too late. She's already pulling a plate from the cupboard and piling on a hefty helping, so I cave. Maybe broaching this conversation on a full stomach will take the edge off. *It's not every day a man is audacious enough to question his father's marital choices.*

Even if doing so may help shed some light on my relationship choices.

Just in case, I pour a glass of red wine and load up a dinner tray, opting to take my food out to the patio.

I could use the extra time to get my talking points in order.

"You sure you don't want to sit with me until Dad gets home?" Mom stops me at the patio door. "Jennifer Ling is doing an exposé on one of those downtown restaurants on the eight o'clock news. Health code violations. Roaches *and* rats…" she emphasizes. Her expression is a strange mix of excitement and horror as she shimmies her shoulders and settles on the couch in front of the television.

It's a hard choice, but…

"Nah, it's nice out. I'll just wait for him out here."

I slide the door open, slip through, and pull it closed. The warm summer breeze is tinged with the scent of salt and the ocean. Even as uneasy as I am, the feel of it washing over my face relaxes me. The tension in my shoulders and neck loosens as I take in the muted city lights in the distance.

Just to the side of the door, there's a six-seater wooden table and chairs where there used to be a wrought iron bistro set. By the looks of the set, it isn't new, but it's new to me.

Settling onto the cream-colored cushion of the chair closest to the door, I'm reminded of how few times I've visited over the past years. How long I've stayed away. *How much I've missed…*

Dad and I don't talk. Not the two of us—never without Mom or Nadia around. It always seemed pointless. And I don't know if I was waiting for an apology—for what exactly, I'm not sure—but some sign or clue that would've helped explain his actions, I think as I swirl my fork into a pile of spaghetti noodles and take a bite. Something that would've let us know we were important to him. I'd been willing to wait forever for him to make the effort, the first move.

But I still can't get the image of my parents on the Fourth of July holiday out of my mind. When it comes down to it, watching them age made it clear: we don't have forever.

Not even tomorrow is promised.

I'm like this for a bit, my thoughts jumbled, alternating between spaghetti bites and sips of wine, until the chime of the alarm system snaps me from my thoughts. It alerts us the front door is open.

I take a deep breath.

There's a rolling sensation in my stomach as I listen to Mom tell him I'm waiting on the patio to talk to him, and he heaves an exasperated sigh.

Before long, the swoosh of the sliding door ratchets up my heartbeat.

"Murphy." The low timbre of his voice causes me to sit up taller. "Don't get up," he says, pulling out the chair next to mine and plopping down with this plastic hardware store bag still dangling from his arm.

"Got yourself a new project?" I jerk my chin to the metal pipe fitting bulging through the thin plastic.

He flits his gaze down to the bag before nodding. "Ah, yes, the never-ending job of being a homeowner."

I twist around, my fingers steepled on the table. Instinctively, I think we both know I'm not here to shoot the shit with him. My pulse quickens as I weigh how I'm going to segue my way into this.

"So, Mom tells me you want to talk…" He trails off, letting me have the floor.

Drawing my shoulders back, I lift my chin.

"We *don't* talk, Dad. That's the problem." I ignore the way he tenses, his posture turning rigid. "We barely see each other on birthdays, let alone holidays and anniversaries. And I know it's been me pulling away, but I think you know where my distance stems from."

He sets his bag on the ground and leans back into the chair, lifting his face skyward. "I know," he says simply, like I'm not tearing my hair out here.

"Look, I know it's not my place to ask you about your relationship with Mom, but I need to understand what happened back then. It's been eating me up, wondering why you wouldn't be there for her. For *us*." I scrape my fingers through my hair. "You have to know it's been slowly tearing our family apart."

When he lowers his head to survey me, I get an empty feeling in the pit of my stomach.

Just tell me.

Deep down, I'm praying he doesn't confirm my worst fears, that he'd been with another woman, or that he was regretting his choice to marry Mom. *Or having Nadia and me.*

I don't think I could bear it if he felt like our family was a disappointment.

Heavy urgency echoes in the back of my throat.

"Dad…" My tone is low and pleading. "I want us to be close again. To rebuild the family bond we lost. I want to believe we can share that again…" I let the words die on my tongue.

As usual, I sense him shutting down.

The Sikes family always acts civilized. We don't question the past or work through our family problems, *do we, Dad?*

But he surprises me.

"Your mother told me you were here a few weeks back…" He fidgets with his fingers. "It hurt me to hear you don't believe we love each other."

Don't make this about me.

"All those years ago… That night your mother was so sick. The fever, chills, dehydration. I took them in stride, managing. But then things escalated. She'd been short of breath, wheezing and coughing, and the sharp chest pains started." He huffs out a sigh. "I thought I could handle it. That I could be strong for her—" Dad twists his lips to the side like he's chewing on the inside of his cheek to keep the memory at bay. *The tears?*

He's got a faraway gaze, like he's back there, watching that night playing before his watery eyes all over again.

The crease between his thick, gray eyebrows deepens, and

a tear streams down his velvety cheek. Quickly, he swipes it away, averting his gaze in shame. But suddenly, I'm the one who feels like the asshole.

It's the first time I've ever seen my father cry, so I'm blindsided by the pain gripping my chest.

"Dad—"

"It destroyed me to see her in that hospital. Weak, fighting for her life. Knowing that I could've lost her…" He trails off, emotion thickening his tone.

I want to comfort him, but I also need to hear this version of everything that happened. I've been waiting too long.

"All the years, the love we shared, the family we built," Dad continues. "I knew I couldn't do any of it without your mother by my side, and it paralyzed me with an unbearable guilt. An agonizing fear. She's the cog that keeps this family running, the glue that holds us together. What would Christmas have been like? Birthdays, holidays, Mother's Day…" He drops his chin to his chest.

"It's okay, Dad."

But he shakes his head.

"In the back of my mind, I kept praying to God that we'd never have to know what it would be like without her. That he wouldn't take her because I wouldn't be able to go on without her. That much I knew for certain. And where would that have left you and your sister?

"Your mother knew it was slowly killing me, that seeing her damn near on her deathbed stole my spirit. So, she told me to go. She needed me to be strong for you and Nadia."

This is my stoic, proud father who never bends or compromises. He wears a stony facade, his steely expression always welded in place. But this… Hearing him tell me how weak he felt seeing his wife, his best friend, and the love of his life lying in a hospital bed, it guts me.

Mom knew. She told him to go.

"Dad, I had no idea…"

A wave of guilt washes over me, pulling me into its undertow.

I hate all this time I've been reading it all wrong. How many times did I let my assumptions about their marriage dictate my relationships with them as parents? Heck, my decisions with women? The fear of being in a loveless marriage rendering me hopeless and alone.

"Listen, I know you didn't know. I didn't want you to see me like that—"

"I would've understood." The words rush out of me, but even as I say them, I know there's no truth to them. I was eighteen. What did I know about love so strong it makes you desperate with despair? He was steeling himself for the worst while suffering alone.

Dad places his big, warm hand on my arm, urging me to meet his gaze.

"I spent every day near the water, praying. For hours, I'd sit there until the stars outnumbered my fears." He deepens his stare. "Murphy, I need you to know that I love your mother more than life itself. We may not express in the loudest, in-your-face way, but it's what got us forty years together. God willing, we'll have forty more. *Please*, never *ever* doubt that."

More than life itself…

His words ricochet off the silence, landing with a thunderous boom in my head and heart. I don't know that's what Rox and I share yet, but hearing Dad's feelings about Mom, I know I want to earn that kind of timeless love.

Down to my bones, I know whether I'm alone or just lonely, it'll all be the same unless I'm with Rox.

"I won't ever doubt it, Dad." The familiar shift as my heart pounds against my chest overwhelms me.

Dad pulls me to my feet and into a full-body hug.

For a beat, I let myself sink into it. Let his warmth seep into the shadowy voids of my heart.

"I love you, son. I'm so proud of you."

Heat pricks the corners of my eyes, and I know it's what I've been waiting for, holding out for all these years. In the same way Mom's words about their love steadied me, Dad's words are a balm to my heart, healing me.

It's a choice.

"I love you, too, Dad," I say, but it blends into a snort of a laugh when I realize I'm bawling, tears drenching the shoulder of his nice shirt. "Good lord."

When I came here after talking to Declan, I expected a stern man-to-man chat with game faces fixed in place. I expected I'd have to claw the answer out of him, and once I got it, it would help me see how far I had to go knowing where I was coming from.

But this, us hugging, crying, saying our I love yous. Now I'm asking for relationship advice? *What universe is this?*

Another chuckle bubbles from my throat.

"This is so surreal. I never thought we could be like this again, Dad."

He's slightly taller than me, so when he presses my head

to rest on his shoulder, I feel like a kid again. Like he's the smartest, strongest man in the world who'll somehow make everything all better.

I squeeze him tight once more, inhaling his warm cinnamon and fresh laundry scent. I think about how many hugs like this I've missed being stubborn all these years—how I might've never experienced them at all.

Again, my breath hitches.

I feel all the emotions I've held back swelling inside me, and I pull away.

"Sorry." I cough to clear my throat, my gaze darting the damp spot on his shoulder. "Didn't mean to..." I jerk my chin to his shirt and wince, heat creeping from my neck to my cheeks.

Dad sniffles and a smile curves the edges of his mouth. He waves off my embarrassment, joking that, as a father, tears have always been the least of his worries with his children's bodily fluids getting on him.

For the next couple of minutes, we stand watching as a smattering of stars dot the sky. We talk about everything from his and Mom's usual trips to the New York house to Mom's art class at the senior center. Dad's been spending the hours she's away on YouTube learning how to fix everything he's broken over the years.

I can't say my heart has ever felt this full.

When I chance the subject of their well-being, my heart beats a little easier knowing they're both in good health. Other than a cabinet full of vitamins, each the size of horse pills, Mom's lungs are getting stronger—she's down to only two to three liters of oxygen—and Dad has added a few laps to his daily swim.

"According to Dr. Malone, I'm in great health..." He trails off, and there's humor blended into his tone. "Might give you a run for your money on one of those paddling boards."

I nearly choke on a laugh. "Oh, yeah?"

He nods, the corners of his mouth dipping as his lower lip protrudes.

"Well, I just might take you up on it..." I chuckle.

My heart leaps at the prospect of Dad and me hanging out, just the two of us. Elation suffuses my entire being. I'm giddy with a caffeine buzz of joy. It's tinged with a bitter-sweetness, though. I want to tell someone. Share the excitement racing through me. Mom, Nadia, Declan, they'll know how this restitches my heart, but Rox... She's the only one who'll make it beat again.

A mix of sadness and fear engulfs me when I realize I might've made the worst mistake of my life.

What if I've lost her for good?

"Hey, Dad? If you're up to it, I could use some advice, though..." I say with a half-hearted shrug.

"Shoot," he says.

I knead the back of my neck and blow out a nervous breath. "I'm in love," I blurt out.

"For what it's worth, if you're asking me, I know you love her. I think we all knew."

I huff out a laugh, but he doesn't even turn to face me.

"You've always been the one who needs time to process your feelings. I've wanted to push you, but Mom always insisted you'd come around when you were ready."

Based on tonight alone, she's not wrong.

"Because I want you to find happiness sooner rather than later, I'm going to tell you not to waste any more time," Dad says. "I'm assuming by the way she ran out of the restaurant, it's Roxanne. She's likely hurting as much as you are, so don't hold back. Make it count. Tell her how you feel and how you can't imagine your life without her—that she's the person you want to spend the rest of your life with."

It's a choice. One you make every day.

A small sniffle from inside the living room snags my attention.

I'd already assumed Mom was eavesdropping through the small crack in the sliding door, but it's the echo of the television that comes in surround sound. Jennifer Ling's sharp voice filters through the resounding jackhammer of my heart.

She breaks stories…

The won't-be-scooped reporter sniffs out scams. Roach *and* rat infestations. But she clearly wants more career-wise. First, with Declan and Harper, she curveballs them with the "are there any wedding bells in the near future," and makes the ballsy move to crash their engagement to break the story. Then with Rox over the crowd-sourcing scam. Though Rox dodged her questions, Ling had even gone as far as prodding at the "famously single sister of the Monopoly Queen" angle, playing up Rox's persona as a workaholic who can't get a man…

But she has one now. She just doesn't know it yet.

My mind shifts and turns, an idea falling into place with the ambitious Jennifer Ling as the center cog making it all work.

I slip out my phone and pull up an app. Expedited shipping is just what I need for the plan I'm forming.

"I guess I'll leave you to it." Dad pats me on the back and moves toward the door.

"Thanks, Dad," I say, flashing him a grateful smile before turning back to my screen. I add two tubs of Red Vines to my cart before finding a bright pink poster board and our favorite classic Trivial Pursuit board game. I take almost an hour to decide how to customize the cards, but I push the purchase button with all the confidence in the world.

Everything will arrive right on time by next Friday.

After I text Declan to ensure Harper brings Rox to Elixir Friday night, I pull up a browser and find the website for Channel 5 Action News. I tap through to the list of reporters and find Jennifer Ling. As I press the call button and let it ring through to voice mail, I breathe an—*almost*—relieved sigh.

"Yes, this is Dr. Murphy Sikes. I have some information related to the Love & Games story you've been reporting on. It's about one of the Sloane sisters, and I know you'll want the exclusive…"

Rox is the woman I want to spend the rest of my life with. I have a week to make sure Jennifer Ling helps me show her.

CHAPTER TWENTY-THREE

ROX

Q: What Japanese tear-jerking workshops are designed to reduce stress and get participants in touch with their emotions?

A: Crying Therapy

OVER THE NEXT week, I wander around aimlessly without my lists. It's disorienting, but mostly freeing. I don't feel the pressure of all the things I need to do hovering over me, ready to be checked off.

At home, I read and stream endless reality shows, stopping to clean only when I can't take the sight and smell of trash a second longer. When the refrigerator gets low, I make a spur-of-the-moment trip to the grocery store, going from aisle to aisle like a strange produce-scented treasure hunt where I discover modern, boldly labeled brands I might never have known existed. I buy outrageous mood munchies to pair with my ever-changing spontaneous bursts of energy.

Even at work, I talk to every customer as they ask for game recommendations, browse books, and buy impulse tchotchkes. I even sell a few dozen Trivial Pursuit boxes just by chatting up Monopoly fans while they get their games signed by Harper and pose for pictures.

I don't know what's come over me when I take a few selfies of my own. Doesn't matter if it's as the Trivial Pursuit Queen or the meme girl from that Jennifer Ling interview.

I have no clue what I want to do next with my life, and strangely, I'm okay with not knowing.

When I'm not at home or work or playing my frantic version of Supermarket Sweep between the grocery store aisles, I've been basking in alone time during the mornings. I walk the boardwalk or let the surf cool my feet as the waves rush the shore. I soak up the sun, listen to audiobooks, and do my best not to let the memory of Murph and me lying in the sand not so long ago push too close to the surface.

I've skipped the last few trivia nights and change up the beaches where I walk to make sure I don't run into him.

I tell myself all I need to do is make it through the summer. Focus on the upcoming holidays, with no plans other than to center all my attention on Harper's wedding. For the five-year store anniversary for Love & Games, I'll take the ideas as they come to me. As for love…

"I got you a blueberry muffin, too," Mom says as she settles on the chair across from me. Careful not to move our game markers, she slides the dusky blue board over a smidge to make room for our coffees and food.

"Thank you." I pull out a travel-sized bottle of hand sanitizer and rub it on my hands. "I am kind of hungry."

We're at a board game café not too far from my house where we meet up sometimes to play and catch up on each other's lives. One of my favorite things about The Sweet Cottage is it smells of tangy cinnamon and buttery vanilla blended perfectly with the robust scent of coffee beans.

It's just my kind of spot.

Warm, airy, welcoming with charm to spare. The atmosphere is chic and easy with petal pink walls and scalloped trim wainscoting like a grown-up lemonade stand. From the time I pass the manicured topiaries at the door, I feel like I'm walking on sunshine, which, let's face it, I can use a lot more of in my life. Between the shelves heaped with games, the glassed-in pastry display anchoring the small space, and the romantic color story, it's like a kid's birthday on steroids—albeit a very discerning child with great taste.

It's not too busy today. There are a few other games in play and two people in line at the register, but mostly the noise level is low with only light chitchat.

"How are you feeling today?" Mom asks.

I give a noncommittal tilt of my head, flipping my palm over and back. "About the same." It's accurate. So-so about covers the range of what I let myself feel so I don't feel sway too much in either direction.

But if we're comparing notes…

Mom and I talk on the phone at least once a day, but it's probably been since June that we've seen each other in person. I can't quite put my finger on it, but there's something different about Mom today.

She's in this relaxed fit dress with a bright, bold turquoise and orange floral print that makes her warm bronze skin glow. She's beautiful with her face-framing highlights mixed in with her dark brown textured curls and green-gold eyes. Though, her usual light makeup has a bit more intention to it. It's subtle, but I notice the bronzer contouring the curves of her heart-shaped face.

And that's not it.

Her brows have been shaped. Her lips are painted a deep rose to match pinch-pink blush and shadow. And she's got lashes. A whole fringe of the high-quality mink variety that cost an arm and a leg to put on but makes them flutter like a heavenly maiden.

"Excuse me… Um, is there anything you want to tell me?" I dip my chin, good-naturedly surveying the light in her eyes.

Mom's flutter game is wild as she bats those babies, feigning innocence.

"I don't know what you're talking about," she says.

But her smile tells on her.

"First off, Mom, a woman does not flaunt lashes like that unless she has secrets to withhold."

She laughs it off, amusement glittering in her coppery brown eyes as she glides a finger along outside corner of her eye. "I just wanted to try them out. I see women all the time looking amazing with a full set."

"And the makeup, and dress, this whole glow you've got going? Still sticking with the no secrets defense?"

She lowers her head sheepishly and shrugs. "Roll the die, Roxanne."

Oh, someone is really trying not to tell me her dirty little secret.

"Ah ha! Deflecting is basically admitting guilt. Plus, going formal with the name is like a telltale sign."

My phone vibrates against my thigh, and I jam my hand into my pocket to fish it out. It's a text message from Harper, probably about the wedding, I think as I unlock the screen.

"Everyone is going to Elixir tomorrow night. You in?"

Uh, no... Why is she even asking? That's Murph's territory.

When Mom reaches for the die, I shove the thought aside and quickly swipe it off the board, locking it in my fist as I flip my phone over on the table.

"Mom..." I drag her name out on a whine until it bleeds into laughter. "You're not slick."

Stubborn as ever, she straightens the teensy brown cheese wheel on the game board then takes a slow sip of her coffee.

"I have a date after I leave here," she finally says.

I gasp as a flush of adrenaline tingles through my body. I'm struck with a blend of wonder and joy. *Throw in a minor panic attack, too.* I'm completely thrown. I thought she was going to say something like she was going shopping or out for wine with her girlfriends. *Maybe* that she was meeting up with an art dealer or gallery owner who wants to pick up a few of her recent paintings...*but a date?*

Honestly, I'm so shocked I don't know how to feel. I've been so caught up in my Sloane women, one-and-done theory, I'd shamefully written her off.

"You don't have to look so surprised." She purses her rosy lips. "I've still got a few things going for me."

"*Mom*, that's freaking fantastic news." I hop up off my chair to pull her into a hug. "Trust me, I know you are damned fierce. You deserve to find someone to share your life with and be happy with."

Settling back in my chair after that outburst, I slouch against the backrest, my arms sagging at my sides as I shake my head in happy disbelief.

The way my mouth refuses to close, it's a wonder a fly hasn't flown in.

"Tell me everything."

Holy shitballs was she holding back. We resume the game, but between questions, I learn Mom is a *pro*.

Turns out, this isn't Mom's first meander into the dating waters. Vanessa Marie Sloane is on her fifth dating site. Everything from matching by age or religion to personal hobbies and interests, and DN-freaking-A. So far, there's been no one serious. A lot of first dates, hell dates, ghosted dates—by her choice. She calls it "putting her feelers out" before diving back in, but I'm loving her no-nonsense approach to trying on personalities and chemistry for size.

Who knew my mom was quietly building a life as a badass huntress and renowned artist on the low?

I sure as hell didn't suspect a thing, but now I'm questioning whether she passed anything on in my genes.

Fingers crossed.

She never gave up after Dad. She took the time she needed to rediscover herself and what she wanted in life, apart from a man.

It makes so much sense. When I think about it, that's what I've been doing all these years alone, including this week. Soul searching.

It's inspiring, really.

Other than Trivial Pursuit and a recent dethroning by

force, I'm the queen of lists. I've read all the best-reviewed dating books and self-help books. I had what I wanted in a man down to the underwear I preferred he wore—*boxer briefs, obviously.* But this slow pursuit, it sounds nice. Not so cut-throat, do-or-die, or 'til-death-do-us-part mumbo jumbo before I've even determined if the feeling is mutual.

A harrowing question hits me in the chest like I've been T-boned by a semitruck: Do I want to try again without Murph or try to be friends?

"Uh-oh, what's that look about?"

I shake my head and roll the die. I move my half-full pink pie marker five spaces.

The question is for a wedge.

Thankfully Mom plays along, falling into the game. She reads from the card, but I'm only half listening. Except, she clears her throat and cocks her head to the side, searching my face. "Really?"

My head is so far from this table in a board game café. Could I try again? What would dating without secretly pining for Murph look like? How would my heart handle it, and would I be settling? Could we be friends?

"You seriously have to think about this question?" Mom asks, snapping me back to reality.

I shove any thoughts of moving on without Murph aside and focus on Mom, who—I peek down at the tiny pink wedge game piece pinched between her finger and thumb—looks downright shocked I haven't shouted out the correct answer to the entertainment question she's presumably asked.

"Sorry, what was the question again?" I square my shoulders to her, determined to be present.

"Red Vines is a popular brand of what type of candy?" she asks again without a glance back at the card.

"Licorice," I say, smiling as she slips the wedge into my tiny wheel. But even responding correctly to a trivia question about my favorite snack doesn't remove the low, somber tone from my voice. *Or the hollow thud of my heart.*

Apparently, even Red Vines aren't even safe from my memories of Murph.

Mom leans across the table to tip my chin up, searching my eyes, reading beneath the surface.

"You seem so lost today, honey."

"Mom, I'm fine. It's fine—"

"Are you trying to convince me or you?" Her expression softens as she deepens her stare.

I don't know whether it's because I've been without my lists or just the fact that I don't have a plan. The truth in her words shakes me to my core. My eyes burn as I avert my gaze. I stare at the wall of shelves stuffed with brightly colored board games, action figures, and themed knick-knacks.

"I miss him," I say simply, but there's nothing simple or easy about how empty I feel without Murph. Every second I got to spend with him felt like a complex network of nerves. Delicate touches, lingering stares, and aligned stars making up the magic we shared. Yes, we were in Vegas, but it had nothing to do with the glittering neon lights or clinking slots. It was a million little things that to anyone else might've seemed trivial, but I felt like we were growing closer, living in a once-in-a-lifetime moment.

But maybe that's all it was.

A moment.

Mom removes our game markers and folds up the board, tucking them back in the box. She scoots her chair around the table so she's at my side. With the pad of her thumb, she swipes away my tears, softly blowing at my eyes. It's a warm, intimate gesture, but it reminds me so fiercely of Murph the last time I saw him at trivia night—the night my world came crashing down.

"Oh, baby." Mom leans in and bands her arms around me. Her familiar citrus and sunshine scent is clean and warm, like my childhood summers, all wrapped up in a whiff. "I know it hurts. You've always given your heart so freely."

"I really miss him, Mom."

A sob hiccups from my chest. Over the past three weeks, I've cried. At night in bed, in my car—a few times in my office at Love & Games when Harper and Nadia were with customers. Only small bouts of streaming tears, always holding back. But there's something about the way Mom hugs me.

The dam breaks and I can't stop myself.

She rubs her hand over my back, soothing me, but the sobs come stronger until I'm ugly crying. *In a public place.* I pull away to wipe my eyes with the backs of my hands, but she stops me.

"You've got to let it out, sweetheart. It's the only way to let your body know it's time to heal."

And so I do.

For what feels like forever, I cling to Mom like life. She

doesn't say a word or rush me along. Nor does anyone else. I let the hurt drain from my heart until I'm empty and nothing but a hollow ache throbs faintly behind my ribs.

When my breathing evens and the sobs subside, I sit up again.

Mom pulls a tissue from her purse and cleans me up, pressing soft kisses on my forehead.

"There. Right as rain," she says, and I think that's going to be the end, but she continues like she was in the middle of a story. "That's the thing, love hurts like hell, but it can also heal like heaven."

I stare at her for a beat, unsure how to apply her words. Is she talking about her and Dad, or a new guy she's been dating?

Like she's privy to my thoughts, Mom tilts her head to me and says, "I'm talking about loving myself *enough* to choose what's best for me." She sets her hand on mine. "I know all about making lists, and believe me, when I met your father, he checked all of my boxes." She presses her hand to her chest, chuckling to herself.

"Ew, Mom."

"You may not want to hear this, but, oh God, that man was my kryptonite—tall, handsome, ambitious. He seemed so worldly to me, like he had his head on straight and he was going places. I just wanted to be along for the ride, so I know. Love didn't cover how I felt about that man, and when we got pregnant, no one could tell me a thing. I was living a real-life fairy tale." She fans her hands out against the air, her warm brown eyes so distant I almost see the lights, too.

"Go on," I prod.

"Anyway, I stopped painting and dedicated every inch of my life to our marriage and family. As far as I was concerned, there wasn't room for anything else. I was going to make this life fit if I had to shove myself into it."

She wraps her left hand around her coffee cup, but she lifts her ring finger and scrutinizes it for a bit, almost like she's searching for the tan line that faded so many years ago.

"Fourteen years I was Harrison Sloane's wife and Roxanne's mother, and I couldn't have been prouder."

I see the light in her eyes flicker.

It's like watching a tragic movie I've seen before and already know how it ends. Even as I enjoy the good parts and the snapshots of the fun times, praying it'll be different this time—that someone pulled a different ending from the cutting room floor, my heart is still heavy. There's still a cloud looming over my head the entire time.

Mom inhales a small breath.

I pinch off a piece of muffin and wash it down with coffee, hanging on to her every word. I know this fairy-tale dream like the back of my hand. I also know how disappointing it is when ever-after isn't so happy.

"Mom..."

"He was unhappy, and I internalized it. I sank into a depression so fierce..." The words fade on her tongue, and I feel for my beautiful mother's heartbreak a little. "Somehow, something had to be wrong with me if I couldn't make him happy. And I'd made it so that my universe revolved around him, so when I filed for divorce, I was lost." She shakes her head. "It took so long for me to realize that I could learn to love again."

My heart races, and my throat tightens.

"Are you saying I should let Murph go or take another shot at this?"

She presses her lips together in a soft smile, the corners of her eyes crinkling. "I'm saying, if you want to take another shot at love with a new person, do it. Or take a second shot with Murph. That's okay, too. Whether you want to keep trying, back-to-back like Dad or take a break to fine-tune what you want before you try again after a while like me, there's no set way to go about finding love. The point is love is always worth shooting for, sweetheart."

I groan because I know what I've got to do.

It's going to hurt like hell seeing him tomorrow, but I must do the things that make me happy—*be* with the people who make me happy. I can't force Murph to love me any more than I can sit still waiting for the day he'll decide to come around. I'll take another shot when I'm ready.

For now, we're just going to fast-track this friendship.

On the table, I flip my phone over, unlock the screen to Harper's text, and fire off a response.

> *"I'm in, but I sure hope you all are ready to come with your A-game."*

CHAPTER TWENTY-FOUR

MURPH

Q: Name the first single from American R&B singer and songwriter Anita Baker's 1986 second studio album, *Rapture*.

A: "Sweet Love"

"IN WHAT MOVIE does Robin Williams play the role of a divorced father posing as an elderly British nanny to spend more time with his children?" Sabita looks up from the game card over to the tables at Elixir. As the teams jot down their answers, she steals a quick glance behind the curtain where I'm waiting to give her the cue when it's time.

Her small nod is my green light for a quick glance.

I take a few breaths, then crane my neck for a better view of the entrance.

Elixir is dark and jam-packed tonight. From where I'm standing—well, hiding outside the audience line of vision for the moment—I don't have the best vantage point of the door. As I peek around the edge of the thick wine-hued velvet curtain, I confirm there's still no sign of Jennifer Ling.

I'm just about to turn back to Sabita and tell her to relax. That Ling will be here any minute. But I notice Rox seated at a table just off the left of the stage. My heart swells when it dawns on me that it's the same table Vick reserved for us that first trivia night.

Rox is huddled together with Harper and Declan, but she's got the same intense expression on her face, probably trying to convince them about an answer before the end of the round. I chuckle to myself as she flits a glance over her shoulder and huddles in closer like she's being careful not to let the people at the next table hear.

Sabita clears her throat, glancing in my direction.

A few more minutes, I mouth, pressing my hands against the air before I look back to Rox's table.

She scribbles on the answer sheet and flips it over. The three of them deflate back against their chairs with looks of pure relief on their faces.

It might be wishful thinking, but as I follow Rox's line of vision, an almost imperceptible tightness hardens her posture as she searches the corners of the room. Presumably—*hopefully*—looking for me. And that's all I need to go through with my plan.

She misses me, too.

"Let's do this, Sikes."

I swallow back my nerves, prepared to get this show on the road with or without Jennifer Ling, when movement at Rox's side steals my attention.

Micah from the bookstore walks up to the table double-fisting drinks. But as he slips into the empty seat at Nadia's table with her best friend, Gwyn, and her boyfriend, Christian, Jacques comes into view—also, notably holding two drinks.

Every muscle in my body tenses as he turns to the table where Harper, Declan, and Rox are seated. Flames of anger shoot through me as he slips into the seat beside Rox, sets a cocktail in front of her, and leans in close to her ear, smiling like he's the happiest asshole on the planet.

"Goddammit."

I want to walk off this stage and leave right now but my feet won't move. I'm angry, annoyed, fucking betrayed looking at them round out the four couples. But how can I be mad? I ended things and took my sweet time figuring out some huge gesture to prove I'm ready. *Am I too late?*

Restless, I clap my hand over my mouth, staring, studying like somehow I'll be able to decipher some deeper connection between Rox and Jacques.

Sabita's voice breaks through the din of the bar chatter and blaring televisions as she clears her throat into the microphone, tearing my attention away.

"Make sure you jot down your answers," she says, but she's looking directly at me with a wide-eyed expression as she jerks her head toward the door…where Jennifer Ling is standing with a cameraman, ready for a "Love & Games exclusive."

Shit. Perfect timing.

Naturally, my mind immediately goes to the worst-case scenario. She's a reporter always looking for the ungettable-get. What if her plan was always to skip mine for the juicier scoop? What if she's been stringing me along this entire time for another exposé on Love & Games? What if she already knows about a new budding relationship between Rox and Jacques and everything is backfiring?

Mentally, I'm cursing myself for staying off social media after that click-bait post they made for me.

I steal another glance at Rox and rake my hand through my hair, clutching it in fistfuls.

My heart wrenches, reminding me how hellish these past few weeks without Rox have been. How much I've missed her. I may be a fool, but I've got to try.

A few second pass, then I give Sabita the go-ahead to end the round.

"That concludes round three, so we're going to take a quick break," she says, hopping off her stool. "Grab yourself a drink and make sure you come right back." She smiles, tucking her lower lip between her teeth flirtatiously. "We've got something *awesome* in store tonight."

Her tone is chummy and relaxed as she walks casually off the stage, waving at someone. It's all very blasé like everything is kosher the way her long inky black ponytail whips side to side.

Oh, sure, this is just another day in the life.

Except, the instant she hits the curtain, she jumps up and down, whisper-yelling like crazy. "Oh my gosh, she's here. Jennifer *fucking* Ling is here." She blows out her cheeks and slowly releases a breath. "God, I want her to do an exposé on me so bad. She's turning into a fucking Midas-touch matchmaker. First, Harper, now Rox… Is it really so much to ask for some hot guy to make a viral video professing his undying love for me?"

I chuckle, wiping my clammy hands over my jeans.

"Let's just hope Rox appreciates this as much as you do. From the looks of things, she's got options."

Sabita peeks her head outside the curtain, taking a single glance at Rox and Jacques. "First, that guy is cute, but he is not you. And second, if she doesn't fall all over herself running into your arms after tonight, I'll be your goddamned rebound." Sabita is dead serious, but also not. Amusement sparkles in her eyes as she bats her wild fringe of dark eyelashes and puckers her rich brown lips.

"All right, we have little time."

"You've got this," she adds reassuringly, firmly shaking my biceps.

The plan is simple. Sabita swaps out the trivia card deck with the one I brought. Vick positions Jennifer Ling behind the tables and handles the logistics, and I, with my bouquet of Red Vines, get ready for my fifteen minutes of fame.

Oh, and pray all of this isn't in vain.

Sabita pivots on her slim black heels and struts back out to her stool in the center of the stage.

"Ow, ow," she howls into the mic. "Are you all ready to have some fun tonight, Elixir? I know I am."

The bar goes wild.

A collective mix of hoots and hollers charge the air, giving me a reality check of just how many people are here tonight. How many witnesses will either have firsthand accounts of my colossal failed attempt at a romantic gesture. Or a rom-com-worthy *profession of my undying love* as Sabita put it so eloquently.

So, yeah. No pressure.

I swallow, rolling my shoulders and taking deep breaths.

"Tonight, we here at Elixir want to thank you for coming out and showing us so much love." It's a shameless plug I'm sure Vick asked her to do, but Sabita clearly doesn't mind milking the attention for Jennifer Ling as she blows a kiss to the camera. "Speaking of love…it just might be in the air this evening, so let's get started on this next round with a new curated trivia deck. There'll be seven questions in total. Your regular six categories: geography, entertainment, history, art and literature, science and nature, and sports and leisure. Followed by a special bonus question…"

Okay. Here goes nothing.

"Entertainment. What classic board game was created on December 15, 1979, by Chris Haney and Scott Abbott, two Canadian newspaper editors, while playing Scrabble and drinking beer?"

Rox doesn't even consult with the rest of her team. She's in full Trivial Pursuit Queen mode as she jots down the answer she's known since she was a child, plugging rainbow wedges into tiny pie-shaped game markers based on a shit-ton of common knowledge.

The rest of the tables aren't exactly scrambling, either, which I'd expect nothing more from a room full of trivia heads.

At the bar, Vick is surrounded by loud, alcohol-fueled patrons swiveling between the cameras and watching sports on the overhead televisions, but he's still as a pole in cement. His posture is rigid, and he looks shell-shocked as he keeps wiping his hands on a small towel affixed to his waist-tied apron. The sweat on his forehead glistens in the low lights. Talking to Jennifer Ling, the star of Channel 5 Action News, as he showed her to her spot must've really done a number on his nerves.

Dammit, breathe, Vick. We've only got a few more questions to go.

I'm genuinely concerned for his health and the stability of the contents in his stomach at this point, but I'm right there with him. Just a couple more minutes before we need to get to our spots—before I'll know whether I'm drinking beer to celebrate or whiskey to drown my despair.

"Science and nature." Sabita shimmies her shoulders, blowing a kiss to the same tall, bearded, lumberjack guy with red hair and bulging eyes that Rox and I saw the first trivia night together.

In fact, his entire crew is here.

The short, bald guy high on his own fumes. The trendy, purple-haired Asian girl with a mean red lip. The broad-shouldered Black guy with his genius-level, thin-framed glasses. They're here, and something about seeing the same faces from that night. Aside from Jacques, knowing Rox is seated at our table. It floods me with the same relief. It lifts my mood, fills my chest with an unnerving giddiness.

Rox doesn't know it, but I'm certain the moment she walked in the door that night I fell in love with her.

Yes, I've been fighting it ever since, but I want that again. I want to feel the air coming alive, zipping blue and gold currents of electricity surging between us. She didn't have to be here tonight. She knew I would be here, but she came anyway, and that's all that matters.

We're both still open to the possibilities, I hope.

"How many miles is it from San Diego to Las Vegas?"

Sabita reads aloud, and a renewed energy fills me up. I can't stop smiling.

Adrenaline courses through me, and my pulse races, my heart skittering.

It was that or a three-hundred-and-thirty-two-mile drive…

I'm so worked up; I can hardly stand still. Somewhere in the recesses of my heart and mind, I think I always knew we were supposed to be together. I don't care if Jacques is here tonight. There's nothing I won't do to give Rox and me the chance I nearly stripped away from us.

She whispers something in Harper's ear before she jots down the team answer. But then, I catch her searching, her gaze sweeping the corners of the room again. There's a bitterness to her smile as she covers her heart with her hand.

Just a few more minutes, sparky.

The next questions are geography and history, both related to our weekend away. What does the term "Las Vegas" mean in Spanish? *We're going to Las Vegas, or The Meadows, if you don't speak Spanish—just a little trivia for you.* Then, "What Las Vegas attraction takes visitors on a world-class, interactive journey that explores the fascinating power struggle between organized crime and law enforcement?" That whole Saturday, we drank mimosas poolside, then held hands and stole kisses around every corner of the Mob Museum downtown.

Recognition glows on Rox's face, and I can tell she's sliding the pieces into place.

The team huddles for a bit, likely discussing the answer to the question, but Rox is getting antsy. She sits up taller, craning her neck to inspect every inch of space. Even though

I can't hear what she's saying, and I'm not close enough to see the light in her eyes, I sense the joy bubbling all around her as a wide smile spreads on her face.

Her shoulders shake, and her beautiful mouth is open. She's laughing, on the verge of breathlessness as she scrutinizes the faces of everyone around her.

"I'm right here, sparky," I mutter to myself.

Taking my cue, I duck into the employees-only door that leads to the back of the bar. As I pass Vick on my way to the front of the house, he still looks like he's pumping himself up for his big assignment, but he flashes me a nauseous, but still encouraging, nod.

Solidarity, brother.

My heart feels like it might cartwheel out of my chest as I sidle up behind Jennifer Ling's cameraman, but there's no time for nerves.

"Name the bestselling enemies-to-lovers contemporary workplace romance novel about two coworkers who go on a strategic reality competition series where the players must choose whether to be themselves or other people all while chasing a cash prize," Sabita purrs into the mic, finding my hidden stare in the darkness. And that does it.

Rox pushes to her feet, shielding her gaze as she disrupts the game.

"Where is he?" Her tone is sharp and accusatory, but filled with amusement as she turns to Sabita, a woman who has clearly and wildly underestimated Rox Sloane's tenacity.

Sabita may know how to schmooze a grimy bar crowd full of trivia heads but is apparently no match for a woman on the hunt for a dogged man in the middle of a romantic gesture.

This is a Red Vine–loving, romance-reading, pizza-crust waster we're talking about. A list-making, trivia head, understand-it-at-the-roots, numbers-and-logic, beautiful, complex woman, and she gets me.

"Uh..." Sabita winces, her shoulders hiked up to her ears unconvincingly.

"Oh, so you just happen to have a new *curated trivia deck* with a question about my favorite novel, *The Blame Game*, huh?" *That's my girl.* She nods slowly. "And love *may* be in the air tonight?" Rox's back is facing me, but her arms are folded over her chest, and I know the *take-no-shit* expression that goes with that body language. *Oh boy.*

Might need to speed this along.

But luckily, I don't have to.

Like the fierce Indian woman she is, Sabita hops off her stool and holds up the next card without taking her eyes off Rox. The entire room goes still, and I swear I hear the old gunslinger whistle music as a tumbleweed sweeps across the stage. It's a duel of well-matched wits between two beautiful women of color unwilling to back down.

Sabita blinks in slow motion, her gaze dropping a millimeter per second to the card. "What recently honored San Diego–based otolaryngologist and trivia genius was an idiot for not confessing his undying love to Roxanne Sloane, also known as the Trivial Pursuit Queen?"

I'm mic'd up, so I move out of the cameraman's hulking shadow. I'm standing a few tables' distance directly behind Rox when Vick, hearing his highly anticipated code words, *Trivial Pursuit Queen*, flips the spotlight on Rox.

"Thank you for joining us tonight here on Channel 5 Action News. I'm Jennifer Ling." She plasters on her television-ready smile. "Earlier this year, the Monopoly Queen answered the call for love to the tune of fifty-six million views and still counting. Now, get ready because tonight it's her sister the Trivial Pursuit Queen's turn. We're here at Elixir Bar and Grill in San Diego where well-respected Dr. Murphy Theodore Sikes, Red Vine bouquet in hand, plans to roll the dice on love with Roxanne Sloane, who you might remember from my *Love, Games, and Scams* segment..."

She turns and every phone, eye, and light in the house lands on me, including a blindingly bright one from the cameraman.

Holy shit.

It's quiet enough to hear a pin drop in this place.

Rox cups her hand over her mouth. Her eyes are wide and unblinking as she slowly shakes her head. Hopefully, in elated disbelief. *Please don't let me be misreading this.* It's a silent prayer that I stop now because it's too late.

She moves. Away from the tables, weaving her way toward the bar, and I think this is it. My heart sinks and my stomach knots. I'm dying a slow, tortured death in what is possibly my worst nightmare.

A collective gasp sounds over the crowd.

But then she corners the edge of the room and I realize she's taking the unobstructed, long way around in excruciatingly slow strides toward me.

Picking up on this, too, the room is alive with cheers, happy sighs, and applause, but I'm cemented in place. All my insecurities flooding to the surface.

What if she's coming to let me down easily? What if Jacques is her choice? What if I really am too late and I'm just standing closest to the exit? A good one-two punch: reject me and make a quick escape, leaving me to tell Jennifer Ling and her legion of followers the details of a broken heart.

As Rox nears, though, the glistening tracks of her tears come into view. Her lower lip is tucked between her teeth and her eyes are searching.

The bar falls silent again when she reaches me.

"Dang, I had this whole speech..." A small bubble of nervous laughter shakes my shoulders as I shift on my feet. "It was about seeing you in Love & Games that morning after the Fourth of July holiday and the first trivia night here at Elixir...dancing during Declan's proposal, the beach, Vegas, all of it. How I needed to process every minute—"

"I know, it was sort of a whirlwind," she says, rubbing the back of her neck.

"I thought I already knew what the other side of happily-ever-after looked like with my parents, and reading your list—"

"Speak up!" a man calls from the crowd.

A flush spreads on Rox's cheeks as her watery gaze drifts to the all the eyes on us before returning to me. "It's okay, you don't have to explain."

"That's just it," I rush to say. "I've always wanted you, but I thought stepping aside was doing the right thing." Panic zips over me as I fumble over my words. "Rox, what I'm trying to say is...you deserve all the love in the world, and I never wanted to take that away from you."

Rox crosses her arms over her chest, and I know I'm

screwing this up. *Bad.*

Off to my right, Declan cheers me on. "Come on, Murph, you've got this, buddy."

"Are you sure?" a gruff man's voice questions in response.

A collective wave of laughter spreads over the bar and I join in, chuckling.

"This was supposed to be romantic and suave," I turn, playing to my audience. "If you'll just give me a minute, I'm trying to lay my heart out for this woman."

I'm met with cheers and swoons and whistles.

Fueled by a tiny shimmer of light in Rox's eyes, I keep going. "All right, now where were we?" I smile at this beautiful, vibrant woman who stole my heart. I hike my thumb over my shoulder. "Is it just me or is this crowd sort of pushy?"

"I don't know, you are fumbling hardcore with Jennifer Ling capturing it live, so…" Rox shrugs.

More laughter rumbles over the bar.

On cue, Jennifer Ling turns to the camera to remind viewers that they're watching a live Love & Games love connection. Then the cameraman pans back to us, and I'm ready.

"Here's the thing, Roxanne Sloane, I'm desperately, sickeningly in love with you. Plain and simple." The place goes wild, but I'm still trying to get the rest out. "I just want to keep telling you that I love you, and never stop telling you."

I reach out and cup my hand to the soft curve of her cheek, sweeping away a tear with the pad of my thumb before I tug her into my arms.

"These are for you, by the way." I hand her the bouquet

of Red Vines, watching as she tries and fails beautifully to contain her smile. "The custom Trivial Pursuit card deck, this whole…production. I did all of this for you. *Only* for you, sparky."

She leans into my touch, more tears pooling as she closes her eyes.

"I'm so in love with you, Roxanne Sloane. I should've known I'd want nothing less than love with you." I brush my lips over hers, planting soft kisses. "I'm sorry it took me so long."

She takes a deep breath and swipes her fingers along the corners of her eyes, her expression brightening. "Are you about done? Because I love you, too." She flits a glance to my lips as she tugs me into a hug, wrapping her arms low and tight around my waist before she comes in for another kiss.

The entire bar erupts in cheers, and light blinds us as I deepen the kiss. This time it's soft and lingers like a balm, sealing the cracks in my heart these past few weeks have caused. I didn't need to process anything. Every day without her felt further away from home.

My heart somersaults in my chest, happiness coursing through me. I'm buoyed, floating on a wave of images of our future reeling through my mind. I want to wake up every day to her bright eyes and the feel of her body molded to mine. I want to take spontaneous trips, play games, and listen to her read stories of happily-ever-afters to me, so I can fall in love with her over and again. I even—and I'll take this with me to my grave—want to make lists with her.

Rox opens her tear-filled eyes. Under the camera light, they're cast with a warm honey glow. "I never want to be without you again."

"You heard it here first. In a Channel 5 Action News exclusive, this is Jennifer Ling, bringing you true love and games." She's beaming straight ahead at the camera as we break the kiss. It might be the angle of the lights, but there are tears brimming in Jennifer Ling's eyes as she turns to us. "Wow. Dr. Sikes. First, let me wish you continued love and happiness in your relationship."

Uh-oh. First?

"Thank you."

The raven-haired news reporter flashes me her trademark megawatt smile before her voice steadies, and she shoots me a severe-looking journalist stare.

"There's been talk about there being more than just games and good times to be had for the lonely and unlucky in love at Rox's small shop. So far, we have one wedding to look forward to. Will there be two?" She tilts her head in question when I don't answer. "As I understand it, there are three owners of Love & Games, one of which is your sister, Nadia Sikes... Maybe there'll be three weddings before long?"

The cameraman pans to my wide-eyed, open-mouthed sister surrounded by Micah at her side, Declan and Harper, Gwyn and Christian, and Jacques and the red-haired woman from Dec's proposal.

Holy hell. No pressure there.

I'd been both dreading and dying to know what curveball she was going to throw at me, if any.

"Roxanne, would you care to comment?"

She's tucked in my arms, still beaming up at me, when

the camera pans back to us. "I have no clue. Right now, all I want to do is be in this moment with the love of my life."

"Okay, we'll let you get to it, then. Congratulations, you two." She turns to the camera. "This is Jennifer Ling reporting, back to you in the studio."

Rox is beaming and beautiful as she finds Harper's and Nadia's faces in the crowd and flashes them a megawatt, *we did it* smile. But she doesn't leave my side. She slips her hand in mine.

"Want to get out of here?"

Laughter creases the corners of her sparkling eyes as we exit, and I tug her close against the breeze. All over again I'm mesmerized, still memorizing the contours of her face, and the way light flecks her loose honey-streaked curls. The thin smattering of tiny freckles dusted over the bridge of her button nose and the slight flush to her pink cheeks. I love every inch of this woman, mind, body, and soul, and I can't imagine my life without her.

"What's that smile about?" she asks.

I give a light head shake before I dip my chin and softly slant my lips over hers. "Nothing… Just…I can't wait to find out what you've got next in your *Book of Lists* for us."

The End

Don't miss the next book in the Love & Games series, *Clued in Christmas*!

Join Tule Publishing's newsletter for more great reads and weekly deals!

Acknowledgements

Let me start by saying, *Trivialized Pursuit* was so much fun to write. Hands down, it's definitely one of my favorites. Not just because I love board games and trivia just happens to be my jam, but Rox and Murph are so much of me. Like Rox, I make lists, overanalyze things way too much, and love extremely hard. On the other hand, I'm like Murph, too. I love my parents, worry about them, and treasure all the moments I get with them. When it comes down to it, I love that this book is fun, emotional, silly, and right from the heart.

Thank you for spending your time with the Love & Games family. Hopefully, since you're reading the acknowledgements, you've loved both Rox and Murph's story as much as Harper and Declan's story and will read and re-read it time and time again.

To my husband, Daniel, thank you for supporting my dream, being my favorite chef, and loving our little family. I love you so much and I'm thankful for you every day.

To my girls, it fills my heart with so much love to know that you're proud of me. I hope seeing me follow my dreams emboldens you to dream big.

Mommy and Daddy, thank you for always cheering me on, and showing me every day what a happily ever after looks like.

To my editor, Roxanne Snopek, thank you again for mixing in the "dig deeper" questions with the cheery comments and laughs. Your work helped me put my best book forward. I love sharing this series with you.

Jane Porter, Nikki Babri, Meghan Farrell, and Cyndi Parent, thanks for welcoming me to the Tule family and making my publishing dreams come true. Special shout-out to Denise, Kelly, Fortune, Lisa, Stacey, Heather, Janine, and Rebecca.

To my Wordmakers family, Tasha, Lisa, D. Ann, Randi, Kris, Ali, KK, Meka, Coralie, and anyone who sat in a Zoom room helping me work through edits and shape this project into a book I'm so proud of, thank you. You are the best group of writing ass writers a person could ask for.

Margo Hendricks, my BWP, thank you for always cheering me on and lifting me up. For reading various versions of this book, thanks to Elizabeth Spaur. Lauren H. Mae, our brainstorming sessions really keep me on track. Joanne Machin, I'm so thankful for your help crafting pitches and queries to help bring this series to life.

Finally, thank you to my romance community, authors, readers, book content creators, my cover reveal team, and my beta readers. I'm so grateful for you all. You make this job fun!

If you enjoyed *Trivialized Pursuit,*
you'll love the next book in the…

Love & Games series

Book 1: *Monopolove*

Book 2: *Trivialized Pursuit*

Book 3: *Clued in Christmas*
Coming in October 2023

Available now at your favorite online retailer!

Trivialized Pursuit Book Club Questions

1. Rox believes that being a Sloane woman means she's got one shot at finding love. Would you take your only shot at love on Murph?
2. Years of watching the relationship his parents shared has made Murph weary about the difference between settling and settling down. How do you think people learn the distinction, if any?
3. Have you ever participated in a trivia night?
4. If you had to trade places with any character in the book, who would you choose & why?
5. Which character could you see yourself dating?
6. If you oversaw casting the movie version of this book, who would you cast as each character?
7. Rox and Murph share many ties. He's her business partner's brother and her sister's fiancé's best friend. Dating feels like risking those relationships. Would you take a chance on love with someone if it meant you could jeopardize, not only that friendship, but relationships with close family and friends, too?
8. Rox is a list-maker. Do you make lists to mark important milestones? What's on your lists?
9. On the beach, Rox reads a romance novel to Murph while they hold hands and warm in the sun. Do you

prefer quiet moments of affection or big explosive sparks of interest?

10. At the beginning of every chapter, there are trivia questions that hint at what the chapter is about. Were any interesting new facts for you? How many did you get right?
11. If you could write one more chapter after the ending, what would you want it to include?
12. If Nadia were to get her own book, who would you want her to end up with?

About the Author

Mia Heintzelman is a polka-dot-wearing, horror movie lover, who always has a book and a to-do list in her purse. When she isn't busy writing fictional happily-ever-afters, she is likely reading, or playing board games and eating sweets with her husband and two children. She writes fun, unforgettable, more than just laughs romcoms about strong women and men with enough heart to fall for them.

Thank you for reading

Trivialized Pursuit

If you enjoyed this book, you can find more from all our great authors at TulePublishing.com, or from your favorite online retailer.

TULE
PUBLISHING

Printed in the USA
CPSIA information can be obtained
at www.ICGtesting.com
LVHW050408161223
766608LV00003B/332

9 781959 988632